# DIRTY TRICKS

With my left hand in the trousers pocket and right dangling loosely at my side, I offered Lanky the easy target, hoping he was part of the majority of people who are right-handed.

I was correct. He grabbed the tempting right wrist and hammerlocked it behind my back. Lanky was to hold while Bulldog applied the harm.

In close-quarters conflict, unless the attacker strikes a stupefying blow, he is seriously disadvantaged by taking the initial grip. Provided the victim knows what to do.

The instant Lanky took me with a firm hold and Bulldog approached with large, threatening fists, I knew the bastards were mine.

# ROBERT PRICKETT

TORONTO • NEW YORK • LONDON • PARIS
AMSTERDAM • STOCKHOLM • HAMBURG
ATHENS • MILAN • TOKYO • SYDNEY

*To my partner in life, Karen Smithson,*
*who made it all possible*

**CANTRELL**

A Worldwide Library Book/January 1989

ISBN 0-373-97090-0

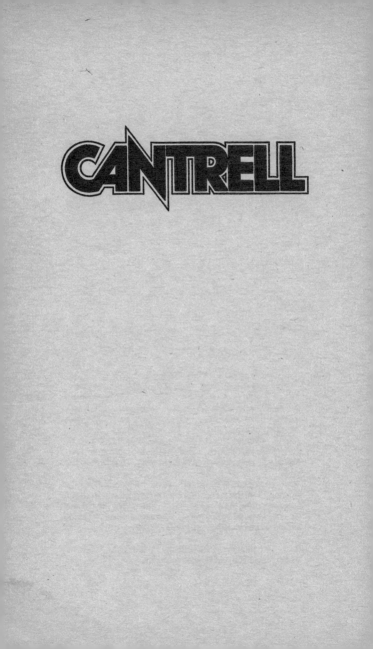

# 1. DEATH

MY NERVOUS BREAKDOWN came after the Israeli war in '73.

It was a simple observation assignment, no harm, no foul, so the three of us took ground in Kusti, a small town in the Sudan. Even then, I was borderline "too old" for active field service, but the seventies were rough and the Company was shorthanded. Besides, it was only a visual and report operation.

We wanted to know if Ugandan troops would enter the fray and escalate the action, so we camped on the only passable road for large-scale movements and watched.

Nothing happened, a big zero, and I felt safe returning to Addis Ababa for a normal commercial flight out. A dumb move, because you can never underestimate insanity during a stupid, desperate war.

The warring powers had agreed to open an air corridor down the middle of the DMZ for Air Italia, for all but Arab or Israeli travelers, and during specific hours. Times were tense, so everyone was constantly challenged and questioned.

At a standard fuel stop in Khartoum all passengers were off-loaded and paraded through the typical customs and passport check.

Carrying an American passport earned me special questions, because officials always suspected members from the Company had infiltrated, and assumed that few sane Americans would be in the neighborhood at the time. After the usual harassment and the ruining of all my tourist film, I was released to board the plane.

It was a crowded flight, and it took me thirty minutes of wandering through the aisles to realize George and James were not with us. From the Agency in Tangier I learned the truth.

Neither of them ever left the country.

The arrest of a foreigner for smuggling concealed firearms through an Arab country at war is similar to a drug bust in Turkey. One can get life. Or death.

James and George were young and green, nervous, and probably felt more secure with hidden handguns. It was not a wet operation and weapons were unnecessary, but I was Control, so the blame was mine. That's the problem with authority, you're responsible for others.

There was never a trace of either man, which kept me awake nights thinking of all the grotesque possibilities. It was too much for my already overloaded psyche, and that is when I cracked.

Working for the Company has very serious drawbacks, but the health-benefit package is fantastic. If you suffer an emotional split, you receive absolute first-class treatment. It's not because they're nice people, because they're not, but once you're in that condition you're vulnerable, and might be vetted to switch.

And you know too much.

After my mental crash, I spent the next uncountable months at a private country estate somewhere in Vermont. It was more rest-and-relax than anything else, along with daily sessions with the resident shrink.

I resisted for a long time, but eventually he convinced me the initial crack had actually begun a year earlier when Kate left me.

Suicidal tendencies since that day, the doc said; I'd put body and soul into every mission without personal regard, but the collapse didn't happen until my two friends were burned in the Sudan. Entirely my fault, and that did it.

Actives are desked long before they get tired and slow, but I was experienced and fairly good in those days, so they had kept me in the field beyond the normal time. After months in the Vermont convalescent home, I was placed on hold while someone at the top decided what to do with this ancient operative.

There is no direct affiliation between the various services, but occasionally a favor is granted, a request approved, so I was transferred via a mountain of red tape to the Buchannon Detective Agency, a pseudolegitimate cover for a covert government organization in San Francisco.

It had survived six different names since its inception in 1942 when the Roosevelt administration needed an independent, fast-response, nonmilitary intelligence system on the West Coast. The Army and the FBI were too busy in those days locking up helpless Japanese civilians to accomplish any significant counterintelligence functions, so the maverick orphan agency was formed.

Over the years priorities altered radically, and each succeeding director blessed the organization with his name, then proceeded to reexamine and reconstruct the overall philosophy. The agency prospered and flourished on changing administrations, burrowing deeper into the quagmire of political hodgepodge, becoming known only to particular senators and key committee members with budgeting powers.

When Buchannon took over, he revamped the entire policy and retired or removed all field actives, wanting strictly an information system, but a year later the Washington gods decided some old salts might come in handy. I happened to be unassigned and completely unattached. Since the agency rarely attempted any rigorous fieldwork, I existed as an insurance policy.

With that, Buchannon and I maintained a strained relationship.

The detective agency was located on the fourth floor of the Morris Building, a triangular-shaped, concrete ugly, which had partially survived the '06 earthquake. When it was rebuilt, the diagonal street across Market resulted in a three-sided structure adorned with gargoyles and other features of nineteenth-century architecture.

An astute observer would have noticed five floors, but only four were listed on the lobby directory. The first three housed authentic businesses, from decorators to artists. Buchannon liked artsy-craftsy people, believing they were just flaky enough to be legitimate, plus easy to verify and susceptible to coercion. Every employee had been subjected to the most thorough and intensive security check, although none was aware of that.

The tenants' respective leases were ridiculously inexpensive, considering the prestigious Market Street location, but they had to abide by one, unalterable rule. Absolutely no outsiders were permitted on the premises. Business had to be arranged by phone and conducted elsewhere.

A photographer once tricked the guard and smuggled in his model. The next day, the man's studio equipment was on the sidewalk. He never returned.

I entered the dingy building and nodded to the guard, a retired police sergeant.

"Morning, Mr. Cantrell," he said in a monotone, and pushed his key, activating the elevator door. The wall buttons were muted unless a particular signal was sent.

I traveled to the elevator's limit, the fourth floor, a typical office with long rows of desks, rattling machines, phones ringing and people shuffling paper. We did employ authentic investigators who performed a great deal of sincere detective work, gathering evidence on cheating spouses, tracking down missing witnesses and finding runaway teens, but all client activity was mandated to take place off property.

Employees were continually screened, and Buchannon's files could reveal how many times a month the staff made love, and with whom and probably if they enjoyed it. They were supervised by a small group of seniors, but everyone noticed a select few like myself who apparently had no function, and were known simply as consultants, although no one ever asked my advice. We also enjoyed the right of ascension to the fifth floor, a place of mystery and, therefore, a source of constant rumor. The others coveted that honor, having no idea what the privilege entailed.

Sitting at my desk, I delegated the morning mail to aspiring heroes, then wondered how to spend the day. The *Times* crossword looked good, but lately I had given up or gone to lunch rather than tackle the tough parts.

Buchannon's secretary buzzed. "He wants you."

I approached the other elevator, located in the far alcove, and passed the clerk who typed reports. Her real job was to key the elevator door for people possessing security clearance. She had been doing this for years and had never been upstairs herself. It was all rather foolish, but that's how we played these games.

That particular elevator traveled from four to five, and no buttons were necessary. I was shot up one flight and stepped into another world.

The fifth floor was space-age, all stainless steel and white acrylic. A gentle hum was produced by numerous ultrastate computers lining the walls. The two-inch-thick, one-way windows were constantly vibrated to neutralize outside sonic detection. Invisible laser beams cut across the floor and, coupled to sensing devices, were monitored on video and thermal-sensing screens. The alarm modules would have made any bank envious.

Personally, I thought it nonsense.

The computer team was headed by Cornwall, the stereotype of a genius electronic hacker. His blond hair looked yellow next to pale skin, and the thick, rimless glasses were always askew. Only in his late twenties, Corny had established himself as irreplaceable, and no one doubted it. He waved slightly as I strolled through. We enjoyed a certain respect for each other, although both fully realized we lived on different planets.

This was the true purpose of the agency, a high-speed information system that continually acquired, deciphered, interpreted and projected data and fed it into numerous banks. The eventual destinations formed an impressive array of intelligence organizations at Langley, New York, Fairfax, Washington, Norfolk and, when the political climate was just right, several others.

Source material came from every conceivable network of communication, then was taken apart and pieced together by Corny's young scientists.

The complex funding was provided through an intricate maze of bureaucratic mystery and bogus departments, all properly budgeted and approved by the highest level, yet sufficiently clandestine and complex to thwart being monitored by overzealous government watchdogs.

At the far end of the floor was Buchannon, behind his monstrous and quite out-of-place desk, old, scarred, walnut and chipped. Instead of working in a private office, he had its partitions removed, preferring to gaze upon his empire of whirring machines, clicking reels and flashing lights.

He disliked fads, claiming only sheep followed others, so when hair was long he had a butch, and as ties changed width, he wore the opposite to the current vogue. Buchannon must have been overtall as a youth and had acquired the habit of stooping slightly, a stance that was magnified by his head, which tipped forward. Cornwall claimed it was from years of looking over the shoulders of too many peons, but with that narrow face and those chiseled cheekbones, I maintained he was a hatchet forever poised in motion, about to strike through an adversary.

Unless summoned, I rarely ventured to the rarefied air of the fifth floor, so we had not seen each other for two months.

"Lost five hundred on yesterday's game," was his opening remark. "Had the Rams all the way and a second to go, some pissy-assed kid kicks for three points. No justice."

Buchannon did not wager real money, but to constantly substantiate his faith in electronics, Corny programmed all statistics, parameters and possible equations for any given sports event, then asked the computer the possible outcome. Neither man knew the difference between a slam dunk and a side out pass, but the game had increased their imaginary winnings from a beginning thousand dollars to a quarter million.

Many times I wanted to tap that data program.

I have long believed people who play with electricity must get zapped once too often, because they all have peculiar idiosyncrasies. Buchannon was a former five-pack chain smoker, and like most converts, was a zealot on the subject. Purified air was circulated through the huge room, but he never stopped finding cigarette ashes on the desk top, which he dabbed away with his fingertips.

"The president of Transcontinental Airlines is named Starkmore," he said, dab, dab, dab. "Three months ago he received a threatening letter saying he was going to lose a plane. At precisely the time indicated, a 707 on the ground in St. Louis blew wide open. It was four in the morning, so nobody was hurt. The loss figures about ten million.''

"Was it a timed or remote detonator?''

"A timer. The bomb was under the cockpit floor in a compartment loaded with electronic gear. The Bureau says it was disguised as a black box. Dozens of them down there, filled with navigation equipment and such. It could have been there for days without being noticed. Ground and flight crews are used to seeing them.''

I didn't like this. Buchannon was not accustomed to making chitchat, especially with me. "Our concern?''

He dabbed at more ash, then examined his fingertip for evidence, ignoring my question. "Standard bang, nothing remarkable, but there were traces of fulminate of mercury.''

"Nasty stuff, but unstable as hell. Damned big pop, though.''

"Yes, more than enough to take out a 707. It's also a bit outdated, but still works. A few days later, Starkmore gets this by mail. That's a copy.''

Starkmore,
Okay, asshole. How'd you like that? The next plane I blow will be in the air with people. If you want to negotiate place an ad in the personals. Say—Mateo, I'm ready to listen.

Mateo

I learned a long time ago it pays to ask dumb questions. How else does one learn anything? "Who's Mateo?''

Buchannon scoffed at the stupid question. "The name has been run through every possible file. Corny came up with several thousand Mateos for our federal friends, plus they provided some of their own. Because of the antiquated explosive, it was believed he, or they, were military trained, probably about twenty years ago. Starkmore ran the ad and received a note to have a million dollars ready. The instructions were quite clear."

"Starkmore paid?"

"He did. Not once, but three times, once every month. After Mateo has the money, he sends Starkmore a note describing where the latest bomb is hidden, and each time it's different. The most recent was a 747 in New Orleans, tucked under a passenger seat where the life vest is stored. It was set for the next day at noon, and could have wiped out three or four hundred people."

"Extortion on the installment plan? That doesn't make sense."

"No shit. Security is impossible with hundreds of TCA planes scattered all over the world. It could be triggered anytime, anywhere."

"And the payoff? How's it made?"

"Strictly amateur night, but so damn simple, I have to admire it." Buchannon nervously checked his slacks for ash. "Mateo uses a legal business courier, or I should say, several of them. God knows how many thousand they have in New York. One is stopped between deliveries, right on the street, and offered a hundred bucks for a quick run. The contact tears a bill in half, gives it to the kid and tells him to pick up a briefcase at the Madison Avenue branch of the Chase Manhattan. He's also given a destination where he's to take the case, along a specific route. Starkmore has been told by letter in advance, so he's waiting at the bank."

"Along with the Feds, I assume."

"Right. The kid shows, gets the briefcase from Starkmore and takes off."

"In front of the Feds?" I asked, incredulously. "They just let him walk away?"

"Right again. Yeah, they look at the kid's map, where he's supposed to go, and radio up to place their spotters. Fat good it's done them so far."

"Let me guess," I interrupted. "The kid never gets to his end point. He's stopped en route and given the other half of the bill, which is exchanged for the money case."

"Correct. He swaps with another innocent courier."

"And the Feds don't know the second leg of the route."

"Or the third, or the fourth, fifth, sixth, ad nauseam."

"Jesus, I don't believe this. The finest agency in the world can't keep up with a silly kids' game of tag?" I said it flippantly, but Buchannon missed the sarcasm.

"Cantrell, have you ever watched them little shits in action? Christ, they go up one-way streets against traffic, through alleys, cut around blocked trucks, down sidewalks, hell, even through hotel lobbies. They whip bikes and scooters around like pros."

"Clever," I admitted, "for a one-shot deal. But our friends should be able to figure something for the next drop. That's incredibly stupid."

"That's just one of the tricks. Mateo has Starkmore convinced he'll detect any kind of tracking plant and let the plane blow, so the Feds are hamstrung to a monitor operation, trying to find the eventual drop."

"Which they haven't been able to do."

"Plus, Mateo adds a new wrinkle every time. Somewhere along the route, out of sight, Mateo's man stops the kid, passes the bill and swaps cases for an identical one. The Feds can't watch every inch, so they spend the afternoon tracking an empty case."

"Cute." I smiled, then hid the expression.

"On the last drop, the tenth courier walked his bike into Macy's and then out came six kids from different exits! Now, how the hell can they keep up with that?"

"I'm becoming impressed. Mateo obviously has no fear of the followers."

"Shit, he's loving it! Rubs their damn noses with every message."

"So, the courier angle has been saturated?"

"Beaten to death. Each one is grabbed later and put through the drill. Mugs, composites, prints, everything. The courier companies are fully cooperating with fliers, meetings with the kids, notices, bureau warnings, the usual shit. But it happens so damn fast. I read several reports. A kid is pedaling along and some guy sticks part of a bill under his nose along with a map. He says to wait there, another rider will be coming in five minutes. If he refuses, he's promised a broken face. He's also warned someone is watching. I tell you, Cantrell, right now I wouldn't doubt anything."

"So, even if the kid is cooperating, he doesn't know if he's the second, third or tenth, or if he's carrying money or the dodge."

"Uh-huh. During the last drop, it was compounded and finally ended with seventeen of those little bastards rolling all over Manhattan, each with an identical case."

"Okay, they can't wire or bug the bikes, so why not a radioactive isotope in the money bag?"

"Like I said, Starkmore is convinced Mateo will spot it. One message said a monitor screen was hidden along the route. The man cannot afford to lose a plane, and the Bureau is following his directives. Hell, they don't want the responsibility, either. If anyone oversteps their authority and causes citizens to get killed, the press will crucify everyone."

"What about the contacts? The guys with the bills?"

"Typical, nondescript, average, beards, glasses, hat, the usual shit. It would fit a million guys. Nothing on known cons, MOs, street snitches, zero. A big fat nothing. It's a new scam with new people."

"How long does it go on? Is there a final figure?"

"Mateo says a year. Yeah, don't look so shocked. It's goddamn insane, but the bastard is pulling it off. And let me tell you, Starkmore is highly pissed. Anything leaks to the media, and he's bankrupt. Who would fly? I hear his top advisers say to shut down the airline."

"Which could also bankrupt him," I interjected, knowing how strange people become about flying. No flight thirteen, or row thirteen, and certainly not planes with a reputation for carrying bombs.

"The rough part is the Feds don't want to stop the couriers, but only track out the final bagman. Wainwright is going nuts."

"Wainwright?" I asked. "Roger Wainwright?"

"Know the man?"

"I trained him for the Company long ago. He dropped out after a few years. His wife couldn't hack the foreign assignments. It's a lousy job for a family man."

"Well, the poor slob is in charge of this mess. Special Agent Wainwright probably wishes he was back with you, sending weather reports from Cambodia."

It was my turn to ignore the dig. "Every monthly payment increases the Bureau's chances of a bust. Why not one big one? Transcontinental can afford it."

"That, Cantrell, is keeping people awake nights. Granted, it makes no sense."

It was a fascinating story, but so far, had no correlation to our particular agency. I waited for Buchannon. When in doubt, shut up.

After a long pause and a few dabs, he continued. "The Bureau is concentrating on the payment sting because it's the most visible and usually where amateurs screw up, but the explosives angle turned something last month. A list of demolition experts trained around two decades ago was enormous, then it was whittled down to a few dozen. One name popped up here in San Francisco—Savino Avalon, an electrician when he works, and all-around bum. On the night before the big bang in St. Louis, he flew to New York with a five-hour stopover in St. Louis. He could have taken a direct flight. Mr. Avalon had more than enough time to plant the bomb."

"What's our source?"

"The idiot used his own credit cards. After a few days in a plush New York hotel, he dropped off the earth. No trace of him."

"Then Avalon appears to be the mechanic."

"Yeah, but it gets better. His girlfriend here, uh, Stella Evans, is a pretty young air brain from Denver. She works the cocktail circuit. Good tips, I suppose, probably a hooker," Buchannon added, classifying everyone. "On the morning of the explosion, her phone bill shows eighteen calls to Avalon's hotel in New York. The first seventeen are only seconds long, but the last one is twenty-one minutes."

"He was out, then she found him."

"Exactly. The news reported the explosion was a fueling error, a freak accident that could never happen again. This was from Starkmore's public-relations people."

"But the Evans girl knew better."

"Yes, and here's the result." He slid several photos to me, and I thanked my habitual skipping of breakfast because I might have lost it. Shown in explicit, gruesome detail were the horribly bashed remains of a once living creature. I think.

Buchannon loved theatrics. "Nice, huh? Two hours after that last phone call, a woman witnessed Evans being grabbed from a Laundromat. The next day her body washed up on the beach after being smashed on the rocks all night."

"Conjecture being she was offed for calling Avalon?"

"Little doubt. Then he disappears. It was probably supposed to look like a straight grab-and-go, rape-and-rob, but no one buys that scam. Every state agency is looking for him."

"I assume the Transcontinental extortion and Starkmore's payoffs are remaining hush. So what pretext is being used?"

"Straight homicide. Nothing complex."

I said no more because I could feel it coming. Experience begets sensitive nerve ends.

"Starkmore has grease, especially with a particular senator who chairs a very important committee on certain budgets. Meaning, the man who indirectly signs our paychecks. When the Feds made a link between this Evans girl, Avalon, Mateo, TCA, bombs *et al*, they moved in hot on the female's death, hoping for anything. Maybe a thread between the cowboys who did it, and New York."

Buchannon waited a minute, which made me uncomfortable. I had to ask. "You mentioned Starkmore's influence."

"There are so many damn jurisdictional gray spots in this, each agency is playing it very tight—federal groups, local police and homicide. Here and New York. Nobody's helping the overall cause. Starkmore is frantic and wants to be certain every possible lead is being followed. Cops are tripping over one another to keep secrets."

I saw the light. "So, with the senator knowing we're independent, competent and not involved, he wants a sort of audit of the ongoing progress?"

"Sort of audit? *Demands* an explanation, would be more accurate. If someone has glitched, he wants to know who and why."

"Look, boss," I said, trying to sound palsy, "a hundred people have pored over this mess. What the hell am I supposed to find?"

"Cantrell, I don't expect you to find a goddamn thing. You don't even have to leave the office. Just sit at your desk and read this pile of shit."

Buchannon pushed an enormous stack of official forms toward me. Goodbye *Times* crossword.

"As near as possible, these are copies of everything filed on this mess from day one, and from a variety of agencies. It was not easy to gather them. Make a summary of everything done so far and create a nice professional report, complete with projections and conjecture. Include some double-talk but be impressive. I don't want to step on toes. Then, we're out of it. The pressure is off the senator, and therefore off us, and it's the Bureau's headache where it belongs."

"Jesus, be reasonable," I protested, my first outburst in ten years. "The girl's dead and buried for months. It's cold. What do you expect?"

"As I told you, not a goddamn thing! Just get the good senator off my back!" The ash-seeking became intense, and I realized Buchannon and I had never had a real confrontation, not once in a decade. He was a true asshole, but a most powerful one, and not to be messed with. Yet it occurred to me he could have pushed it much harder, and just possibly he had the same reservations about this aging child.

"Cantrell, we were forced together by circumstance, but I have no complaints. How often do I ask you for something? Just give me an impressive report, and we'll probably both retire before it's necessary again. Okay?"

I stared at the haphazard pile. "Couple of days?" He smiled.

Paper used on the fifth floor is constructed with an internal bond, sensitive to emitted sound waves at the elevator door, which will not open if triggered. This seemed like ordinary paper. "Am I cleared to take this off the floor?"

"It's been censored in places regarding Starkmore or the airline. Go ahead, I don't care if you sleep with it."

Back at my desk, I pondered the massive file until lunch, my eyes returning to the morgue shots, which ruined the appetite. I've witnessed my share of violence and caused some, but I've never gotten used to it.

I nibbled on a ham and Swiss, gave up and thought about the reports. The investigative thoroughness was incredible, considering the demise was that of an ordinary citizen. Of course, the Feds didn't really care about Stella Evans, they wanted a lead to Mateo. Every speck of dust had been bagged and tested. The inventory from her house alone ran a hundred typed pages and included details about her garbage. Avalon was apparently a frequent visitor, overnights often, although he seemed to roam between motels.

It was a beautiful day, so from curiosity as much as frustration, I drove out to the Richmond district. The current occupant of Stella's rental was dubious about letting me in, but my police inspector's license convinced her I was no threat. Buchannon always provided excellent papers.

I roamed from room to room, taking worthless notes while she carefully observed. It was a standard two-bedroom, single bath, garage underneath, very ordinary, and I learned nothing.

That had been on impulse, but the real purpose of my visit was the house next door and the neighbor who identified the body. Mrs. Nevell had been grilled many times by the blues, then the Feds, but I still wanted to get her impressions firsthand.

There was no reason for secrecy, so I introduced myself. She was sixtyish, with pictures of the grandchildren and dainty glass figurines on the mantel.

Mrs. Nevell invited me into her kitchen, and while brewing tea, rambled on for ten minutes about the horrible crime, and I did not interrupt. She loved the attention.

"Did you know Miss Evans well?" I eventually asked.

"Not personally, if you know what I mean. Oh, we were close neighbors and such, but Stella kept to herself. Mind you, she wasn't stuck up or anything like that, but a very private person."

"Did you know her boyfriend?"

"Sam? Hardly at all. We said hi, but that's about it."

"Did you ever see other guests? Friends? Relatives?"

"Nobody. 'Course I'm not nosy, so I don't see everything. But Stella did tell me she was an orphan and didn't have anyone close."

I asked several questions about Savino Avalon, but it was clear Mrs. Nevell knew very little.

She sighed a long moan. "The funeral was so sad. There were only a few of us from the neighborhood and four people from the restaurant where she worked. Even Sam wasn't there. The police said they couldn't find him."

"The report states she came to your house two days before the, uh, tragedy."

"I remember exactly because it was our forty-fifth anniversary. We had a small barbecue in the backyard for some friends, and I saw her car pull up. I asked her over for champagne." Mrs. Nevell smiled. "You know, Stella really did have a good time."

"Was she nervous, upset, or act unusual in any way?"

"On the contrary, like I told the police, Stella seemed quite happy." Mrs. Nevell suddenly jumped up. "I almost forgot." She opened a drawer. "These were developed a few weeks ago. Herb is a marvelous photographer, but he keeps film in that camera forever."

She handed me a stack of three-by-fives and explained who every person was and a personal tidbit about each guest. "Here's Stella," she said proudly.

Herb was indeed a gifted amateur, and Stella Evans was not a pretty fluff like Buchannon had said. This was a remarkably beautiful young woman. It was an extremely close shot, full face, showing a warm, vivacious yet secretive smile and perfect white teeth. Her high cheekbones were set in an oval face outlined with long black hair, not straight or curly, but a gentle wave that seemed to surround her. Stella must have had Gypsy blood in her background because those huge dark eyes seemed to leap out and burn into the soul.

The picture haunted me, recalling what she had looked like after being pounded on the rocks for a day. I felt sick again. "If you have the negative, may I keep this?"

"Certainly," she offered graciously. "I was planning on having an enlargement made, anyway. To remember her. Lord, such a sad thing."

With no purpose in mind, I drove four blocks to the Laundromat. It was narrow and about sixty feet long, with a rear exit. According to the reports, the witness was just entering the front when she saw two men at the far end dragging the screaming and kicking Evans girl out the back. The woman had the presence of mind to run through and catch a license number as the car raced away.

It was stolen and found abandoned days later. Dozens of latent prints were found but none of value. One smudge might have belonged to a local shooter, but he could not be found.

It seemed everyone who dealt with Mateo disappeared or died.

I looked over the parking lot, then drove home to my tiny Diamond Heights apartment. I rewound the tape and listened again to Mrs. Nevell while comparing official notes, but found nothing. I always record interviews secretly because people often freak at the sight of an exposed, running machine. Even worse is taking notes, because you miss the real story while concentrating on writing. A recorder gives me the chance to study their faces for nuances, gestures and hesitations.

But everything was right, so I erased it.

Exhausted, I dumped the massive file on the table, took one last look at the photo of the strikingly enchanting Stella Evans, then gagged my way through a TV dinner. After the late news, I poured a deep, hot bubble bath, my great indulgence. Soaking and armed with three inches of very expensive Napoléon brandy, I stared at Kate.

Her picture had been carefully sealed to prevent water damage and taped above the faucets. It was my own private world, and I was never quite certain if that photograph kept me sane or drove me closer to the edge.

I toasted her several times. "Where are you right now?" I asked, feeling melancholy. "No matter who you're with, old girl, he'll never love you like I did."

It was a decade since I had seen or heard from her, but the pain would not leave. I ached all over each time I repeated the ritual, but I could never stop. It was my one last grasp at sanity.

Other than reactionary muscle response, neurophysiologists have determined it takes four-tenths of a second for outside stimuli to reach human conscious awareness. I stared at Kate more intently than usual because something was drastically wrong.

It was like standing near a railroad track, hearing, seeing, feeling the monstrous freight train approaching. It takes forever, but when it passes, the world stops as the roaring hurricane strikes.

Suddenly, the locomotive screamed right through my brain, and although the water was very hot, I began to shiver.

I just realized someone had murdered the wrong girl.

# 2. HOMEWORK

JUMPING FROM THE TUB, I ran naked to the dining table, dripping sudsy water on the carpet. I went through the reports again and again.

It was inconceivable that a hundred trained investigators could possibly make such a blunder. I had to be wrong, but as I evaluated the information with a different attitude, seemingly insignificant but vital details jumped at me. I circled them in red, and the number kept growing.

Trembling with cold, I threw on my robe and examined the material once more, trying to pinpoint a logical reason for the monumental error, then found it.

The first officer on the beach scene made the initial report, a highway patrolman more accustomed to traffic problems than bodies washed up on the sand. His efforts were exemplary under the circumstances, but with no identification, the girl was named a typical Jane Doe.

According to the dates, it was five days before a sharp-eyed detective connected the kidnapping of Stella Evans and the body. Homicide then took jurisdiction, looking for leads to the killer.

Federal agents were researching demolition experts, hoping for the airline extortion tie-in, but it was another three weeks before they made an association from Mateo to Avalon to Stella Evans.

By then, the body had been identified, autopsied and buried. Through necessity, the Feds took all their information regarding the body from the earlier data.

The initial mistake was relayed like dominoes from one agency to the next, each assuming previous material to be correct, primarily because they were seeking the wrong information. A classic case of not seeing the forest for the trees.

So who was killed? And where was Stella Evans?

After fitful little sleep, I arrived early next morning and rang Buchannon. "Must see you right away," I said, and was granted a presence. "I might have something," I told him.

"Like what?" he asked as I approached. "Did somebody blow it? Who's to blame?"

"Nothing firm, but there's a good possibility of . . . a serious oversight," I began, then decided to withhold for now.

"Shit," he muttered, irritated with my independence, but knowing I had the field operative's right to remain mute temporarily.

"I need Cornwall and a good legman from the fourth floor."

Buchannon considered that. "Okay, you can have Barry Dirkson, but only until you produce or I cancel it. Same with Corny."

I thought about Dirkson. Good man, young, eager, probably my replacement someday. He had been exposed to field training beyond the normal detective work, and this was a logical exercise.

"Remember," Buchannon cautioned, "this is strictly hush, and only to audit the homicide of Stella Evans. Nothing to be said to Mr. Dirkson about TCA or the extortion. He's not cleared for that. Corny did the code work on inbound messages so he knows, but avoid the topic if you please."

"Understood," I agreed, surprised it had been so easy. I had been prepared to divulge my suspicions if he refused.

Buchannon spoke a few words into his phone, and minutes later Barry Dirkson made his grand entrance from the elevator. A first-timer is quite noticeable, attempting to appear casual and nonchalant, but unable to prevent himself from staring at the electronic superroom. Dirkson came at us cautiously, quick glances to either side as if trespassing, violating the innermost secret kingdom.

He reminded me of the reserve quarterback, standing all season on the sidelines, not wanting the starter to be injured, yet knowing that was his only chance to play. Intuitively, I dislike overanxious players.

Dirkson was tall, square shouldered and lean from those required gym sessions. He actually took that stuff seriously. His thirty years were denied by the clean-shaven boyish face and eternally affixed grin. A likable enough young man, if a bit too Joe College and regimented.

Buchannon had a skill for selecting raw talent, and that alone indicated Dirkson was qualified. Still, I would have preferred to see him experience a few years and bruises before sharing a serious mission with him in the cold.

But not to worry, I told myself, that was all behind me.

Corny approached the gathering, and Buchannon acknowledged rank by addressing him first. "Cornwall, delegate everything until further notice. You and Dirkson will temporarily report to Cantrell. He is Control, as of now."

"Uh, Mr. Buchannon," Dirkson began hesitantly, having only talked to the great man a few times in five years. "I was assigned to finish up—"

"Drop it."

"Yes, sir," he stammered.

Strike one on the kid. I would later explain he never questions Captain Marvel unless he has nothing to lose. Like me.

I led the two downstairs into the coffee room and closed the door. Everything on the top floor was wired. "Is this place clean?" I asked Corny. He nodded. "Good. First, let me bore you with old shit. But I want it clear, I am Control, meaning you both report any and all findings to me and me alone. I will convey upstairs. Understood?"

I then summarized the death and investigation of Stella Evans, along with my theory that another female had been killed and misidentified. I produced several pages of the file and explained the red-circled items.

"I have learned about this woman, her styles and preferences, and nothing matches with the dead female." I pointed to the inventory. "Look at the report on the wash found in the Laundromat."

Dirkson scanned the pages. "It says here everything was held unclaimed, then the FBI had it reviewed more than a month later. What's the FBI doing on a local homicide?"

Take away his strike one, the kid was sharp. "I'll explain later. Compare that with the list of her personal garments at home. Stella's a natural type, preferring soft hues and earthy colors, like browns and greens. Nothing flashy. The wash load had bright colors—red, orange and purple. Also, there was a partially filled clothes hamper in Stella's bathroom. How many people go through the hassle of a Laundromat and leave dirty clothes behind?"

Corny spoke for the first time. "Maybe that's all she could carry?"

"Stella had a car. Now, Corny, do you wear underwear? Shorts?"

"Huh? Sure."

"Do you own more than one pair?"

"Of course."

"There was a single bra in the laundry load, just one, and none anywhere in the house, clean or dirty. I cannot believe that any woman who wears bras would own just one. I maintain Stella Evans did not own bras or wear them. Period. The dead girl did. Stella had several pair of ordinary cotton bikini panties, very plain, but those in the wash were nylon. Different styles completely."

Dirkson and Cornwall stared at me, uncertain if this was merely coincidence, a misinterpretation of explainable variances, or I was going senile.

"And the sizes?" Corny asked. "Any correlation?"

"Mostly in the medium ranges. A few numbered sizes, but mixed, nothing conclusive either way."

Dirkson had continued to study the lists. "Why didn't homicide or the federal investigators find this significant? They've been on this for months."

Good question, and to acquire dedicated assistants, I had to convince them. "Because they were not looking for it. Their job was to find the perpetrators, not identify a body. That had been done. Remember, the body had been properly ID'd, and completely established. Why go over accepted facts? They had no interest in her belongings or in reviving any question of her identity because she was dead and her boyfriend had her triggered. *He* is the target, not her."

"Makes some sense," Dirkson agreed.

"Thanks," I replied gruffly, as if I needed collaboration.

"What about the ID?" Corny asked.

"It's very weak," I said, "but that's my department."

Dirkson was looking from one list to another, occasionally shaking his head. "I just don't see how experienced cops would miss this, if it's really important."

I sighed patiently. "Spot a man looking at his watch and immediately ask him the time. He'll look again even if only five seconds have passed. The first was reactive habit, but it didn't register on the conscious mind. The same with these reports. They've been studied a thousand times, but nothing registered, because they were searching for leads to the whereabouts of Savino Avalon, not meaningless junk like unmatched underwear."

It was obvious they were not convinced, and I was becoming irritated, unaccustomed to being challenged as control officer. Getting old and set, I thought.

"Look, there's one item after another. The wash load had expensive designer jeans, but Stella is unpretentious with ordinary jeans from Sears. Nothing matches, nothing."

Corny was thumbing the medical reports. "What about pathology? How could they have glitched so badly?"

"That was my biggest problem, but I spent an hour placing the events in order, and I'm certain of what happened. But that's also my problem. There are some loose items to confirm."

They were still dubious and with good reason. It was very thin, and all conjecture so far, but I purposely held back the zinger for the moment. It was too soon.

"Consider common sense," I urged. "Maybe there's a logical reason for this, even washing a friend's clothes as a favor, but there are flaws in that, too. Hell, we could pick it apart and find weak explanations for everything, but think on this very carefully. Stella Evans has just learned her boyfriend is deeply involved with a serious federal rap that could get him twenty to life, easy. She tries to phone him in New York time and time again and finally connects. Shortly after that last call, she simply loads grocery sacks with clothes, leaves behind her basket and drives four blocks to do some wash. Corny, thinking logically, do you buy that?"

"Females and logic are not necessarily synonymous," he joked, "but no, I don't buy that. In fact, it's the one aspect that gives your theory the most credence."

"Fine," I pounced, not wanting to lose that bit of faith. "Dirkson, you dig out her neighborhood. I know it's been thoroughly covered, but don't forget, the first teams were scrubbing for leads on Avalon or the alleged perpetrators. You're digging for Stella, anything about her, and especially her female friends. The victim had Evans's car. Also, take a missing-persons angle from the top. Runaways, errant wives, the lot. Try for a connection with a missing female about the same build and age, around five-nine, mid-twenties, during the same period."

He nodded, feverishly taking notes.

"Corny, you'll love this. Where does a scared girl run when she realizes someone's trying to kill her? When she's probably terrified and needs safety? Right. Home. If for no other reason, it gives her a psychological edge. Concentrate on the Denver area. Look for an entirely new person. New accounts, addresses, banking, car loans, registration, insurance, magazine subscriptions, anything at all. Don't forget new employment, social security numbers, bar and restaurant jobs. Remember, you're looking for a woman who did not exist more than three months ago. If she has a past before that, it's not Stella. She will seem to have just been born. A whole new identity."

Cornwall breathed a long gasp. "What do you want after lunch?"

"Corny, let's not be modest. You feed data into the biggest computer systems in the country, and it's no secret you can tap most of them. Put that magic to work, and consider it a challenge."

He removed the crooked glasses and gave me a myopic grin.

"One more thing, Corny. We both know that right after I leave now, Buchannon will question you. You would never compromise yourself, nor would I ask it. Tell the truth, but only what you're asked. Okay? Just say I'm convinced the key to the murder is in her past, in Denver, and that might lead to Mateo. That much will be true.''

He thought long on that. "Seems okay to me.''

"Who's Mateo?" Dirkson asked.

Damn kid didn't miss anything. "In good time. One more thing, Dirkson. Stella's credit cards were used after the murder. The cops figured they were fenced. Dig into that, plus anything financial about her. If I'm right, and she did a rabbit to Denver, how'd she pay for it?''

"Assuming you're right," he replied, "why wouldn't she just hide right here in town?''

"Possible, possible, but I've studied this girl and all the interviews with acquaintances. Stella's a loner, and I think she'll go to ground, preferably someplace she's familiar with, and that has to be Denver.''

I had to know the next answer. "Corny, is my home phone tapped?''

He laughed openly, a rare event. "Believe it or not, even Mr. Buchannon has reservations about snooping on agents with class-A security.''

"What about mine?" Dirkson snapped, glaring at Cornwall.

"Sorry, nothing personal, you understand," Corny explained. "But I'm not class A myself. I have the loathsome task of listening to my sister talk to her boyfriends.''

"Okay," I instructed. "You both call my home whenever you have something, no matter how trivial, and no matter what time. Use pay phones only, not from your houses, and especially not from this building.''

"Why the secrecy?" Dirkson wondered.

"Everything I officially have will be given to Buchannon because our purpose is to provide information. He'll initial it and Corny will send it, and if I'm right, within minutes I'll be invited to the federal building for a million questions.''

"If you are right," Corny added, knowing something of organizational jealousy, "the Feds are going to look damn silly."

"Exactly, and if that's the case, you can bet we'll be pushed out, and they'll take the credit after blaming somebody else for the glitch.'' I leaned over the coffee table and whispered. "This is a very, *very* big deal, and if we provide anything concrete, I don't think we should miss out on the credit.''

Motivation comes in many forms, and these were young, aggressive men with a large future. Corny was already at the top, but there is always ego, and his type of research is usually unrecognized. I had ignored attaboy letters in my file for decades, but it works for some.

It took an hour in pathology to find my man. The autopsy report was signed by doctors, but I didn't want medical mumbo jumbo. No, I needed the lab technician when the identification was verified.

The scrawled initials belonged to a young Oriental, who no doubt knew every homicide detective in the city, so I used my bogus FBI badge.

"Yeah, sure, I remember that one. I've never seen that many people interested in a non-VIP. Big-time, huh?''

I gave a conspiratorial wink. "Yeah, big-time.''

"Giant drug ring or something?''

"Or something. Tell me, the reports had no indication of a fingerprint match. Why not?''

"She was a Jane Doe for days. It's SOP, sending prints to the FBI, as you know. They have everything from military to state licensing. No match anywhere. Kind of unusual, huh?''

"Not everyone gets a driver's license. It's pretty common these days, especially for younger people. I think it started back in the Nam days when kids were burning draft cards. Never get a card or a license or a social security number. How about the dental records?"

"The same. We shot the X rays, and the police sent them all over the Bay area, but there's a lot of dentists around here. There is no national record system. You know, it's a myth people can be traced that way. You need a set of X rays, then a person, and sure, I match them. But it's not the same as fingerprints. Just having X rays or just a person, and you have nothing. Almost impossible."

"There was a positive ID from neighbors, the Nevells."

"Right, and that's when we stopped looking. There was no need to continue. They had a positive make, so why bother?"

"I see. Your initials say you were present."

He became nervous. "Hey, is something wrong? Yeah, I was there but that's SOP, and so were two detectives and another cop. They verified everything, you know, I just watched."

"Nothing's wrong, but I'm stuck with the follow-up. No sweat." He calmed slightly, and my right hand was keying the pocket recorder. "Tell me about the reaction of the Nevells. How long did they view the body?"

"Hell, I don't know. The usual."

"Five seconds? Five minutes? An hour?"

"A few seconds, I suppose. The old lady was really shook. She almost passed out. The husband had to hold her up when her knees went."

"Did Mr. Nevell actually view and identify at all, or was he concentrating on helping his wife?"

"Of course he observed! That's the law. *And* he positively made the ID!" the young man snapped, thereby protesting a bit too much.

I vividly remembered the pictures of the bashed victim and seriously doubted if her own mother would have recognized her. I was completely convinced the body was not Stella Evans, but more nails in the fence make it stronger. It was time to call in a marker.

LIEUTENANT MATHEWSON of robbery and I went back a long time, and we unofficially exchanged favors. If he needed out-of-town information, he could get it through normal channels, but with antiquated telecommunications, waiting time, paperwork, requests and police priorities, it often took days.

One call to me, and Corny had it in five minutes. The lieutenant owed me one.

"Matt," I said over the pay phone, "I need a favor."

"You got it."

I gave him the names and dates. "Two suits and a uniform were present during a positive ID on a Jane Doe. Would you approach each one individually and ask if he is one hundred percent confident the Nevell couple made a positive ID? Absolutely positive? Unofficial, Matt. Call my home and it'll record. I promise to erase it."

"Consider it done."

It was perfectly logical the Nevells made a hasty mistake. Stella's red Pinto was abandoned at the Laundromat. A woman claimed to see her being abducted by two men. Stella never returned home. The police came to the Nevells and requested them to identify the body of Stella Evans. They were *told* it was their neighbor, and everything supported that idea.

Ergo: as I thought, the ID was a sham.

It was also quite understandable how the killers could make the same mistake. Avalon had made the hit contract from New York to local cowboys who did not know Stella, either. By best estimate, it was less than two hours from the time she talked to her boyfriend to the snatch. Obviously, a very rush job. Avalon feared her panicking and calling the blues so he ordered a quickie kill. No finesse, no time for it. Anyone fitting Stella's description, even vaguely, coming from her house and getting into her car, must be the right girl.

Everyone on this deal had fouled out.

After I dialed my home, the recorder came on, and I keyed the replay for messages. Dirkson had said he was canvassing the neighborhood for a second female and decided to try the evening, after the work crowd came home. That was good thinking, but zero progress.

The remainder of my afternoon was spent running down useless leads, ones already pounded out by earlier investigators. I expected them to be nonproductive, and they were, but it had to be done. Driving back on Market, I saw lights in the upper floor of the Morris Building. Being on premises after hours was authorized for only a select few, and I knew Corny was working late.

It was after ten, and this tired aching frame was screaming for rest, but I didn't have the heart to crash while my assistant was still hacking away.

Entering the building after it was secured was quite involved. Only Buchannon, myself, Cornwall and two others possessed the specially designed key. I opened the stainless steel box beside the front entrance. Inside was an alphanumeric microprocessor display. After keying the inhibitor, I entered my own complex code. The system knew who was knocking at the door and disabled a few alarms. One entry mistake and all hell would break loose. Rumor was, the first floor could be saturated with Mace. I didn't doubt it. Buchannon loved gadgets.

The door opened, and immediately infrared sensors and motion detectors began tracking my every step. I knew Corny upstairs had been alerted and was watching me on video. It was possible to key up codes at the hidden elevator panel, but Cornwall saved me time by clearing through from above. Inside the elevators, an emitter/sensor could detect any ferrous object with a greater density than .25 lbs/in³.

I often wondered how much this cost the taxpayers. The system could rival anything in existence.

"Hungry?" I asked Corny. "I can make a deli run."

"Naw," he answered, not turning away from the terminal.

There was no need to ask for progress. I could tell.

Over his shoulder he moaned rather than spoke. "I have thirteen hundred and eighty-odd new female identities shown in the Denver area over the past three months. So far," he added glumly.

"Thirteen hundred and . . . I don't believe it!"

Corny spun around, glaring. "Have you ever heard of such things as marriage and divorce? Women change surnames all the time. How about girls living with the folks and then striking out on their own? The info banks consider these new people, just created overnight. This doesn't even count Lord knows how many moved to Denver."

"Jesus, can they be checked?"

"Of course, but one at a time, boss, one at a time. I've eliminated a few hundred by age or ethnic background, but I still face the majority."

"Damn it to hell!" I growled, not having expected this. I watched him work for a while, with no idea what was happening. "Did the man approach you?" I asked Corny.

"The first possible chance he had. I explained your theory about Mateo and Stella and the possible connection in Denver. It satisfied him, I guess. He couldn't find anything in the reports about Denver and figures you might have something going by identifying this Mateo guy from there." Corny looked at me. "Luckily he didn't push it, Cantrell, because I would have told him everything. I have no choice. If he thought there was any possibility the Evans girl is alive and we were holding out, well, I wouldn't want to be in the same room with him."

"Understood."

"I sure hope you're not expecting some miracle. Let me tell you, I've already got a handful of untrackable names. Roughly ten percent. That means more than a hundred when I'm through. Surely you didn't think I'd push a few buttons and out pops the magic one?"

"I don't know what I thought."

"Well, it doesn't work that way. Look, I'm going to try something different. Instead of a direct link with names and past IDs, I'm resetting for an association. You know, similarities and such."

"That's your department. Whatever works," I said helplessly.

Then Corny did something that to the best of my knowledge no one had ever witnessed before. He took a crumpled pack of cigarettes from a drawer and lit one. He smoked like a twelve-year-old, no inhaling, blowing out quick little puffs of smoke, and holding the cigarette between finger and thumb like a schoolgirl. The exhaustion and frustration showed on his face.

"Cantrell," he began slowly, "what I'm trying to say is, this most likely is a dead end. My loyalty is known, and I'll stay on this until instructed to abort. You're Control and I follow orders. But I have to be honest." He hesitated a minute. "We don't have much going for us. Everything is weak hypothesis, disjointed and flawed. I've thought of numerous explanations for the laundry business. I even applied very liberal constraints and parametered all data through modems to the Hewlett-Packard probability tank. It's the best in the world. And it's not very impressed, either. Sorry, boss, I had to say it."

I patiently explained the erroneous identification from the Nevells and the lack of fingerprint or dental matchups.

He shrugged his shoulders sympathetically, and it was time for the zinger. I had purposely avoided it, knowing Buchannon would push Corny, and this would definitely go to the Bureau within seconds. Five minutes later, a dozen agents would descend on Denver.

"Corny, listen to me. After the so-called positive ID by the Nevells, everyone ignored Stella because they were assured she was the victim. Mind-set. Once convinced of something, people resist opposition and overlook anything contrary."

"So, Dr. Cantrell?" he asked sarcastically.

"So, Mr. Cornwall, Stella Evans has very dark eyes, and the murdered girl's were blue. Now, stick that in your probability tank!"

# 3. DIGGING

Leaving the agency and suddenly pumped with enthusiasm, I stopped at cocktail lounges where Stella Evans had worked. Turnover was rapid, and most employees had never heard of Stella, but a few recalled her enchanting looks.

The last I visited was her most recent and my final hope for anything useful. I found the night manager in the upper-class, expensively priced establishment and made a mental note to ensure Corny was checking such places in Denver. They would be her logical choice.

The manager was undoubtedly impressed with local law, so I used the San Francisco Police Department credentials. I was prepared for most contingencies. The man cooperated but could not offer much. He was merely the boss and worried about profits and books, and didn't have time to know his people beyond the workplace.

"She must have had one special friend. Who would that be?"

"Linda, I suppose, that blonde over there." He indicated a tall, stunning beauty in a tight, floor-length dress, slit up the side. Nice.

"I don't want to interfere with your business," I said to him, "but I must talk to her. It won't take ten minutes. Could you send Linda over when it's convenient?"

Common courtesy has two advantages beyond ordinary politeness. One, nightclubs are frequented by cops expecting special favors because of tin badges, and two, I didn't want him upset and complaining downtown. The blues had no one assigned there, and I could be in deep shit. Buchannon had juice, but impersonating an officer was frowned upon by certain departments. Deception was acceptable as long as you got away with it. If caught, you stood alone. Carrying funny paper had its risk.

It paid off, and she stood beside me in five minutes. "We can talk back there," she said, pointing to an empty office.

"I understand you were Stella Evans's best friend."

She lit an extralong cigarette, and it looked ridiculous and out of proportion to that pretty mouth. "It really breaks my heart," Linda said, sighing, "that she considered me her best friend. God, she must have been so alone. I hardly knew her. We were work buddies, I guess you'd call it. We never saw each other away from here except one day for lunch, and that time we just made female gossip. You know, we talked about creepy customers and jerk bartenders."

"Did you ever meet her boyfriend, Savino Avalon?"

"He came in near closing sometimes, and they'd leave together, but no, we never talked."

"Did he ever come in with anyone else?"

She thought a moment. "Not that I remember."

"How about Stella? Did she talk to anyone else? Another employee? Relatives that dropped by? Acquaintances? Another woman?"

"I'm really sorry. I'd like to help, but I've been asked all this before. Look at this place. It's only Wednesday and packed to the walls. I never have time for anything but my tables. I don't see what happens."

"Well, thanks anyhow. Uh, I promise this is no hit. You close in thirty minutes, and there's an all-night coffee shop a block down. I'll be there if you'd like coffee and pie."

Linda stared into my face a long minute, undoubtedly the way she had done with a thousand men before. "I might just like that," she finally responded.

It was more than an hour before she came into the coffee shop. "Sorry, I should have mentioned we have to bus our tables before leaving."

After the customary small talk, Linda lowered her voice. "What I said earlier about it being sad, well, I was thinking about Stella's funeral. There were Tina, Marty, Babs and myself from the club, a few neighbors, and that's it. God, that shook me."

"I got the impression she preferred seclusion."

Linda ordered banana cream and tea. "You know, you may be right. I've never known such an independent person in my life."

The woman then related tiny episodes about Stella, anecdotes that filled in her overall character. I had hoped for just that. To Linda, I was no longer a bothersome cop investigating a crime, but a man making chatty talk on neutral ground about a mutual acquaintance. Cocktail waitresses usually know enough dirt to put dozens of people behind bars, and they naturally become anxious about contact with the law.

As I expected, Linda knew a great deal more about Stella than she realized. "And this one time," she continued without any prodding from me, "Stella's car battery went dead. Sam was supposed to be a super mechanic, but she would never ask him for help. She took the battery out with pliers, hauled it to a gas station in a shopping cart for charging, then put it back in. All by herself! I told her she was nuts, but Stella was too proud to ask anyone for help."

"Or simply too independent." I thanked Linda and left two numbers in case she thought of something else. "Anything at all," I insisted. "It's really important."

Investigators fail or succeed depending on their degree of empathy with the person, whether the target is friendly or enemy. One must identify and think like the prey. Sometimes it takes years to learn this, and many never do. It's a special skill, a gift perhaps, and it becomes the undefinable talent that cannot be taught at the academy.

In the titanic struggle for control of the African desert during World War II, General Patton did not simply research Rommel's strategies, but also the man's personality, which had enormous impact on his tactics.

All my directions and theories were based on interpretation of Stella's mental and emotional profile as I judged it. She was a loner, a survivor, independent, and trusted no one. Infinitesimal scraps of data were meaningless when viewed in isolation, but collectively, each fragment formed a larger picture. While the blues chased a killer, I was tracking the victim. A puzzle. My kind of game. We were playing on Cantrell turf now, and I would find my girl.

My girl, I thought to myself, what an odd notion.

It was late, but this aged frame needed another ritual. In the hot suds, I toasted Kate's picture. That was two nights straight, meaning I was becoming quite depressed. "Did you leave me, old girl, or did I drive you away?"

Women should not become involved with men whose lives are hush. It rarely works. Females possess an insatiable need to know everything about their man, from his first screw to the previous girlfriend. In this rotten business, we are trained and conditioned to become nonpersons, to blend unseen and unknown with no past. It stinks.

I switched on the message recorder. Lieutenant Mathewson did not identify himself. "About the matter we discussed today. One thinks he's superdick and was part of the original hunch concerning the two females being the same person. He got a pat on the back, so naturally he's fully convinced it was a positive make. I pressed the other two and both admitted they'd hate to bet their badges on the ID. I don't know what you're up to, Cantrell, but I do know a little about this mess. Take care, old buddy, it's tender ground.''

Five seconds passed then came Dirkson's voice. "I have a little something, nothing big, but too much to record. I'll call you in the morning at eight."

"Shit!" I cursed. It was almost 4:00 a.m. Before crashing, I recalled my word to Matt and placed the cassette in a degausser for erasing.

It seemed like only minutes later. "Morning," Dirkson said happily at eight sharp. I hate cheery people in the morning. There is something unnatural about it. Being grumpy, I unloaded.

"Dirkson, don't ever do that again! I gave specific orders to update me on anything you turned, regardless of how trivial. I don't care if you yak into the recorder for an hour. You are just one cog in this operation. What if you had a stroke in the night? You report the instant you have anything. Understood?"

There was an awkward silence, then he calmly asked, "Is that why you're keeping everything from Mr. Buchannon?"

Smartass punk. "Okay, your point. What've you got?"

"There is definitely a female friend. A few doors from the Laundromat is a pizza parlor. The Evans girl sometimes came in with a tall, young, dark-haired female while they waited for the wash. The pizza cook doesn't know her but remembers because the two girls played liars' dice to see who changed the clothes from washers to dryers."

That would fit Stella's personality. She would not accept any kind of assistance or advantage herself. "Did the second girl ever go in alone or with anyone else?"

Dirkson waited before answering. "I didn't think to ask that."

"Take away your point. Anything else?"

"I talked with the eyewitness to the abduction. She viewed it through a dirty window from seventy-two feet. I measured the place. Her ophthalmologist says her distance vision is fair. One more thing. She told her story straight through, almost word for word from her original affidavit. The woman has it memorized, but when I asked random questions out of sequence, she got confused and contradicted herself."

Memory is a funny thing. It becomes conditioned by reflection and repetition, and after she'd told the story many times to anyone who would listen, her recollections were enhanced, distorted, and errors firmly planted. Attorneys frequently interview their key witnesses one last time before a trial. Testimony secured months, even years earlier, is suddenly embellished with lucid details never mentioned before. Many cases fly right out the window.

"Anything on the missing credit cards?"

"Like you said, that trail's been beaten to death. The cops figure the two cards were taken by the hit men, then fenced. All the clerks have been quizzed. Zero. Everything bought was under fifty bucks, so no authorization was necessary. Signatures are crude, but clerks never check. They've been shown photos of known card buyers and passers, but nothing yet."

"The one photo they didn't see was Stella, because she was supposedly dead. Try one of her."

"Will do. According to store charge codes, she moved around the departments and outfitted herself. Mostly clothes, notions, one bag."

"Good work. Wring out the pizza cook about the second girl and any possible third parties. Get an artist's workup of her and pass it around."

"Right, and uh, I'll call in."

Pieces of the puzzle were locking together, but we still had only my hunch Stella would return to Denver. That worried me more than anything. I knew she was alive, but where? How far can a girl run? I remembered Cornwall's discouraging statistic of more than a thousand new females in that area. If she was not there, and we had to scour the country, I would have no choice but to notify Buchannon to flag other agencies and increase our resources.

At times like that, I honestly wondered why I was doing it.

In the office, I pondered my options. Stella had obviously charged to the limit, then destroyed the cards. She was being quite clever, this little lady, making it appear that professionals used her credit in a quick buying spree, then dumped the evidence. Stella had also ignored her checkbook. The account showed two hundred dollars that was untouched. Using it would have indicated she was still alive. Tricky, tricky.

Based on the large tips I saw Linda earn the night before, Stella must have done okay, yet lived modestly and spent little. Where did she throw it? On drugs? Doubtful, there were no signs in the house and homicide had checked that angle thoroughly. On Savino? Possibly, but not likely. If my theories were correct, I was certain Stella was a hoarder. Was it hidden in a sock? A safe-deposit box?

I was considering these possibilities and how to dissect them when I felt a slight shudder. Buchannon was paging me. How long did I dare hold out?

"Cantrell," he said without hesitation, then left me standing there waiting while he completed some mundane task. I think he read that in a management book, and it signified to me who was God, as if I didn't know. "What gives?" he finally asked.

"Meaning?"

"Meaning, tell me what you have, in detail, now."

I took a breath. "I'm convinced the key to Stella Evans lies in Denver, which could springboard to Mateo and extortion, but I have nothing hard yet."

"You think Mateo knew her there? That's why she was offed? Avalon, too? Maybe a team that went sour?"

"I don't know, but that's a possibility. Corny may have something soon. Which reminds me," I said, and slid a travel voucher for five thousand dollars under his dabbing fingers.

"Well, we are really going first class, aren't we?"

"If it turns my way, I will have to grease the skids."

"Keep very accurate records," Buchannon mused, as he signed the chit. "I will need Cornwall tomorrow, so you have only today. It's best to perform some miracles. Our senator friend would like an update. Do not disappoint me." He paused, Buchannon's way of indicating something profound was coming. "You could have Corny and Dirkson indefinitely, provided there's progress. If it's good, well, you know what I mean."

I did. "Let you know," I said, and walked away.

Buchannon had said something that I had purposely blocked from my mind, but had to eventually face. There was always the possibility that Stella Evans was not innocent, but directly involved with the TCA extortion scheme. She might have said the wrong thing to Avalon on the phone, and he ordered her termination. When she realized the situation, Stella did the rabbit. Possible, possible.

I passed by Corny. "How many to go?"

"Four hundred and fifty-six."

"Shit. Yeah, I know, one at a time."

"The problem is much of the info is on hard copy, not programmed. To eliminate a name, I have to backtrack on each one, trying to find some past detail that was recorded on a prior data bank. Bounced checks, refused credit, a driver's license, something. A single name might take me ten seconds or an hour. Or I might never crack it. I think you're going to have to leg it for a final screen."

"I'm ready to go. Just give me a list."

"I'm still working on the association angle. Friends, neighbors, anyone she knew, based on the skimpy info I have. School records, city directories, and if they were foolish enough to add their name and address to one of those census questionnaires. That's always a good source."

"I thought that shit was for population figures."

"It is, mostly, but if you believe that's the only purpose, well, I have a gold-colored bridge for sale, good price, been in the family for years. Special discount for seniors."

"I hear you," I mumbled, losing faith, particularly since I did not understand how he performed this magic.

"Ah, Cantrell, I apologize for doubting your…ability," Cornwall said sheepishly. "Thinking about it, I understand now why you didn't want me to know about the eye color. Buchannon would have stormed the palace. I should have realized this was more than unmatched laundry. Sorry."

"Corny, I wish I could take credit for brilliant deduction, but it was a fluke. Her neighbor gave me a photo, and those eyes wouldn't let go. Hypnotic. I had just been studying the pathology report, and the truth slapped me in the face. Five minutes later and I would have missed it. Pure luck."

Standing up and feeling tired, I patted him on the shoulder. "A fluke," I repeated. "Besides, she might not have run to Denver."

"What then?"

"Then, my friend, I swallow all pride and confess to Buchannon."

"Don't worry, we'll find our girl."

It was some time later I felt a trace of satisfaction. Corny had said "our girl," meaning this was no longer an exercise in analytical computations. Stella Evans was more than digital information on little chips, and Corny was locked into the challenge. Like me, he had become determined, committed, obsessed with the chase.

On the top floor, musical tones signaled outside calls for specific individuals. I heard my tune and grabbed a phone. It was Linda from the nightclub. I told her I was busy and would call back shortly.

There were no safe phones in the Morris Building, so I dialed from a pay booth on the corner.

"I've been thinking about Stella," she began, "and what we talked about last night. I tried to explain why she didn't trust anybody. You know, about when she was young."

"I know a little. Her mother abandoned her. The father was career Army and bounced Stella through girls' homes like an orphan. After a few years, he stopped writing and later was presumed dead sometime after his discharge."

"Right, at least that far. I shouldn't tell you this because I promised, but maybe that doesn't matter anymore. Once you got beyond her protective wall, Stella would do anything for you. I had trouble with my old man once, and she said to stay at her place anytime, whether she was there or not. Stella really didn't know me that well, but she trusted me. You see?"

"I think so."

"But what I want you to know is why she was so introverted and private. Scared, I guess. Promise you won't write this down?"

"My word on it."

"I just wouldn't want anyone to think . . . well, anyway, she ran away from that last home at fifteen and thumbed to

San Francisco because that's as far as she could get. Then
she sort of . . . worked on the streets."

"You mean she hooked."

"Yeah, but she had no choice. She worked at a lunch
place, a diner, for pennies. Even the YWCA won't let you
stay more than thirty days without paying. I suppose it's not
important, but I wanted you to know how rough she had it."

"I wasn't judging her."

"I know, but if you keep talking to people about her past,
well, I figured you'd find out, anyway, and it might look
bad or something. Doesn't matter, I guess, but those first
two years were hell for her."

"I appreciate your honesty. Linda, let me ask you a
question. I have no interest other than finding out what
happened. Could Stella have kept a stash of money someplace? Is that common?"

"Oh sure, we all do it. Jesus, with the tax laws you can't
deposit tips in a bank. Most of us blow it, but probably not
her."

"Any idea how much she might have had? It could help
me."

"She got good tokes. I'd guess a few thousand. Stella
didn't waste money."

"Just one last question and please think carefully. In your
opinion, what were Stella's true feelings about Savino Avalon?"

"Boy, that's tough. She was so closed up about private
stuff." Linda reflected a moment. "Well, I didn't like the
creep. I can spot takers a mile off. I don't think she really
cared for him, and she was so hip it surprised me that he interested her at all. He was such an obvious phony. I suppose she felt safe with him, you know, like we both wore
wedding rings at work to keep off the charmers. Sam
thought he was using her, but it really was the opposite, if

you know what I mean. Stella wasn't lez or anything, but she really didn't like men. She didn't trust them. Yeah, that says it. Sam was the beard for Stella, and he didn't even know it. He was the reason she couldn't go out with other guys. But Stella could control him, so she was safe. Does that make sense to you?''

"It sure does. Thanks again, Linda, and if— Wait! Stella let you stay at her place. Did you have a key?''

"No, there was a spare taped under the window box.''

Everything fit into the loop, physically, emotionally and psychologically. The patterns merged complete, but I had had one reservation that Linda unknowingly solved.

Somehow, Stella had known what happened to the girl at the Laundromat, so she ran, but first she had to retrieve the money cache from the house. Her keys were found on the ring in the Pinto's ignition, so how did she manage the money? The key under the window box!

Stella's purse was never found, presumed stripped and dumped into the ocean. The assumption was correct but the identity wrong. The unknown girl's purse went down, but Stella had her own because she later used the credit cards. However, she still needed a key. The spare.

After an endless day, I went home and stared at the wall a great deal, making lists, cross-lists and possibilities. Dirkson checked in with nothing. All my ideas about identifying the dead girl zilched out. Zero. No one was missing that fit her description, meaning she was completely alone, or perhaps a hooker from Stella's past, or maybe new in the city or, hell, dropped out of the clouds. I had no idea.

Aching all over, I finally dozed, snuggled in a favorite recliner with an old comforter tucked at the ankles. Heaven. The phone rang at 4:10. Living alone is hell enough, but waking an insomniac deserves capital punishment.

"This better be goddamn important," I mumbled, ready to kill.

Corny said just three words. "I found her."

# 4. STELLA

"A POSITIVE?" I ASKED, coming awake quickly. "No doubt?"

"Ninety-nine point nine probability with almost zero deviation factor. It's her. And Cantrell, this was no fluke," Corny bubbled, "I deserve all the credit."

"Yours, now tell me how."

"Well, after thinning out the obvious and still having over two hundred names, I went to my association idea. Friends, neighbors, and the like. I patched into the HP 5000."

"Corny," I interrupted. "Come on."

"It was the marriage thing that screwed me, changing names and all, so I backtracked to maiden names, then compared on that. There is a Sheila Harrington today who used to be Sheila Billings until six years ago. Schools getting government support keep great records. One lists a Billings, S., along with Evans, E., at the same time many years back. I assume they used the proper Estelle, rather than Stella."

"So?" I prompted, anxious for the punch line.

"Two days after the murder, Ms Billings develops a sudden interest in San Francisco papers. She subscribes to both and has them mailed."

"Checking up on local killings."

"I figure so. Nine days later, she opens a checking account under the same name. Billings."

"Wait. Didn't you say she used to be Billings, but now is Harrington?"

"That's my point. There is still a Harrington, mother of two and working in a dress shop, but after six years of non-existence, the Billings lady suddenly comes up again as if she never left."

"I'm getting the picture. Instead of creating a new person, Stella takes on the identity of someone who used to exist."

"You got it. She's complete with school records, doctor's files, birth certificate, driver's license, even old parking tickets. Clever little shit, ain't she?"

"Jesus . . . would her new identity have surfaced on your first list?"

"Hell, she wasn't even on it. I could have searched for years. I was looking for new people, and the Billings name goes back two decades."

I should have figured it. Stella was streetwise and knew all the tricks. I must never underestimate her, I thought to myself. "We're assuming this person is our Stella. Any possibility it could be another female using the Billings name?"

"Possible, but the odds are astronomical. She's working a cocktail lounge, started eleven days after the killing, and filed a social security number that has two digits transposed from her real one."

"Meaning?"

"Meaning, unless someone is really on a deep search, they'd never attach that number to her real name. It's an old trick, usually to avoid income taxes, but if caught or challenged, the innocent little lady claims she must have accidentally written it down wrong. Just mixed up a couple of numbers, that's all. Cantrell, the lass is sharp."

He gave me several more details that were being recorded as I dressed and listened to the external speaker. "Corny," I asked when he finished, "who is Control?"

It caught him off guard. "Ah, you are."

"Right. And you were instructed to follow my directives unless countermanded by Buchannon himself."

"Ah, yeah, right," he responded, unsure of the conversation.

"Put all the data into access with your own secret password. I don't want your whiz kids retrieving it. Next, and most important, go home and take the morning off. Don't answer the phone for any reason. Go sailing or something, but avoid contact with everyone."

"Buchannon will have my head. And yours."

"No, he won't. You're too valuable, and I'm too old. He'll rant for a while, but do nothing. At noon sharp, you go in and tell him everything, but not a minute before that."

"Cantrell, you're nuts. I swear, he'll tear my face off and have you jailed. I know he will."

"I accept full responsibility for everything. It is my problem."

"Oh Jesus, Cantrell, this is not going to work."

"Look, Corny, at one minute past noon, Buchannon will have it all, and fifteen minutes later the Denver PD will arrest Ms Evans. Our boss will be a hero, not you, not me."

"But wasn't our job just to find her?"

"Yours, yes, but mine goes beyond that. I'm going to get there first."

"Why? *Why?*"

"Call it personal. Corny, we accomplished more in a couple of days than a hundred goddamned investigators from six agencies could produce in *three goddamned months*! Doesn't that give us the right for one shot? One lousy crack at it? All I'm asking is time."

"What will you do?"

"Talk to her. Once Stella's locked up, that's it, and no one will get near her. I want to find out about Mateo. That's all,

but I need a little head start. What's another few hours after they've messed around for months?''

"Now I know why I took up computers instead of fieldwork. You guys are crazy."

"I admit to a degree of maniacal tendencies. Comes with
the job. Corny, I can't order you. I'm asking."

"You're forgetting something. I'm calling from the office. This has all been taped."

"So, you designed the system. Untape it."

"Hey, my God! You're asking too much, way too much."

"Corny, I've made my pitch. It's in your hands. All I ask,
is if you're going to report before noon, tell me now, and I'll
go back to sleep. There's no chance for me to make it." I
held my breath. It was a terrible ploy, putting Cornwall in
that position, but my only shot. I also knew Buchannon
would blame only me, so Corny was not in serious trouble,
but his loyalty was being stressed.

"It's four-thirty," he finally said. "I've been at this over
twenty hours. The same yesterday."

I waited.

"I could use a little rest." He yawned. "Maybe the bay
will be gusty. Good sailing weather."

"Yesterday's news predicted the best possible sailing."

"Haven't had the sloop out in months," he continued.
"If I didn't show up here until noon, I guess the world
wouldn't end."

"Thanks, Corny," was all I could say.

It was a true pleasure waking Dirkson. In careful language, I instructed him on several tasks that would take
hours and keep him out of touch with the agency. He was to
report to Cornwall after lunch.

I piled shirts on the bed and prepared the subterfuge. I am
not a particularly violent man; in fact the sight of blood,
especially mine, makes me ill. My nature is not a magnani-

mous one, nor do I harbor any extraordinary benevolence toward fellow humans. No, I just didn't want to get hurt. These old bones take longer to heal every year.

After breaking down the Ithaca sawed-off shotgun, I carefully wrapped each piece in lead foil to distort the shapes. I replaced the normal stock with a chopped, pistol grip. The Walther 9 mm automatic was trickier, but folding over the lead made it unidentifiable.

Airport security is a joke, which all agents and terrorists fully realize. The X-ray monitoring guards are trained to spot the shape of a gun and little else. Disguise it slightly, and they're easily fooled. They provide a presence deterrent rather than a true safeguard from professionals. The foil would show strange patterns, but it was highly doubtful anyone would challenge.

On United's earliest flight, I studied a Denver map and plotted the location of Stella's apartment. Time was going to be short, very short, and I regretted not asking Corny to hold a few more hours. Assuming normal traffic, I had forty minutes to overwhelm her. Maximum.

Assuming, of course, Stella bought the story.

At Stapleton Airport I rushed to the Hertz quickie service and drove away in my reserved Ford. The apartment complex was in suburbia, outside Denver toward Littleton. It comprised several large buildings, and I lost seven precious minutes finding C-312.

Stella was a loner, so I was initially surprised she would select a crowded, densely packed area, then realized it was precisely the kind of place she could disappear into, and become surrounded and swallowed by buffers of strangers.

For the past hours I had planned my opening gambit. I had several contingency plans, including if she had visitors or a boyfriend at home. My only real fear was her absence;

however, Stella worked late so hopefully would spend the daytime hours relaxing.

It was almost 1:00 p.m. local time, meaning an hour to noon in San Francisco. This was going to be close. Blow the meet, I told myself, and kiss off any advantage I might have. She was intelligent, resourceful and loaded with savvy.

A tough combination.

Seconds after ringing the bell, I saw a flicker of changing light pass across the viewing peeper. She watched me.

I held my impressive credentials near the tiny glass eyeball. "Special Agent Cantrell, United States Justice Department," I said loudly. "Just a few questions, Ms Billings, that's all."

Using the USJD as a front has certain advantages and is generally successful every time, the greatest attribute being most citizens do not actually understand what it does, but it sounds important.

The door opened a crack, held by a thick chain. "Badge please," came the soft, unemotional feminine voice. After I handed it through the narrow opening, the door slammed shut and I waited. This was going to be tough, I thought, and quickly revised my kindly, rational, understanding approach. It would never work on this lady. Blitzkrieg attack was my only hope.

The chain rattled, the door opened wide, and she stepped back ten feet. Stella was barefoot, wearing a stained and ragged green robe clutched tightly across her stomach with crossed forearms. She did well hiding it, but Stella Evans was scared. Good. My one chance.

"Is anyone else here?" I asked with a simple smile, and she shook her head. I sat down without permission, to appear relaxed. Physical power would not threaten her, no, it was the symbolic authority of the badge that terrified.

Stella said nothing, waiting for my move, having experienced police before. Never say a word unless you must.

Mr. Nevell's amateur photograph was very good, but as the saying goes, it did no justice to this young woman. Even dressed in her knockabout grungies, this was not an ordinary creature. Stella Evans, by any standard, was a magnificent beauty. I recalled the conversation with Linda about the relationship between Stella and her boyfriend. I would volunteer to play beard for this lady any time.

"I am not here to harm or arrest you, or I would have by now. I came to ask a few questions, maybe offer some advice, and help if you want it. You are in very serious trouble, Sheila Billings, or Sheila Harrington, or Stella Evans, or whatever name you're using today."

Give credit when due. She didn't even flinch.

"There is a murder investigation in San Francisco, and everyone thinks you were the victim. Of course, you already know that. Let's see, for starters that's withholding evidence and testimony in a homicide, felonious interstate flight to avoid prosecution, possibly conspiracy and maybe accomplice to homicide, and certainly accessory. A second-year law student could get you five years on that alone."

I waited a brief moment to let that sink in, then continued softly. "They will consider a plea bargain, but only if you know the precise location of Savino Avalon and testify against him. You've been a naughty lady and made fools out of some very important and powerful law agencies. They do carry grudges, I promise."

She stared at me, not with anger, fear or any detectable emotion, but those magnetic, hypnotic eyes never left my face.

"Then, there's Mateo and a matter of blowing up airplanes. The prosecution will easily tie you in, so add extortion on a grand scale, willful destruction of commercial aircraft and a dozen other skyjacking violations, all against federal laws and very, very heavy. Make that twenty years."

"I didn't do any of those things," she finally said, whispering.

"I may regret saying this, but for what it's worth, I believe you. But the facts are, your future is bleak. I guarantee one thing, they will concoct every possible charge against you."

For the first time, Stella showed a glimpse of weakness. The perfect olive skin paled slightly, and her arms clutched tighter over the robe. "What do you want?" she asked. "Why are you here?" Quickly becoming the suspicious, crafty female again.

"I work for an organization you've never heard of, a sort of distant cousin to the State Department. I'll explain sometime, but not now." I looked intently at my Seiko. "In fifty-one minutes, my boss will learn of your location and inform the FBI. Their Denver agents are downtown so they'll ask police for assistance. That should take nine minutes. The nearest cruiser will be here within another ten and hold you for the Feds. One hour and ten minutes, tops, will mark the end of your freedom."

"I can explain everything. I had nothing to do with any of it. I didn't even know!"

"Sure, you can explain. From a jail someplace. You'll stay locked up until the girl's death is solved, Avalon's arrested, Mateo is stopped and the extortion plot is squashed. I should mention they've been on this for three months and made zero progress, so it could take years. Even if they run out of charges, they'll hold you for protective custody. Indefinitely. Someone wanted you dead, remember? And you're a key witness."

Now she wavered and sank into a chair as the rigid exterior began to fade. Incarceration frightened her more than anything, and I recalled Stella's early years in guarded schools.

Seeing her terror manifest, I proceeded with the distasteful task of capitalizing on her fears. "You have four choices, none attractive, and no time to ponder them, plus you have absolutely no bargaining position. In other words, this is it. One, walk out right now and run. I won't try to stop you, but you have no chance. Some nasty men want you dead or the Feds will arrest you. I found you, so can they.

"Two, call the police and turn yourself in as a material witness to a San Francisco homicide. They'll hold you, then turn you over. Same results as the first option. Three, do nothing and someone will be here in approximately—" I glanced at the watch "—sixty-three minutes. In any of the three choices, there will be a monumental jurisdictional dispute, but while they sort it out and take their own sweet time doing it, you'll be in jail. Promise."

I emphasized the latter, recognizing her intense anxiety over probable restraint.

She stood and began pacing, the quick flash of fear subsiding and angry survival instincts taking over. "You said four choices. Don't shit me, you're holding the worst for last. Sure as hell, it's the one you want. The reason you're here. So stop fucking around and get to it."

Cinderella had an acid tongue. "You're right on both counts. But with luck, you'll be free. In five minutes we leave here together with whatever clothes you can throw on. Nothing else. I will hide you."

"Why?" she demanded.

"Because you know things about Avalon and Mateo and the murder and probably the extortion from Transcontinental Airlines. You must, because your boyfriend wanted you dead. I want that information."

*"But I don't know anything!"*

"Four minutes and thirty-five seconds from now I leave, with or without you."

"I swear it! When Sam threatened me I panicked, and Cindy showed up and I didn't know and she just wanted to wash and Sam said—"

"Four minutes and twenty-four seconds. Every tick puts you closer to jail." It was pure chickenshit and I well knew it, but there was no time to negotiate.

Stella shuddered, took a deep, resigned sigh. "What do I do?"

"It's a corny old movie line, but true. Trust me. Do exactly what I say. We leave in four minutes and—"

"Stop that!" she screeched, then buried her face in trembling hands. "You said we had an hour."

"That's when they arrive here, but if you're not around, they'll throw a screen over the airport. We have to clear that before it's too late." That was enough said. It was too complicated for explanations, but I knew Agent Wainwright, and he would immediately secure all outbound flights.

"Believe me," I added. "There is not a second to spare. Come with me now, and you can drop out any time you want. That's my only promise."

Stella gazed at me the same way her friend Linda had, wondering, sizing up and placing more value on experienced intuition, and her ability to maneuver, deal and survive in a man's world.

"Okay," she agreed. "But if I don't like it, you'll take me anyplace I choose."

"Done, now *go*! Now! *Now!* Jeans, blouse, jacket and your most comfortable shoes, and that's all!"

She ran into the bedroom, and I coaxed her with several shouts to hurry. Stella ran down the hall, wearing one tennis shoe and carrying the other.

"No time for bathroom junk."

"At least some brushes?"

"We'll buy everything you need." I took Stella's wrist and tugged her toward the door. "Did you grab your money stash?"

She looked at me defiantly, without comment.

"Good," I said, "but you won't need it."

We scampered across the massive lawn dividing the buildings. "How did you find me?" she asked.

"Later," I told her. In the Ford, I pushed the speed limits but watched the mirror. A ticket was the last thing on earth I wanted.

"Where are we going?"

"Las Vegas, greatest city in the world to get lost in, assuming we get through the airport before they take up positions."

"Is that where I'm going to hide? Vegas? Will you be there? What am I supposed to—"

"Stop," I snapped, then added softly, "please. I was serious about trusting me. I can't answer questions now, I have to think ahead." Reaching into my jacket, I gave her my legitimate identification card from the detective agency. "There is a twenty-four-hour emergency contact written on the back. He's a highly placed government official named Buchannon. An asshole, but honest. It's a direct line to him even if he's on the pot. Any time you want to cash in, just call. You'll be picked up and protected."

"In jail?"

"Most likely, but also safe. So bear with me and please be quiet. Agreed? Fine." We pulled in front of a Western clothing store I had spotted earlier. "Ever been in here? Okay, pick out some boots with the highest possible heels. You have five minutes. If you can't manage that, I'll pick them for you."

We dashed inside as I yanked her along. "I'd say you're a size seven jeans and thirty-four blouse."

"Usually, but I have to try them on. Some things run large and—"

"Get the damn boots! Fancy ones, expensive, and don't forget the heels."

I found a gaudy, orange blouse with swirls of colored filigree across the chest and shoulders, decorated in brass snaps and gold piping, and a suede cowgirl jacket with beads and dangling leather strips.

Bizarre and perfect.

Four minutes and no Stella. I ran through the store and found her sitting with several boots beside her. The clerk was forcing one on. "Does it feel okay?" he asked.

"Well . . . ?"

"It's perfect," I interrupted. "Do you have it with more heel?"

We carried them to the counter and Stella giggled. "You have to be kidding! I wouldn't be caught de—" She stopped.

The brief humor evaporated. "Total this," I told the woman, "and let's see that hat." Without being gentle, I wadded Stella's hair and plopped one hat after another until we had a reasonable fit.

"There's a drugstore on the corner. Buy the brightest lipstick and the biggest, darkest sunglasses they have. Meet you in the car in precisely four minutes."

Her anger flared, as I knew it would. "Wait! I am getting sick of your frigging timetable! I am not a goddamn train schedule!"

I wanted this over before we got to the airport and on display. I grabbed Stella fiercely by the shoulder and hissed in her ear. "This frigging watch just might keep your ass alive! You can call Buchannon any time. Now go!"

I paid $430 and selected a large rhinestone necklace at the last minute. I grinned at the clerk. "Daughters. You can't make them happy."

Stella was approaching the car, and we jumped in without comment, both pissed, nervous and scared. Good signs. Makes the prey sensitive and alert.

Avoiding her vision, I glanced again at the time. We were several minutes ahead, even allowing for traffic.

"Would you at least tell me why this ridiculous Halloween outfit? I thought the idea was to hide. Christ, I'll look like a clown. Everyone will notice me."

"That's the idea. I want people to stare at your clothes because that takes attention away... Look Stella, face facts. You are sharp, and there's no way to hide that without a new face. I want them fascinated with the garish outfit. Same with the boots. You're five-nine, and we can't make you shorter. Instead, we exaggerate and emphasize the height. With the hat and heels, you'll look six-three."

"Jesus, I don't think I can wear this."

"You can and you will. Carry your clothes and my suitcase. I'll drop you in front. Avoid uniformed employees, and keep looking down. In the very first ladies' room, change into the new stuff. Here's a dime for the stall."

"Where will you be?"

"Taking care of this car." I handed her a roll of bills. "At United's counter, buy two first-class tickets to Vegas, round trip, but leave the return date open. I checked, there's space. Drop the wad on the counter, and let them count it. Money means nothing to you. Be loud and brassy. Show off. People stare at money. Check my suitcase, then go through security to the gate. Got it so far?"

"Yes, sir," she answered without enthusiasm.

"Listen closely to this part. After the metal detectors and security, check in at the gate and get both boarding passes.

There's always another ladies' room nearby. Lock yourself in a quiet stall until the last call to board. Remember that, you'll hear the speaker announce last call, and *don't* come out before that. It's important."

"How much time do I have to wait?"

"I figure about thirty minutes."

"Thirty minutes! What the hell was all the damn rush?"

"Stella, you are hot property. You obviously don't realize how much. When your location is relayed to the Bureau, it's only a matter of minutes until they clamp the airport. Hiding in the john may be unnecessary, but good insurance. The timing is very, very close. It was all I could do to get this much."

"If you're wrong?"

"They'll grab us here or have a welcoming committee in Vegas."

"You have it figured to a gnat's ass."

"That's why I've buried so many friends, but I'm still alive. Any questions?"

Stella thumbed the roll of hundreds. "There's a couple thousand here. What's to stop me from buying a single ticket to Miami and leaving you cold?"

"Absolutely nothing. Go ahead." We neared the airport. "In your San Francisco house, the left jar on the spice rack is marked oregano, but it holds an ounce of high-grade Colombian. Street value, maybe two hundred bucks. Leisure stuff. The Crown Royal bottle is filled with cheap whiskey, cut with port wine to mellow the bite. It's probably for Sam because you prefer white wine, usually Chablis. You're wearing cotton bikini panties, cut high on both sides to the waistband and the label is Night Lady. How'm I doing?"

It was unnecessary to ask because her expression said I was on target, and it bothered her. "I could write a book on you, but it's been done already. A data bank has everything from day one. There are no secrets. So run, I gave you that option. Go ahead, but you'll be had in hours."

"I did okay until now," she scoffed. "Three months to find me."

"Because nobody was looking for you! Don't you understand that? They've got a condition red on their hands, and suddenly your existence becomes known. Jesus Christ, Wainwright will pull out all the stops. Right now, you are their only hope!"

I calmed myself a minute, knowing that anger would only harm the situation. But I was frustrated that she really did not understand what they would do to her. "Stella, I'll be quite honest. The odds of us pulling this off are low, but we have a good chance if you listen to me. This is my kind of dodge. Hell, I wrote the drill those guys will be using."

She looked uncertain. And scared. "I still don't know why you're doing this."

"I'll tell you soon. Let's get this part over with. We need each other. Okay?"

We stopped directly in front of the main entrance. Stella attempted a weak smile and got out, carrying her things and my bag. She suddenly turned back. "Where do I put my old clothes?"

Jesus, Cantrell! I swore to myself. I missed telling her that. "Carry them on board in the sacks from the store. You'll need it all later."

Before leaving the Ford in the parking lot, I felt behind the interior mirror. Rental agencies subtly identify their vehicles, so passing officers can spot them. No one would pay an expensive rate and leave the car unattended for days. The small green sticker would be a tip-off, so I peeled it away.

Walking to the terminal, I felt pangs of guilt. I had coerced Stella, overwhelmed her with fears and could not guarantee her safety. She would definitely be better in a federal lockup, but I truly believed I could pull this off.

Besides, her personality would simply not fit the confined environment, and therefore I was helping her. Or so I told myself. The biggest dangers were all the unplannable details that could go wrong.

However, what bothered me the most was knowing if it turned out to be a tie game, I would have to use Stella Evans as bait.

# 5. RUNNING

WHEN I REACHED the terminal, Stella was not in the ticket line. She was either already waiting in the ladies' room, or had not yet purchased the seats. I wandered toward the gate, trying to acquire a feeling for normal security, and stopped short of the metal detector and passenger screening table. There were three guards, a young woman and two men in uniform, all working casually.

When the heavyweights arrived, several would run a blanket sweep through the rotunda and outer gates, including waiting lounges and planes. Extra power would then be assigned at the security clearance point where everyone heading to a flight passed. It was a perfect bottleneck.

I hoped they would take only a cursory glance through the rest rooms. Faith, Cantrell, faith.

Turning, I saw Stella walking toward me, looking a bit silly in that garb, but the theory worked. Even I stared at her clothes. I walked directly at her, and within speaking distance, said, "Follow me."

Pausing at the magazine concession, she stood beside me, thumbing through *Mother Earth News*. It didn't quite match her appearance.

"Everything okay?" I asked.

"Uh-huh," she muttered. "But I look like a masquerade leftover."

"It'll do," I countered. "The search will be for you, but they'll have my picture. When the Feds show, they'll question the airport security guards."

"You can have my hat," she offered, attempting a light-hearted remark, but the tension was obvious.

"I'll go first," I continued, ignoring her comment. "Follow me by twenty feet. When I get to the counter, do something to attract attention. I don't want them to remember me. Here, I can't be stopped for metal." I stuffed my ring, keys and change into her purse.

"And that goddamned watch!" she demanded.

I reluctantly handed it over, and she gave me the ticket. "Last call for boarding will be five minutes before departure. Don't come out until you hear that announcement. Everyone should be seated. Okay?"

We both took deep breaths as I casually strolled off. There was a short line, and I was tempted to glance around but thought better of it.

As I reached the security archway, I heard a crashing noise behind, followed by Stella's fishwife screech. "Son of a bitch!"

All eyes focused in her direction, and I scampered through the tiny aisle without a single glance. After quickly moving several feet, the temptation was too much. I looked back.

Stella must have bumped a middle-aged family man and then dropped her purse upside down. There was a slight incline and the contents scattered, rolling away, as the apologizing gentleman on his knees gathered her possessions.

She'll do just fine, I thought to myself.

In the men's room I deposited a dime, then shuddered. Damn, what if Stella didn't have more change? I'd given her just one coin for the initial change of clothes but forgot the repeated ladies' room gimmick. I briefly stepped into the corridor, but she was not there, so I assumed everything was okay.

I reentered my tomb for the next half hour, thought about the problems we faced and several times considered dropping the entire project. Maybe I really was too outdated for fieldwork. A has-been. A dinosaur. Hell, I was called that a decade before, and by more than one person.

When things don't go as planned, I get very nervous. All should be under complete control, so one can think ahead and not worry about correcting errors on the spot.

It was Stella who had asked about her old clothes. I had forgotten to explain they would be needed later. What if she had dumped them? It was a small enough detail, we could buy more, but that was not as planned.

Then, I'd forgotten to determine if she had another dime. Jesus, Cantrell, catch up to the game or quit. Nervous, nervous.

They announced first call for boarding, and I waited an eternity. From habit, I looked at my naked wrist fifty times and cursed Stella for taking the watch. Every time someone entered the rest room, I painfully tugged both feet to the toilet seat in case it was a blue, looking under the stall doors.

Suddenly, I was outraged at my own stupidity! It had just occurred to me that since Stella had handed over my ticket at the newsstand, I was not checked in at the gate and would have to obtain a boarding pass. When the Feds figured that we skipped, ticket agents would be shown photos of me, perhaps determine Las Vegas, and if they moved quickly enough they could be waiting for us. Dammit to hell! Was everything going wrong?

Sweat formed on my forehead, and I realized the Company may have been right. We hadn't even started, and I'd already glitched several times.

Luck is fickle and can drop on either side. My first good omen came when they announced last call for boarding. That meant five minutes to taxi, so I stayed put while counting to one hundred, then opened the stall door and walked briskly toward the gate. I found myself ten paces behind three uniforms and two suits, all cops, studying passengers sitting in lounges waiting for flights.

A quick glance aft confirmed that the security aisle down the corridor was covered by four guards, watching everyone. Those additional hundred seconds had saved my bacon! I would have been caught in the police sweep.

We strolled in the same direction, and as they passed my gate, I quickly stepped to the Jetway. A young ground hostess glanced at my ticket. "You don't have a seat assignment," she accused, as if I'd stolen the Holy Grail.

"The sales counter said I was the last passenger. I'll just take whatever's left."

She shrugged her shoulders, disapproving that procedure had been bypassed, but reluctantly tearing off a stub from my ticket. "Have a nice flight," she monotoned, her conditioned response.

Dashing down the empty Jetway, I heard one engine spooling up. The flight hostess stood at the 707 cabin door and glanced at my ticket. "She told me to find a seat," I explained, nodding toward the ground hostess at the other end of the tunnel.

During that brief moment, I spotted two uniforms approaching my flight, fifty feet away. People were still in the aisles, arranging coats in the overhead rack, so I politely but firmly maneuvered my way through, smiled at Stella sitting in first class, then continued toward the extreme aft end of the plane. Another hostess, assisting an elderly lady, asked, "Seat, sir?"

"Thank you, I have it," I said. Act as if you know what you're doing, and generally people won't bother.

During those past few days of researching Stella, I had also studied the Boeing 707 and airline procedures, trying to figure different methods that Mateo might utilize to plant his bombs. I knew the three aft lavatories would be locked on the ground, so my pocket knife was ready as I reached the tail section, just beyond the galley.

The hostesses were busy as I placed my blade into the slot of the door latch that said Occupied, slid it sideways until Vacancy appeared, then stepped inside and relocked it. I knew those two cops were going to walk the aisle, checking faces. They couldn't have a photo yet, but my physical description had no doubt been forwarded.

There I was, hiding on another toilet seat, but this time I recognized that an incredible piece of luck had fallen my way.

Willie Sutton, the infamous bank robber, had no fear of being shot by the police because he never allowed firearms on his team. His only worry was a kid happening by with a squirrel gun and putting one between his eyes. The unpredictable, uncontrollable fluke.

Only this time, it worked in my favor.

Normally on commuter flights, one is given a boarding pass at the check-in counter, and a seat number is peeled from a master list, then stuck to one's ticket. The two blues would follow standard procedures, leaving one man at the entry door to ensure no one slipped by, while the second walked through the plane. He would also carry the seat assignment list, but no passenger would be missing because my sticker was still on the clerk's page at the counter. Coming on late had done it!

More engines began spinning, and I felt the lurch as the ground tug pushed us into dispatch position. I knew the flight hostesses would be strapped in just outside my door, two feet away.

There is no seat belt in a plane's lavatory, so I braced my knees against the narrow bulkhead, but it was unnecessary. The takeoff and ascent were smooth. When we stabilized at altitude, a hostess made the usual announcements while another unlocked lavatory doors for passenger use. I re-locked mine, waited ten minutes, then entered the cabin and walked directly to the first class barrier. As I stepped through, a hostess immediately approached me, and I showed her my ticket.

"I sat with a friend a minute," I explained. She examined my ticket closely, figuring I was a gate-crasher into the elite section, then nodded approval. I found two empty seats and gestured to Stella.

She moved next to me. "What happened? I saw you get on, but you kept walking."

"Later. Did the cop stare at you?"

"Just for a second." We ordered drinks, wine for her and a needed brandy for me. "I'm sorry," she said, handing me the watch. "About bitching. It happened just like you said. Right on time."

"I know the head of the investigative group on Mateo. A crackerjack agent named Roger Wainwright. I used to work with him and hopefully remember how he thinks. Roger's good and wouldn't waste time sealing off the airport once he saw we ran."

"That's good, that you know him, I mean."

"I trained him a thousand years ago with another agency. Trouble is, he knows me, too."

It was several minutes before we spoke again. I had to start thinking ahead. Luck goes both ways; I must depend on skill.

Stella looked pleased. "I've never been to Las Vegas."

It was too soon for the truth. Let her enjoy the idea. "Answer time," I said, then angled in the seat so my VFW lapel button was aimed directly at her. I wanted clear reception for the tape.

Before switching on, I cautioned Stella. "Just answer my questions, okay? No ad libs or anything else."

"Yes, sir," she responded, once again half-humorous, half-miffed.

Knowing she would wander, I held my finger over the pause key. "First, tell me everything about the dead girl."

She looked at me a second, then came the tears. "God, I feel horrible about that. But I didn't know! Honest! I have nightmares every night."

I remained silent as she purged herself. I was the first person she'd been able to talk to, and Stella had carried a monumental load these past three months.

"Am I to blame?" she finally asked, gaining stability.

"Only if you knew someone was there to kill you and you sent her instead. Don't look at me like that. Of course, you're not to blame. Now, who was she?"

"Cindy Cummings, but she changed her name all the time. I don't know if it's right. That's common in my business if you move from place to place."

"To avoid taxes?"

"That, plus other reasons. I hardly knew her. Crazy, isn't it? If she were a friend, I could cry and grieve it out, but she was almost a stranger. I feel so terrible."

"Details," I prompted, "from when you met her."

"She worked at the lounge a year ago for just a few nights. Cindy lived with this creep in the Marina Green. Their apartment didn't have a laundry, so we agreed to share the misery." Stella managed a weak smile. "I offered to pick her up because she didn't have a car, but she liked riding the bus."

I interrupted several times for names and data, but it threw off Stella's concentration, so I shut up and let her talk. Time enough later.

The hostess brought another round and gave us menus. "Eat well," I suggested. "It might be your last good one for days."

"So, she'd call or drop in twice a month. We'd take my car down the street where..." Stella paused, becoming emotional.

"Not yet," I cautioned. "In a minute. Tell me about Savino Avalon. Everything, from the beginning."

It was a standard story, nothing unusual. They met at a friend's party six months earlier and began dating casually. She knew so little about him that I became irritated, for the most common answer to my questions concerning her boyfriend was, "I don't know."

Then I recalled Linda's earlier explanation. She said Stella tolerated Savino because he was no threat to her and provided a partial shield from the outside world.

Stella said he slept over one or two times a week, worked at a television and repair store occasionally, but not full time, and was a jerk. He liked to parade her through nightclubs, which Stella despised, but endured the childish display for his friends. It was a cheap enough price to pay for emotional security. With a permanent male friend, no one bothered her.

Stella began talking about Mateo, and I stopped her once again. "We'll discuss him separately." I switched off the recorder as our dinner arrived.

We made small talk during the meal and enjoyed London broil, lean and sliced with a surgeon's scalpel, asparagus tips smothered in hollandaise, a crisp Italian salad tossed right there, followed by a choice of desserts. It was magnificent, and totally sated as we were, it took a while to get Stella back in a conversational mood.

"Now, tell me about that morning," I urged, and keyed the recorder, noticing the huge dark eyes becoming misty again. "Keep the emotion out of it. Just tell me what happened. Like a book report."

"That's damn easy to say," she whimpered. "Okay, I guess it started when I heard the morning news. Believe it or not, I stay pretty well informed. They talked about a plane blowing up. Nobody was hurt. I didn't pay much attention until they repeated it an hour later. All of a sudden, it hit me! They said Transcontinental and St. Louis and it was Tuesday! After that, things are kind of a blur." Stella looked at me. "Do you know what happened? Sam and Mateo were just talking about it, and they argued about Tuesday and St. Lou—"

"*Stop!* We'll get to Mateo. That morning only, what happened?"

She gulped her wine and calmed slightly. "I knew they did it. Just like they said. I kept calling Sam in New York. God, I must have called a hundred times."

"Eighteen," I told her. "How did you have the number?"

"Information. Sam left a note with the hotel name. Said he'd be gone a few days."

"Anything else on the note?"

"Usual junk. Be a good girl and go straight home from work. That kind of crap. You had to understand Sam. He was insecure and jealous, always afraid I'd go out with someone else. As if I wanted to date anyone, including him most of the time."

"Why did you?"

"Why? I don't know. Sam was no problem, I guess. I could handle boys like him. He was . . . okay, I suppose."

"Then you reached him on the phone?"

"Yes, finally. Mr. Cantrell, I honest to God don't remember much of that. I kept asking if he did it, and he kept screaming at me. I'm not certain if he admitted it, but he yelled over and over, so I knew he did. I told him never to come back, or I'd call the cops. Then I slammed the phone."

"You were on the line for almost thirty minutes."

"It was the same thing over and over. Just yelling at each other. I couldn't believe it. Maybe I kept waiting for him to deny it."

"And then?"

"I'm not sure when, but Cindy showed up carrying her wash load and banging on the door. She had tried to call but my line was busy."

"What did you tell her?"

"Nothing. I couldn't talk. I gave her my car keys and said I was sick. After that, I wandered around the house a million times, trying to decide what to do. I kept looking at the phone and thinking about calling Sam again. Jesus, I didn't know what to do!"

"Stella, go slowly now, and tell me every detail."

"I looked at the clock and realized Cindy had been gone way too long. I figured the starter cable got loose again. It does that, and you have to wiggle it around. After worrying about Sam and all, then Cindy being stuck, I decided to walk down and rescue her. Actually, I think I had to get out of the house or I'd scream. I expected to see my car with the hood up or something, but there were cops all over the place."

"And?" I gently prodded.

"I just stood there with the crowd. Probably a hundred people. There was a big ribbon stretched across the curb. I'll never forget the words. Crime Scene. Do Not Enter. SFPD. One lady said a woman named Stella Evans had been kidnapped. Jesus, I just froze."

The hostess came near, and I ordered after-dinner drinks while Stella composed herself. I tried to imagine the incredible stress suddenly piled on her in a matter of hours.

Learning of the explosion, accusing her boyfriend, and then someone kidnapped in her place.

"I was staggered. My head buzzed. Please understand, I had to be alone a minute. I really didn't mean to run. Not at first. I walked toward my house, but a police car was in front. I was actually thinking about calling Sam and telling him, when it dawned on me. Maybe I already knew, but it just sank in. I remembered his warnings on the phone. He said if Mateo heard my threats, he'd have me finished. Then, I realized what he meant. Somehow, they thought it was me. But Jesus, it was only a couple of hours later. That's all!"

"People with connections move fast. What then?"

"Uh, I was on the corner, just standing there, and this bus pulled up. The driver opened the door and asked if I wanted on or not. Real nasty, like I made him late. I rode to the end of the line, went to another, and rode around like that for hours. I didn't know who to trust."

"Your purse?"

"I had it with me. Habit. Finally, I thought of Sheila in Denver. We went to school together. I just remembered her all of a sudden, so I called. It was desperation. I didn't have anyone in town except Sam."

"How did you know her married name?"

"That was funny. I got a wedding invitation years ago. It was weird because she was marrying a guy named Harrington, but added a note he wasn't like the Harrington we knew in school."

"Who was that?"

"One of the teachers. A lecherous old fart who used to look down our blouses. I couldn't forget that name, we joked about it, so I called every Harrington in Denver until I found her."

"So she said come along, what then?"

"Nothing much. I went to the airport and bought a ticket."

I stared at her. "First, you charged some clothes and a bag."

"Oh yeah." She shrugged. "I forgot."

"Stella, you must help me. That's our only chance. I must know everything."

"Sorry," she murmured, then detailed stores and purchases.

It was completely immaterial at that point, but I was trying to condition her memory reflexes. Stella had been through hell, mentally and emotionally, and had intentionally blocked some of the horror from her mind. I had to get every detail about Mateo, and was then just triggering her brain neurons to stimulate the appropriate cells. Pure conditioning.

She waited. So did I. Finally, I prompted her. "The money? How did you buy a ticket? How did you get to it with the cops there?"

"It was with me," she answered, without conviction.

"You carry that kind of cash in your purse? A couple of thousand?"

"Yes. No. What difference does it make?" Stella gazed out the window at the approaching Nevada plains. "Okay, okay, I'll tell you, but I don't see why it's your business. It's personal. You take a Kotex and remove most of the center absorbent cotton and roll hundred-dollar bills up tight, then stick them inside the gauze. I learned that in girls' schools. You couldn't leave anything lying around for a minute or it'd be gone."

"Damn clever," I admitted.

Stella blushed, which pleased me. When was the last time she felt comfortable enough with someone to show embarrassment?

I gave her precautions about Vegas. It was possible Special Agent Wainwright was a jump ahead, assigning agents to meet us. There was little doubt he would eventually figure it out, but hopefully too late. The Denver police believed themselves to be on top of it, and yet we had slipped through their airport security screen. But Wainwright would track us to Vegas, easily enough.

During the limo ride to Caesar's Palace, Stella was bubbly and excited. "Look who's playing at the Sands! Can we see a few shows? My treat, I have money," she said with a wink.

I still avoided telling her the truth.

# 6. RED HERRINGS

ARRIVING AT THE HOTEL, Stella was in ecstasy. We had purposely stalled at the airport, so no one riding in the limo came off our flight.

I leaned toward her. "I'll take the suitcase. Wait until there's no crowd at the counter. Slip the registration clerk two twenties and ask for a nice room. Be extravagant and pay for three nights in advance like someone who just scored and has nothing to hide."

"Will you follow me upstairs?"

"No, there's a gaming room off the lobby. I'll be near the entrance. Don't go to your room. Can you play blackjack? Good, come in and try your luck. After you lose a couple hundred, leave, and I'll follow."

"What if I win?"

"We'll split it."

"I have a question. Shouldn't we check in together, like a couple? It might look better?"

My respect for Stella's instincts was growing, but this was no time for compliments. Stella had to accept my decisions without hesitation, a trait she was obviously unaccustomed to, but it was vital. I gave her my frustrated look. "No! If Wainwright's people get this far, it's because they've figured it, and to be honest, I'll be damn disappointed if we stiffed his entire bureau with one simple move. Now, are you ready?" I snapped.

Stella returned my glare with her whipped-puppy look, and I did not wonder why she normally controlled events. She was quite the actress.

After I'd been resting my butt on that suitcase for thirty minutes and had shooed away three bellboys who wanted to help, Stella finally left the table and walked to the elevator. Other people got on, so we entered the room before I could speak. "Hope you enjoyed that," I said stoically.

"Your cut," she scoffed, handing me almost two hundred dollars. "We played in school. Bunch of amateurs down there, throwing their money away. The dealers must crack up at some of those bettors."

"So, you're a real pro."

"No, Mr. Cantrell," she said with a grimace, dark eyes flaring. "I'm about the slowest learner you probably ever met. Not too bright, so I have to work hard at it. But when I do manage to grasp something, it sticks to me forever, and I make it work."

"Good, 'cause you're going to need it. We both are. Now, show me how to make this room appear like you slept here all night."

"I don't get to stay?" Stella pouted, her expression changing in a split second. She moaned again and walked across the luxurious deep carpet, touching everything.

"We're not even staying in Vegas," I explained.

"Why? No, don't say it. I know, trust you." She checked the other rooms. "My God, look at this!"

All four walls and ceiling of the enormous bathroom were covered with gilded mirrors. A gigantic round marble tub filled the center, sunken to floor level, sloshing with continually bubbling hot water. Beside it was a bottle of complimentary champagne in a silver ice bucket.

I called her to the living room window. "See that yellow truck down there? After you've messed the room, change into your Denver grungies and stand beside that truck in one hour. Pack the fancy clothes in the sacks."

"What are you going to do?"

"Find new transportation."

"Make it two hours. Please? You said we have a long, miserable night in front of us. I'll never see a tub like that again. I have been cooperating."

If they were not waiting at the Vegas airport, we had them faked for a while, and another hour actually wouldn't hurt. There were a lot of hotels in town, which would take days to check. "Hour and a half," I answered, compromising. "No later."

It was vital to get messages off to Buchannon and quickly. If the Feds caught us, Wainwright could make life rather distasteful for us both. I had to cover our collective ass. Heading for the lobby, I did have one humorous thought. I wondered about Buchannon's outburst when he saw the room receipt. Hundreds for a bath.

Assuming I got the receipt to him.

Special schools for agents are the finest in the world, intense, thorough, demanding, but many things they don't teach. Anyone who survives this clandestine business very long, living on the fringes of violence, must learn tricks on his own. One is a safe mail drop. I have several, but my favorite is an ex-corporal I met in Nam. He was my assigned guide as we determined Charlie sympathy within civilian populations.

We became friends, and after his discharge, he returned to his hardware store in Cleveland. I tested him for a solid year before gaining complete faith. An error in judgment could be catastrophic. Two or three times a month, I mailed him an envelope containing another one, plus some money. He kept the money, ensured no prints were on the preaddressed inner envelope, and mailed it from the central post office, thus providing a Cleveland cancellation. Such things come in handy.

The envelopes all came back to a box in San Francisco under a code name. I had each letter scrutinized with microscopes, magnetic foil breaks and laser-tested fibers, to see if they had been tampered with.

Always clean, untouched, so I had used the ex-corporal for years.

To avoid being bothered by wandering cocktail waitresses, I carried two drinks and a keno ticket to a quiet table off the lounge. There was nothing earth-shattering on the tape containing minor data from Stella about the murdered girl, so I added a message in clear.

Buchannon,
This might help Dirkson identify your mystery Jane Doe.

Cantrell

The second communiqué was more vital and quite secretive. The Venetian code is so simple a Boy Scout can use it, but so difficult that without certain keys and codes, it literally cannot be broken. No one knows the exact origin of the system, but the city of Venice has been given credit for using it when they were under siege hundreds of years ago to send messages to their allies. Since then, countless armies, intelligence organizations and high school pranksters have used it.

We were told the KGB once cracked a message using the Voltig Q-1000 cryptographic computer in Minsk, but that was never confirmed. Even so, breaking one code is meaningless because the cipher is progressive and constantly changing. Keying one would not help the next.

The two half-dollars looked ordinary, except the tiny serrations on the outer circumferences had been carefully polished away. With extreme precision, the alphabet had been inscribed with tiny indentations equally spaced around the coins. The letters for each coin were in random order, drawn from a hat by our Mr. Fergus, and he changed the letters at unknown intervals.

I rubbed cigarette ash around the edges of the coins so the letters had better definition, then, wearing my strongest reading glasses, stacked them together like poker chips and rotated them until the *W* on each was aligned, my particular identification for that period. I then rotated the top coin eight letters, the arithmetical computation of my birthday, which confirmed the message source.

The first letter of my signal was *B*, so I located that on the upper coin and read the aligned letter, *K*, from the bottom. After noting each corresponding letter, the coins were rotated one space so no letter affected another, and repeats and patterns meant nothing. *STELLA* in one line might read as *MJKLO*, and in the next become *WPRIR*.

Cipher computers, no matter how sophisticated and complex, need some form of logic, frequency or discernible pattern to formulate the millions of possible combinations, but the Venetian code is triple blind and progressive. Unbreakable.

The top line to Buchannon was gibberish.

KEOVVPWLOTMZLAPQRIDSKMGNEKTOD-
PERTALQPGKIIEL

Fergus would have identical disks, and knowing my beginning point, would decipher and relay the message to Buchannon. It was up to them to insert the word breaks.

BUCHANNON/ONLY/CONDITION/ZEBRA/RE-
PEAT/ZEBRA/I/HAVE/STELLA/     CAN/ID/
MATEO/CANCEL/FEDS/WILL/CONTACT/ALL/
OK/CANTRELL

I went through again from the start to double-check,
thereby avoiding a drawback to the code system. If you lose
track or make a mistake, it becomes garbage since each letter is derived from the prior. It's slow and cumbersome for
long messages, plus invariably I dropped the damn coins,
lost my place and had to start over. But you can't have
everything. Even secrecy has its price.

After rinsing off the ash, I finally found blank envelopes
in the stationery section of the hotel. I addressed several,
then stepped outside into the late afternoon.

All clandestine agencies have strict rules governing behavior and practices of their field operatives, and one of the
most stringent is tampering with the safety or property of a
citizen. Verboten. We often bend regulations as circumstances dictate but avoid violating that one if humanly possible.

When boosting a car, we always take rentals, and the
company quickly replaces it for the customer, then puts the
license on a hot list. There were dozens in the huge lot, so I
had a great selection and picked a new Chevy with a light
coat of dust. Hopefully, the renter was having a good
enough time not to miss it for another day.

The three-needle jumper clip from my pocket was
snapped to the ignition bundle, and I was off. Time from
door open to start: fifty-one seconds. Slow, Cantrell, getting much too slow.

Stella was beside the yellow truck as I pulled up. "Please
no talking or questions for five minutes," she said. "I'm still
in heaven."

I peeled off the rental sticker as we drove to a stereo store. "Wait here," I told her. Inside, I found an employee working alone and offered him the cassette of Stella's conversations.

"I need two copies of this," I said, and gave him forty dollars. He returned from the back room in minutes. My recorder used a simple phase scrambler that is easily decoded, given the right equipment, which I knew he did not have.

In the car I instructed Stella which item went into each envelope, as I located a post office with coin-operated stamp machines. Miles out of Vegas, she asked me, "What were those for?"

I began to tell the truth, a rare commodity in this trade. "I've taped some of our conversations. One to my boss, another to my own desk and the last to a personal friend, in case I sort of disappear."

"Disappear? Like where?"

"That's the point. Off the earth. It's happened before. I work for an honest organization, usually, but if you fall from grace, they can also become a very bad enemy."

"Sounds lovely. Like some bartenders I know. I'm almost afraid to ask where we're going, but if we sneak through another airport, you wear the clown's outfit, and I'll play the straight."

I couldn't help but laugh. Under different circumstances, Stella Evans was probably quite a woman, at least to someone half my age. Or less. She was bright, astute and usually candid.

I disliked breaking the speed limit, but fifty-five on the desert highway looked suspicious, so I kicked the Chevy to seventy and blended with the sparse traffic.

"Ready now?" I asked. "It's time to talk about Mateo. First the name. Is it a code or—?"

"The whole thing was like little boys playing with secret passwords and burning notes. It all seemed so damn juvenile. Each guy took the name of the city where he got the best screw in his life. Dumb, huh?"

"So Mateo?"

"You know, San Mateo on the peninsula."

So that was it. Mateo was a place from the past, not a name. It certainly would not be listed on any file. Even Corny couldn't find that one. "Other names?"

"There was Wayne, I think that meant Fort Wayne. And York for New York, and a few I never met. Sam wanted to be Frisco, but Mateo said no so he picked Seattle."

"Why did Sam want Frisco?"

Stella gave me her long, impatient sigh that I recognized. Dumb question, she was gesturing.

"Because he was patting my ass at the moment and trying to make points with me. After his friends left that night, Sam expected me to ask about his great lay in Seattle, as if I cared. He kept apologizing that I was really his favorite. I suppose now you want the details?" she snipped.

"I asked for a reason!" I said harshly, suddenly irritated. "Maybe you weren't his only girlfriend in San Francisco. Maybe there's another lady who might know his location."

"Sorry," she muttered. "I forget this is a tough business. But sometimes when we're just talking, things slip out— Hey! Are you taping this?"

"No, I have a pause button. Any time you get close to something personal that has no impact on our problem, I key off."

"You son of a bitch! How the hell do you know what's personal to me? I don't want private stuff ending in some damn file in Washington!"

"Stella, I promise you—"

"No more, that's it!" she announced, then folded her arms.

I could not tell if this was real anger or another pouting act. Stella was so difficult to read. But I needed her full cooperation.

We drove for several miles in silence, both wanting to remark on the incredibly beautiful desert sunset, but neither would speak. "Stella," I finally said. "This is bullshit. We'll be in Reno in a few hours. Once in the city limits, you have until the first phone booth or a police station. I'll drop you at either one you like. We used to say in school, 'talk or walk.' Your choice."

"Times must have changed. I heard it as 'fuck or walk.'"

"Nothing's changed, but all I want is conversation."

She replied with slow, carefully chosen words. "Cantrell, I know the difference between Plato and Socrates. I can find Kathmandu on a globe, and I understand square roots. I'm no frigging dummy, but what did that ever get me? Nothing, that's what. I can wiggle my rear, smile at the boss and have a job. I can sulk and pout with the best of them, and I usually get my way. It's called making do with what you have."

"Understood. Your point?"

"Just don't expect me to drop a lifetime of conditioning, okay? I'm not used to telling anything to anybody, most especially people associated with the law. So, if you want my help, it works both ways. I have the right to determine what's on that tape some damn clerk will type up for the world to read. Fair?"

"Fair enough, as long as I get everything about Mateo."

"Done. Give me the recorder."

"It's connected inside my pocket. The wire runs through a belt loop up to this lapel tack. I can't just hand it over."

"Well, genius, you figure it out. That's my offer. The ball's in your court, and I'm not pouting now, just waiting."

I silently cursed the little bitch, as I slowed to twenty and snaked the apparatus from my clothing. She played with the switches a minute, experimenting with her new toy.

After that, Stella was extremely cooperative, answering each question clearly and directly. She held the VFW pin to her mouth like a microphone, and after practice, learned to key out when she swore.

"We don't want Washington to be embarrassed," she said with a wink.

Amazing woman, I thought to myself. So damn unpredictable.

"They were like planning a panty raid on the girls' dorm. Maps, charts, notes, whispers, giggles. I stayed in the front room and watched TV, when I was there. Sam was miffed that I never asked about it."

We covered Mateo's description in detail, but there was so little to work with. Forties, swarthy, five-ten, salt-and-pepper hair and a few other tidbits, but nothing I could really use. No scars, accent, speech patterns, skin splotches or anything to trace or recognize.

"So, two or three times a month you'd come home and he was there with Sam. Ever see the car he drove?"

"Never. There are cars all over that neighborhood at night."

"But sometimes you overheard him complaining about the lousy food on the flight, so he came from someplace by air. Ever mention an airline? A city? A restaurant? Can you pick out any special days, like Mondays?"

"Like I said, zero. Sorry."

"How about the TV? Is there any program or movie you recall when he was there? Anything we could check? Maybe something that happened earlier at your work? Or with a friend? Did you ever buy something on a day he visited?''

We continued in that vein a long time, but without much information. ''Stella, we have a guy named Cornwall who can solve any puzzle, but he needs something to begin with. Dates, cars, flights, arrivals, airline, hell, anything!'' It was my turn to sulk. There was nothing to go on.

''You keep saying they were playing a game. Why call it that?''

''That was my impression,'' she answered, ''plus I know Sam. His type of thinking. Always a quick-rich scheme, and the more illegal the better. He watched robbery movies and then told me how it should have been done. 'No real pro would do that,' he'd say. Sam came into the club one night, and within minutes, said how he could rob the safe and not get caught. Always something, he never stopped.''

''As you said earlier, lovely people.''

''Yeah, that's why I thought it was a game, and he found a few other nuts to join in and play make-believe Dillingers.''

''Yet Mateo's reason for coming over was not attached to this game?''

''No, Sam said he was a traveling salesman, and they were old friends. San Francisco was part of his route.''

There would be plenty of time to quiz her later, so I let it go. She could concentrate another time.

''How long will we be in Reno, or is this another quickie stop?''

''You're learning. Maybe enough time for you to hit the tables again, but not much.''

''Will your FBI friend trace us to Vegas?''

''No doubt. And they'll eventually find the car I dumped at the airport. Trouble is, there's no way to know when.

He'll backtrack a dozen times, and maybe even glue some pieces together, but this dodge in Reno should work.''

A pro chasing another is always fascinating, particularly if they've worked together and understand how the other thinks. A game of chess between fierce competitors, only with higher stakes. It was the little wrinkle that both hoped for, and mine was very simple, yet effective.

Many Reno hotels provide bus trips to attract gamblers from the Bay area into Nevada. You board at any number of places around six in the morning and ride to a specified hotel, which offers free lunch and dinner, and they often throw in a small stack of chips to keep you on the premises. You're free to watch stage shows or gamble, the latter being the preferred attraction. An hour after midnight, the chartered bus reloads, then returns to point of origin. The elapsed time was twenty-four hours, and one had to be really excited about gambling to endure the grueling trip. However, the price was incredibly low, often less than thirty dollars, and the popularity of these sojourns was astonishing.

Invariably, the riders to Reno were more numerous than those returning. Some simply could not cope with another long bus ride after a brutal day, and stayed over at the hotel. A few might hit big and want to remain, or come home on a flight. Many could not break away, once sparking the gambling fever. There were always empty, unaccounted-for seats on the return trip. Certainly, the hotels encouraged this practice, which gave them more time to capture pocketbooks.

After eating chili burgers at a Reno diner, which did not thrill Stella at all considering the number of fine local restaurants nearby, we had two hours to waste.

When Stella heard my instructions, I could see the involuntary shudder, but she kept the promise and did not complain, so I let her play the tables in a small casino until midnight.

"You didn't stake this," she said. "Do I have to cut you in?"

"Keep it," I growled, watching her wad a stack of tens into her jeans.

I had selected the Sahara Hotel because of its size and popularity. A few minutes past twelve, we walked into the crowded parking lot, which was dotted with a dozen tour buses. The drivers were just arriving, checking their rigs and kicking tires.

Stella took a breath, sighed weakly and said quietly in the darkness, "In my younger days, I did some kinky things for a dollar, but I've never picked up a bus before. I'll give it my best shot." She approached them, talked to a few individually, then returned.

"We're set." She smiled. "Just like you said. The first two were nerds and the next was heading north. We're on that number 15 to San Carlos."

"Perfect. And?"

"Like clockwork. I told him you scored at roulette, and I want us out of here tonight. I gave him two hundred for a pair of seats. Before he could say anything, I gave him another one for his trouble."

The American hundred-dollar bill, instrument of negotiations, underground movements, briberies, and common currency for people living on the other side of midnight. "You did great," I repeated. "The money will go straight into his pocket, illegal as hell, but he'll forsake his own mother before admitting it to anyone and risking his license."

We boarded early and took rear seats. The driver nodded, then quickly looked away. We were nonexistent. For the next half hour, the passengers arrived. Some bragged, many whined, most were partially or fully drunk and all had a story to tell.

Everyone ignored us.

At precisely 1:00 a.m., the door slammed shut and we roared away. There were still a dozen empty seats.

The trip was one of the most miserable I have ever experienced. Stella was hurting, too, but never said a word. While we were crossing the Sierra Nevada, my ears kept popping, giving me a horrendous headache.

Stella slept fitfully, a few minutes at a time, and would occasionally hold my wrist to see the time. "Shit," she'd groan, then twist around for another position. She finally dozed on my shoulder, producing another throbbing ache.

After five torturous hours, we pulled into a small shopping center in San Carlos, thirty miles from San Francisco. A tobacco shop advertised all-night, round-trip gambling sprees to Reno, leaving at six and returning twenty-four hours later. I asked Stella if she'd like to try one, and her expression was not complimentary. Words could never have said it better.

Most of the passengers drove away in their own cars, parked there from the previous morning. Some people were picked up, but I was astonished how many men were adjusting shirts and ties, preparing for a day's work. God, was I ever that young and strong?

As I expected, a few late-shift cabbies were there, hoping to snag a winner with more cash than sense. I flagged one and told him the airport Hilton.

"Do I get to sleep now?" Stella mumbled, from her zombie state.

"We'll eat first."

"Screw it. All I want is a deep hole for two days."

I used my George Wade identification, which was solid and unknown to the agency, and registered as Mr. and Mrs.

I had to kick Stella's foot to bring her conscious, then led her to the room.

She sank immediately onto the bed, fully dressed, and was sound asleep. I considered the large overstuffed chair, then said to hell with it. I rolled her over slightly, and lay down beside her.

As I drifted away, the mind confirmed a nagging thought. This was my last field operation. Absolutely. A young man's game, and I then recognized a notion I had been nurturing for years. I was over the hill. Burned out. Done. No more. Outlived my purpose. All the clichés came to me.

There was also a very sudden nervous twitch as I considered what might happen next. It was a long way from over, and I prayed for the strength to see it through.

I could rest a few days, but then things would become very tricky.

# 7. TO GROUND

I COULD NOT BELIEVE how much Stella could eat.

It was early afternoon, and she ordered enough for three and devoured most of it.

Waking early, I rented a car using the untraceable Wade name, then phoned numerous property agencies, explained my preferences and arranged several appointments.

We drove south, away from San Francisco to Santa Clara in the heart of Silicon Valley, and found the first rental company. They had nothing of interest, nor did the next six, but the last showed us a little bungalow behind a much larger house.

It was very private, set deep among huge willow trees with sprawling limbs drooping to the ground. Prying neighbors were virtually shut out by the massive vegetation, yet it was within walking distance of a shopping center, which Stella loved.

"It's called a mother-in-law house," the agent said. "Popular in California. Uh, where you from?"

"East," I replied. I signed an agreement and paid a month's rent plus security. The owner lived in the big house but dealt through an agency, not wishing to be bothered with collecting rents.

New luggage looks awkward, so we found some battered pieces at a used clothing store, then went on a spree. Clothes, bathroom supplies, books and magazines, food for three weeks, kitchen necessities and a portable color television.

It was the first look of calmness and peace I had seen on Stella since we met just one day before. I realized she had been very nervous but carried it well. My dad once told me, "To make a woman happy, take her shopping for anything." Probably true, but it was more than that. Stella was trusting me. She felt safe. I could see the difference.

I stayed six days. With separate bedrooms, we had sufficient privacy to avoid getting on each other's nerves, but we did have to arrange a shower schedule. Stella was an average cook but managed a spectacular lasagna.

"Used to work in Italian dinner houses," she explained.

Stella cleared the table and made coffee as I washed the dishes. We spent hours talking about her past, as I maneuvered into chats about Mateo.

"Time for business, huh?" she would say.

"Every little bit helps." We repeated the drill dozens of times; each new session would produce a minuscule piece of information that she had overlooked. Stella realized Mateo was left-handed, always wrote with thin-line felt markers and was a Boston Celtic fan, all of which meant nothing, but I had to build the picture. Hopefully, we would meet soon.

"Stella, through all the hours you witnessed them checking over notes and charts, didn't you get the least suspicious that it was serious?"

"No, I really didn't. That's why it was such a blinding shock that morning. Please remember, I was not in love with Sam, nor did I care for his friends, so I paid very little attention. In fact, I rather enjoyed having Mateo there because everyone ignored me, and I could do my things in private, and Sam didn't bother me."

"But he never discussed later what they talked about?"

"Never. I just picked up bits and pieces. You see, they'd argue and get loud until Mateo would shush them. They mentioned TCA several times, and 707s and names of cities. They had a very hot debate the last time. Sam insisted on Chicago, but Mateo said it'd been changed to St. Louis whether he liked it or not. Sam was really pissed. That was the real tip-off, when I heard the news about a 707 blown up in St. Louis. Otherwise, I probably would not have associated it. I mean, who would believe it could happen, and planned over my dining table?''

"I'm sorry, but it's difficult to imagine all this was going on and you simply ignored it."

"Well, I'm *sorry*!" she shouted, her first signs of anger in days, "but that's what happened. I didn't give a damn what they were doing."

That was our last evening. I had pushed her hard, but Stella always recovered rapidly. I truly hoped I would not have to use her.

"I'll be leaving in the morning. Anything you can think of? Do you need anything? Money? Food?"

"I think you've purged me. No, I'm set."

"Fine, just one final little task. Sit over here and hold this." I aimed my cheap instant camera and took several shots. Naturally, Stella did not care for any of them, gave me advice, and I shot a few more before she was satisfied.

Suddenly, she became very serious. "Cantrell, will you get in trouble over this? Hiding me and all?"

"Yes and no. Buchannon will raise hell and make a dozen idle threats, but I have them over the proverbial barrel. He has the tapes and messages by now and some very large problems. Whether he wants it or not, I have thrust him straight into the limelight. He's contacted the Bureau for certain, and they're in shit, too. They know you're alive and with me, but afraid to do much. If they notify San Francisco Homicide, a bunch of amateur cops get into the act, start sending out your description, and sooner or later some sharp newsman picks it up. Then, look out."

"What happens?'

"The dominoes start to fall. Real fast. Our top law agencies plus high-level forensic labs failed to ID the right body. The local papers will have a good time, until someone wonders why the FBI is concerned over a simple local killing. A few words, a couple of bribes, and Lord knows where it might end. An avalanche. All hell will break loose if anyone connects the TCA bombing and president Starkmore making extortion payoffs to keep his planes from exploding. A mess, first class, particularly when it hits the evening news. Right now, a few dozen people are looking for scapegoats, and wondering what I'm going to do."

"Which is?"

I ignored her question. "That's why you are relatively clean right now, and not charged with anything official. Yet. Court reports and warrants become public very fast, and lawyers and newsmen hang around city hall like vultures looking for juice."

"Why do you feel safe? I mean, you keep saying how dangerous these people can be."

"In one message, I put the term 'condition zebra,' which is very complex. Zebra stands for *Z*, or the last letter, meaning last resort. The actual policy is fifty pages long, but breaks down to a security breach. When a field operative such as me calls that signal, it indicates I believe there is an internal security leak, and I am not responsible to report in. With a leak, my progress might be passed on to the wrong party. To put it another way, I am completely on my own. This takes Buchannon off the hook. He won't be chastised for losing control of his agent."

"Protecting your ass, in other words."

"Right, mine and the boss's. Only the operative who called it, or Buchannon, or the director in Washington can clear the Zebra condition. No one dares cancel it for fear of repercussions, but this way, it's my ass out there, and they're not worried about that."

"So temporarily, you're hands-off material?"

"Right again, except the Feds would risk it to grab you. They don't care about Buchannon's problems. He has to convince his boss at the top, who says the right word to another Washington key man, who I hope tells the field boys to lay away. They'll watch me damn closely, yes, but shouldn't touch for the moment."

"It all sounds very dicey," Stella said, "and complicated."

"Not really. I'll never understand how a cocktail waitress can remember a dozen drinks at once."

"Simple, you learn little tricks."

"Now, you have the idea. I have tons of little tricks."

We looked at each other for a moment, both feeling quite awkward. "Well," I said with a shrug, "you sleep in. Take care...and, uh, you know, follow my instructions. Do you remember them all?"

"Cantrell, if you make me repeat them once more, I will scream."

Stella hesitated, then threw her arms around my neck and planted a hard kiss on my cheek. "You be careful, old man, and be back here safe. Promise? See you in a few days?"

I sat on the bed for an hour, thinking about the meeting with Buchannon, all the things that could go wrong, and again wondering if I was in over my head. My acting ability was still there, because Stella seemed convinced of my confidence, but I knew how much was show and bluff. I felt like hell. A lot depended on my boss, and if I had judged right how much he wanted to become a hero. I had to convince him he was not at risk, and had nothing to lose. The only flaw in that, was Buchannon's ego. I had damaged it severely by going off on this stint without his approval or knowledge, and he was a vengeful ass.

"Yes?" I said to the soft tap at the bedroom door. She came in. She possessed one of the most enticing figures I have ever seen, with long legs, slender waist and, judging from her sweaters, perfect apple breasts. Stella did everything possible to hide it. She was wearing another ratty floor-length robe, threadbare, faded and patched, that she had bought at a nearby garage sale for a dollar. It made her look all the sexier, but I will never understand why.

"I've never thanked you for all you've done for me. I'm not good at saying that. It always made me feel indebted."

"You're welcome. No matter what happens, it was my pleasure."

"I know you're in trouble, and I really don't know how much."

"No sweat." I smiled. "I'm an old pro."

"One question, or maybe an answer to a question you've never asked. When I first came to San Francisco, I did things. Since you know everything about me, I guess you know all that, and they're probably written down somewhere on a report."

"No, those details meant nothing, and they died with me."

"I just wanted to say, I'm not proud of working the streets, but I'm not ashamed, either. I never asked for handouts. It was that or move drugs. All those homes for wayward girls are bullshit. They file reports and want your name, and the first thing they do is contact your home. I'm not sorry for what I did, if that makes any sense. Uh, I just wanted you to know that."

"There is something you should understand about me. I have shattered the Ten Commandments, not once but many times. Over and over. I'm no saint by any standard, and I learned a long time back I have no right to judge anyone."

"Well, after one week, you know more about me than anyone on earth. You even know where I hide my mad money, and I've never admitted that to anyone. So you're special."

"Now, I thank you," I said sincerely. "That is nice to hear."

She turned to the door, held the knob, then looked back. "What's funny is, I was trying to think of an excuse to come in here and say that, then I almost forgot my excuse. I wanted to tell you something that just happened. I was watching TV about a big storm coming down from Canada, and I remembered. It just flashed on me. Another name. Trudeau. Mateo said it over and over, dozens of times, whenever they met. But an important name, not just another member. Maybe they were planning on blowing up Pierre Trudeau's plane or something? Maybe kidnap him or one of his family?" She caught my dazed look. "Just a thought," she mused.

"Okay," I replied, my mind spinning but not wanting her to notice my reaction. "I'll pass that along."

Stella left quickly, but I hardly noticed her absence. I stood, very agitated, and paced the room. A hit on the former Canadian prime minister or his family was ridiculous, out of the question, but considering the events and weaving together details, another possibility far more terrifying came to mind. I said the name several times. Trudeau. Trudeau. Trudeau.

I didn't sleep that night, weighing the staggering implications.

# 8. SURFACE

IN THE MORNING I rechecked my armaments, turned in the rental car and took a cab to San Francisco Airport where I stored the suitcase in a day locker.

I dialed the Buchannon Detective Agency and held my breath. After identifying myself to his secretary, I naively expected immediate connection to the Great One. Considering I had put the entire department in turmoil these past days, my call should have provoked a reaction.

Instead, I was placed on hold, but not for a trace. Corny had very sophisticated systems that could display my number and location in a blink. No, Buchannon made me wait as a show of power. He did not want me thinking I could disrupt the smooth ebb and flow of his empire, then receive an audience at my convenience.

The secretary returned to explain it would take a few minutes, so I decided to play his waiting game. "Forget it," I told her. "Tell him I'm coming in right now."

I left the cab a few blocks from the building to see how they would play this scene. Buchannon had obviously alerted the Bureau, and they had plenty of time to set up a tag team. The FBI people were masters at that.

My Condition Zebra code protected me for the moment because I was holding the most valuable witness in the country, but the next five minutes would determine my fate.

Strolling casually to the Morris Building, I wondered who would finger me. He was standing at the corner reading the *Wall Street Journal*, a common enough practice in the financial district, and he turned a page as I passed. It was uncalled for and unprofessional of me, but the temptation too great, so I walked back to him.

"That was clumsy," I chided. "Amateurish. You won't survive with moves like that."

Barry Dirkson lowered the paper and said nothing, just looked embarrassed.

"Around here and right now, it doesn't matter, but if you ever play hardball with the heavyweights, they'd spot you a block away. Barry, you would be cold meat."

"It was a quick assignment." He grinned. "No time to set up."

"My friend, don't ask me why, but I like you. Since this is no doubt my last venture, let me tell you this. Hone your instincts, and forget the classroom textbooks. They weren't written by successful field agents."

"I'll remember," he said sincerely.

"How many are on me?"

"I really don't know."

"Second mistake. Always insist on knowing who's on the team."

There were probably several agents around me now with photos of this errant employee, but a positive make is always better. A person carries himself slightly differently from anyone else, and those noticeable traits cannot be described on paper. A man can alter his face, but not his walk, and they might have to track me at night.

Inside, I was treated like a leper. The word was out, and even though most did not understand the seriousness or implications, I was definitely persona non grata. The guard, secretaries and even clerks looked the other way. People fear guilt by association.

After being keyed through various security points, I briefly wondered if all my coded entry numbers had been changed. It would figure.

I walked directly to his desk, staring straight at him every step across the vast expanse of the fifth floor, then sat down without permission, a violation of normal manners. Buchannon said nothing, just waited, probably thinking of how many ways to castrate me.

"I have Stella Evans," I opened. "She's safe."

"Tell me about Zebra," he countered, ignoring my comment.

That would be his top priority. Screw the original problem, which was an FBI headache. Buchannon had been asked only for a minor assist, and now his group was deep in the mire without his approval or desire.

"Look!" I said loudly, charging to the offensive. "Everything about this project has been mucked from the beginning. Top Feds have been on it for months, and I found the girl in three days. The whole damn operation was run by Curly, Moe and Larry. There just might be a leak!"

It was pure crap. We both knew it, but it gave him an out, and I was counting on just that. He pondered and considered his position. If I was wrong it was my fault, but if I was right, he dared not lift the Zebra Condition. Until then, I was free to operate as a lone entity without agency interference. Either way, he was clean. My responsibility.

Buchannon was empowered to override me and cancel the code, rescinding my security "challenge," but the repercussions were enormous. His superiors in Washington would come unstuck. Our entire charter was ultrahush, ultrasecret, intentionally buried in a quicksand of bureaucratic red tape. A departmental leak from me or anyone to the outside world, in Buchannon's eyes, was comparable to a nuclear plant going to critical mass. He could and would use that argument to explain why his field agent had gone awry, and had best be left alone.

"If there is a leak," I said softly, augmenting my situation, "bringing in the girl might be fatal."

"She would be protected."

"Sure, like they protected Varisnoff." It was a cheap shot, but I was already on a gamble. Varisnoff was a defector I had brought in from Bulgaria, and through agency policy, I had turned him over to the Feds. He was dead in five days.

"Entirely different circumstances but let's not waste time debating your non sequitur. What are you going to do?"

As quickly as that, I had won. "Through her, I can get to Mateo."

"How?"

"Do you really want to know?"

Buchannon thought about it. The more he knew about my plans, the more vulnerable he was to criticism if I botched. Conversely, if I was successful, he would grab a lion's share of the orchids, no matter how little he was involved. It was crucial for my mission to keep him in a no-lose situation. I needed his full cooperation.

"Your ass is out a mile," was all he said.

"I have contingency plans," I replied confidently. "If anything happens to me, the Evans girl will call you personally. It's all arranged."

That pleased Buchannon, and I quickly dismissed the notion the bastard would have me burned so Stella would surrender to him. The possibility had occurred to me, but one has to have some faith.

"Do you want a field controller with you?"

I certainly did want a backup and immediate contact where I was going, but anyone he selected would constantly report my activities to the fifth floor. "Not for now," I answered.

"I want twenty-four-hour progress reports."

"No," I said, and we stared at each other like hungry dogs over a bone, each outflanking the other. "If you hear from her, it means I didn't make it."

That seemed to satisfy my boss. "Did the Feds get everything I sent you?"

"Of course," he scoffed, dabbing at his desk top for stray ashes. "In case you've forgotten, that is the primary objective, to provide information to other friendlies. And I told them you were definitely not in Cleveland, which is one of your forwarding services."

Buchannon smiled, enjoying games as long as he was the cat and someone else the mouse.

I stood, preferring to signal the meeting's end, rather than have him dismiss me. "Make certain the Feds know I'm clean with this office. I must have free rein."

"You are withholding a crucial federal witness."

"She hasn't been charged with anything, and with your help, they'll lay off. If they get to Mateo before me, she'll come in and testify, but for now, they've got to hold back on me."

"You're asking a lot, Cantrell. How much grease do you think I have with the Bureau?"

"And I'm risking a lot, because I know you've got the pull through certain Washington powers."

"Temporarily, I guarantee, only temporarily."

"That's all I need, just a little edge."

Buchannon had already thought out the potentials. "Okay," he mused. "For now."

Leaving, I nodded toward Cornwall, and he grinned back. I wanted to thank him for his technology, but Buchannon would probably think we were cohorts again. No sense putting Corny on the spot.

Barry Dirkson was at his desk one floor down, and I asked if anything had turned up on the dead girl.

"Zero. We don't know if the Cindy Cummings name is legit. Probably not. Just a drifter, I suppose. A poor little nobody."

"Your third mistake this day. There's no such thing as a nobody."

Outside, it took thirty seconds to spot the first tail and a minute for the second, but there would be others. It felt rather comforting being surrounded by a barrier of federal agents. I made no attempt to lose them. Everything in its own time.

In the cab back to the airport, I realized there had been no need to play my hole ace. Had Buchannon refused help, I would have been forced to tell him Stella's theory. Her idea of snatching Pierre Trudeau was nonsense, but Buchannon would have choked over my idea. For the moment, that was my private leverage.

I picked up my bag, checked it through, boarded Trans World and noticed my new friends had dropped off except one. Others would join him later, and his job was simple contact.

After a boring six hours, we landed at JFK, and I approached the baggage section. As my suitcase rotated on the carousel, I carefully observed the two locks. When latched, typical key slots are parallel to each other, but after locking mine, I can turn the left slot a few degrees. If they're exactly parallel, I can see someone has opened it and knows the contents.

This was the acid test. The welcoming agents had snooped and witnessed my firepower. The Ithaca scattergun was as illegal as hell, and I was not licensed in New York for the Walther. Plus, I hadn't red-tagged the suitcase in San Francisco as carrying arms. All very serious state and federal violations.

It was only by departmental cooperation that I had been untouched so far, but they could grab me on other statutes, press heavy charges and keep me on ice until I traded Stella. And Buchannon could do nothing.

Except for my gamble. Special Agent Wainwright knew my methods. I hoped he feared I had a signal system with Stella, so that if I fell, she would go to deep ground out of the country. He couldn't risk that.

Ironically, I had no such back door for Stella.

Confirmation arrived when I grabbed the tampered-with bag and walked away without interference. My bluff and Buchannon's clout had worked.

In Manhattan, after a handsome tip, I instructed the cab driver through a maze of several alleys behind hotels until locating one that was satisfactory. It must have given my tailers some strange thoughts.

I checked into the Monarch, a middle-class touristy place, and insisted on a third floor room in the rear. The window opened and provided a perfect view to the alley below.

I wandered the streets for a while, had three bagels and beer, then returned. They were experts, and to the ordinary eye nothing had been touched, but my tiny dabs of Vaseline had all been smeared. They had already checked my bag at the airport, but tossed the room anyway. It was a silly game we all played. I knew what they were doing, and *they knew* I knew, but went through the drill anyway.

The following morning I dressed slowly, working the strategy in my mind, knowing it would be improvised and altered with necessity. After all these years, I still had gut butterflies.

The Transcontinental Building is an enormous structure, and according to the wall directory, President Starkmore's office was on the fifty-fifth floor in the executive wing.

"You're getting a bit old for this active shit, ain't you, Pops?"

I turned to the voice and there stood FBI Special Investigator Roger W. Wainwright.

# 9. FEDS

IN A CORNER BOOTH of a nearby diner, we joked, lied and bragged about past victories and defeats. Finally, he came to the subject.

"So now you're baby-sitting a bunch of kids playing with computers?" Wainwright kidded.

"They let me out to run a few errands," I told him.

"Sure." He reacted, sarcasm overriding his usual calm. "Tell me, old fart, why this nonsense? This Mateo crap? It's not your fight."

"Well, like MacArthur said about Korea, maybe this is one last battle for an aging warrior."

"Bullshit. He only got fired. You will very likely get creamed, and by any number of people. Cantrell, you have a lot of new enemies. There's only one thing keeping you alive and on the street. You have the girl hidden someplace, and remembering your sneaky ways, she's probably impossible to surface."

"Maybe I'll get lucky and have a stroke. Save you all a lot of trouble."

"Believe me, that can easily be arranged." He ordered Danish with the coffee, and we flipped for the tab, automatically recalling that game from twenty years earlier. "Cantrell, you could have been one of the best."

"Roger, you used to tell me I was the best."

"I worked for you, remember? What else could I say? Look, Lone Ranger, I'm serious. After your... problem in the Sudan and the Company kissed you off, any agency would have grabbed up your talents and experience."

"Another glory bunch? No thanks."

"Come on, Cantrell, don't be such a damn prig. Hell, with your knowledge of counterinsurgency? Methodology? Infiltration? Networking? Christ, you had the influence. Yeah, the Company ghouls were assholes, but you could have pulled strings for the Secret Service! Defense Intelligence? Justice?"

"Thanks, pal." I was growing tired of this. "You know I hate regimentation. And the service? Ha! In Dallas back in '63 there were over fifty agents working the inner circle, and they still got to him. An impossible job, not my kind of vocation."

"You said they got to him? Don't tell me you buy the conspiracy theory?"

"And don't tell me that you can peddle the lone gunman idea with a straight face?"

"Touché. Well, what about the Bureau? You could have become an adviser or instructor."

"Are we talking about the same agency that describes pencils as 'manual inscribing instruments'? Get outta here."

"We're the best, you know."

"Once maybe. Roger, you have eight thousand agents, and what do you clowns do with them? Cracking the largest systems of organized crime in human history? Hell no, you fools deny they exist. Instead, you assign a hundred people to tempt congressmen into cocaine-buying stings. Jesus, anyone's vulnerable if the stakes are high enough."

My old buddy, with whom I had shared many a tight circumstance, was getting pissed. He was a very loyal type, but then, we had never agreed on much.

"Sorry, Roger, but you know my feelings. You guys watch your old television stories, and it's gone to your head.

The Mossad of Israeli intelligence is the best in the world. Why? Total dedication. KGB is second. They recognize and fulfill logical priorities. You're tied for third, but I won't mention with whom because I don't want to get punched.''

Roger shook his head and sighed. "You goddamned old dinosaur. Never have changed, have you? Always spitting into the wind.''

"I hate overly powerful government groups who are autonomous, answering only to their own kind. You guys were tops once, but the Second World War ended that, when real crime took a rear seat to Hoover's pet projects and paranoia. The Bureau has never recovered.''

"You bastard." He grinned. "You're still a shithead." He refilled the cups, relations strained from our overstepping of diplomatic grounds. "So, with your background, you end up in a think tank, baby-sitting whiz kids and their computers.''

"They let me go out and play, once in a while. Speaking of which, am I okay today?''

"Your clearance is so damn fragile, one blink and you're meat. Count on it." He waited a moment, then continued. "There are so many charges hanging over your ass, you'd never see daylight again. Assuming you'd survive the first ten seconds. I shouldn't tell you this, but your reputation in certain circles is keeping my people off your back. The bureau believes you've marked a trail for the girl. She'll go deep, and we'll never find her. I confirmed that you were capable of that. Any truth to it?''

"You're right. I'm capable.''

"Shithead," he muttered, with a noticeable tinge of respect or frustration, I couldn't tell which.

"We tracked you and the lady from Denver to Vegas, then it got murky. I suggested they check stolen cars reported within twelve hours of your arrival and where they eventually turned up, but then dropped it. I knew you'd pull a wrinkle and didn't want my boys sucking your smoke across the country. If you had the girl, you'd show up sooner or later."

"Here I am. So, what are your instructions?"

"What are your intentions?"

"Impasse." I smiled.

We stared at each other a long minute. Roger Wainwright was one of the few Bureau chiefs who knew anything about the Buchannon Detective Agency, and its association with Washington. To most, we were another pain in the ass. Even so, we had no real clout, supposedly information and nothing more. But Roger was aware that when things got really shitty, Buchannon would send out a sheep to either win or be slaughtered, and with no fanfare. Whatever the outcome, Washington was clean, and Americans could sleep at night knowing their protectors played righteous ball.

"Cantrell," Roger spoke softly. "I owe you a lot. More than I could ever admit. You brought this pup through the early days, Cuba, Bolivia, Algeria. You remember Havana when it was open season on gringos? And our butts were on the line?"

We returned to the TCA Building in silence, but once inside he grabbed my elbow and pulled me into a foyer. "Goddammit, Cantrell, I'm trying to save your bacon! I owe you, son of a bitch! Give us the girl and go home. You've already made your damn point. The Bureau, Homicide, cops all over the place look like idiots because of what you uncovered. Dammit, you've won! Don't you understand that? Go back and wrestle a desk or something. Become a consultant or retire or whatever, but get the hell *out*!"

"Can't," I said simply, not wanting him to know how badly I wanted out.

"Face it! You're too damn old for today's game."

"Thanks, Roger, I appreciate what you're saying. I really do. But what the hell."

He released the iron grip. "Okay, Pops, here's one for free. Mind you, I can't help if you get into a bind, which you probably will. But Miller, that big guy over there in the blue suit, is one of mine. He has additional orders straight from downtown. If you mess up the Starkmore payoff, or wreck any contact with Mateo, he'll put one in your spine. Count on it, baby. The only hope to nail Mateo is our way, and if you screw it, look out."

"Thanks," I muttered, feeling queasy.

"There's more. Miller was the assigned agent in San Francisco when your Miss Evans was accepted as the dead girl. He was convinced, and reported same. You have shattered his credibility. Need I say more?"

"Right. My triggerman does not love me."

"Exactly."

"Have you received all the data I gave Buchannon?"

"It's being digested now. I can't believe that's all you dug out of your girl after a week."

"A long story without much plot. She simply didn't know what was going on, didn't like Mateo and paid little attention to him."

"That's about the biggest stack of crap I've heard. Cantrell, you bastard, you have lots more, or you'd never be trying this stunt."

"Maybe I am getting senile."

"No shit. What now?"

"Now, assuming your Mr. Miller will allow it, I'm going up fifty-five floors to see Mr. Starkmore."

"He won't stop you. For now, you're just another citizen. But don't push it, my friend."

"Later," I said and turned, but he grabbed me again.

"Since you probably won't survive this dogfight, at least tell me why. Huh? This hero bullshit is not your line. I really want to know."

I gave that long thought. "Roger, I honestly don't know. Maybe it's a scared lady whose life has been turned upside down by a boyfriend who tried to kill her. Or maybe I hate turds like Mateo who upset the natural order of things, terrorists and bombers and maniacs. Or hell, Roger, it's probably like I said. One last chance for an old warrior."

"Shithead. So, you're going ahead?"

"Watch me."

# 10. SETUP

WAINWRIGHT ACCOMPANIED ME to the private elevator as I stole a quick glance at Miller, standing in the lobby and looking quite capable of nailing me. And enjoying it.

Roger blocked the door open with his foot. No one else apparently had the authority to use this executive elevator. It was empty. "Cantrell, you're a citizen, and I can't stop you from seeing Starkmore. But I told him of your *unrecognized* status in this matter."

"I'm sure you did. He probably thinks I'm a leper after your description."

"Close." Wainwright grinned.

"What exactly did you tell him?"

"Precisely the truth. That you're from a nonactive department of our government, that you have no connection with mine and that you are meddling outside your minuscule authority."

"Thanks for the torpedo. I'm amazed he's seeing me."

Roger looked slightly amused. "You know, so am I. Buchannon probably knows someone in D.C., with grease. Figures your five minutes with Starkmore can't hurt."

I smiled and stepped inside. As the door closed I tried to calculate Wainwright's cooperation, meager as it was. But he wanted the girl and perhaps I might drop a hint to Starkmore about her location.

Our game of minds was still on.

The express shot me fifty-five floors with gut-wrenching speed, and opened to lavish carpets, enormous plants, massive desks, soothing background Muzak, all ventilated with antiseptically purged air. I wondered how these people survived the environmental and cultural shock when they returned to city streets among the mortals. Or maybe they lived up here forever.

I introduced myself to an exquisite Oriental woman, who announced my presence into a hidden device. I spotted four video cams and realized Mr. Starkmore was probably observing me right then. Twenty seconds later, the lovely lady ushered me into the executive world.

Everything was larger, grander, plushier than anything on the floor. Rank hath its privileges, and this was obviously top dog. There were no less than twenty television monitors on the left wall displaying news and stock information from around the globe. The sound was off, but the pictures were a strange kaleidoscope of color.

Mr. Starkmore was precisely what I expected, and my heart sank a notch.

I had hoped for a man, but was confronted by a Harvard M.B.A., no blood, just accounting ink in the veins, a flawless executive. Precisely one-half-inch of cuff extended beyond the custom-made jacket sleeves, links and tie tack were matching gold, and his slightly creased, tanned, fiftyish, rock-hard face with graying temples looked right off the cover of *Esquire*.

We cautiously shook hands. "Mr. Cantrell," he said in a firm voice.

"Mr. Starkmore, I understand my counterpart has discussed my involvement with your...problem."

He walked behind a huge desk and sat down, motioning me to a chair. "I don't think counterpart was exactly Mr. Wainwright's definition."

"Roger is trying very hard to discredit me before I even begin, but ask yourself, why am I here? For that matter, why does the Bureau even allow me to see you?"

"I don't know. Subterfuge in business I understand, but this is out of my realm. He was quite vague, only emphasizing that you have no authority and I may cooperate with you or not, entirely at my discretion."

"That sounds like my buddy," I said sarcastically.

"Then perhaps you can explain it to me."

"You see, there are certain government groups with information and abilities not shared by others. Occasionally, we cross paths."

"What government groups?" he demanded.

I was losing him. Roger had done a fine job of character assassination. "That's not important," I countered firmly. "As you know, there are numerous federal entities that are household words—FBI, Secret Service, CIA. They receive the publicity for several reasons. But certain key projects and objectives can only be obtained through the use of more ... let's say, clandestine organizations. Particularly if the problem is sensitive, such as yours. I'm assuming you prefer no media coverage?"

"Are you kidding?" He roared. "Our stock would drop like a turd."

"Yes," I confirmed. "If people knew some maniac was planting bombs on your aircraft."

Starkmore calmed. "You know about all that?"

"I assure you, I know far more about it than anyone else."

Starkmore looked dubious.

"I have top-level clearance and the promised cooperation from the Bureau."

The man was still unsure of this development, probably accustomed to a room filled with consultants.

I had made my point, and it was time to thrust, not with a gentle finesse but straight power plays. "Mr. Starkmore, the Bureau has been screwing with this problem for three months and accomplished nothing. Every passing day increases the odds some newspaper will catch the story."

He visibly paled.

"I think I can get Mateo for you."

There was a stunned silence. "How?" he finally asked.

"Because I have information from a source and a plan the Bureau does not have and can't get, and that is the only reason I have been allowed up here."

I let him absorb that a minute. "The FBI will continue their efforts, naturally, but it's your airline and your money and your problem. Just listen to my idea. What's there to lose doing that?"

"Nothing, at this point. I can hear what you propose."

"Is that your private bathroom?" I asked, nodding to a door. "Good, let's talk in there." Before he replied, I led the way and closed the door behind us.

Inside, I cranked both water taps on full and flushed the toilet. "Sir, your office is wired six different ways. If you belch, people in Washington know it."

He glanced nervously about, no doubt thinking of private conversations held in the recent past. "Now?" he asked.

"Continually," I answered. "It's standard routine for them in these cases, but the water will cover our voices," I added in a conspiring tone. It was us against the other team. Spies everywhere.

I let him ponder that a moment. "You realize that Wainwright had no objection to our talking? I want you to understand I can do things the FBI cannot, and they know it. They also know if I fail, there's no harm done. If you'd like to check further on that, we have a mutual contact in Washington. You asked a senator for help. Well, that's me."

Again I paused to let that sink home. The next was the gamble I had to win or go home. "I want to get a message to Mateo during the payment tomorrow, and there's only one way to do it. I need to tape a letter to the outside of the briefcase as the courier leaves the bank. It has to be done on the street."

"I don't understand."

"If it's inside the case, Mateo will realize the Bureau knows the message. It's a bluff, which I think might connect, but only if Mateo's people see it happen. It must look realistic."

"What do you want me to do?"

I thought he'd never ask. "After the money is counted and packed and about to be given to the courier, tell Wainwright emphatically, I mean with real authority, that you have given me permission to stop the courier for ten seconds and say something to him. That's all."

"Just that?" Starkmore asked, flushing the toilet himself, enjoying the subterfuge.

"That's a whole lot because Wainwright will have a fit. His men will stop me if he doesn't okay it, because they will cover that boy like a blanket."

"I'll tell him right now!"

"No, no good. That would give him twenty-four hours to prepare and thwart my move. He'd probably have me arrested for jaywalking. It must be at the last possible moment with no time for Wainwright to think or call for instructions. I've got to catch him unprepared, so your timing is critical. He has at least one overanxious agent looking for an excuse to shoot me."

"Honestly?" Starkmore shook his head.

"It's an old grudge, you might say." The hot water was steaming, building a thick mist. Starkmore didn't seem to mind. "Well?" I asked. "I just might pull it off, no guarantees, but your help is vital. And if I do screw up, there's no harm done."

"Except to you, perhaps."

"I get paid for it."

"Pardon my question, but aren't you somewhat senior for this kind of assignment?"

"I'm no hero, if that's what you mean. And I'm not suicidal."

"What's in the letter?"

"An invitation to meet."

"Sounds doubtful to me. What will you do if it works? Arrest him?"

"Let's just say, if I make contact, your problem will be over."

Starkmore was on his turf now, negotiating, wheedling, seeking the optimum advantage. "Since Mr. Wainwright magnanimously allowed this discussion, I can only assume your credentials are impeccable. Although I do not understand all this secret department stuff, maybe I do detect a glimmer of personal motivation. Somehow, I get the impression this is voluntary on your part. If so, I would like to know why."

He caught me off guard. I was prepared to logically debate all aspects, and even divulge parts of my operational plan, but this question snagged me. "Mr. Starkmore, there are a dozen good reasons, but none sufficiently demanding to justify it, except one. I want that bastard."

He hesitated, then smiled. "I do not understand your personal motives, but I might comprehend the drive behind them. A long time ago, a friend took my girl. Married her, in fact. He also scored higher in final exams, graduated above me and made more money for several years. He was even a superior athlete. Hell, I had a dozen reasons to hate him. I wanted to get even, and did, but not for the expected reasons. No, I hated him because he once embarrassed me in public. Just once, but I never forgave him." Starkmore smiled. "Ridiculous, isn't it? But purely personal. Mr. Cantrell, your reason is the same. Purely personal."

I grinned at him. "Sort of."

"Well, that I understand. Okay, I'll do what you ask."

"Don't mention anything about a message. Just instruct him to keep his clones away from me, and that you have approved my actions."

"You have it. Uh, good luck."

As I left, Roger was waiting for me at the receptionist's desk. When his wiretap in Starkmore's office had zeroed out, he must have panicked and followed me up the fifty-five floors. "Just what the hell was that all about?" he demanded.

"I was complaining about his airline's food. It sucks, don't you think?"

"Cantrell, you miserable son of a bitch! You've dug a hole, and I'll bury you in it. I'm calling Washington to revoke your clearance."

"Gotcha," I replied, and waited for the elevator.

Starkmore appeared in his doorway. "Mr. Wainwright, come in here. I would like to discuss your listening devices in my private office."

Roger was angry because the bathroom was the only area in Starkmore's empire not bugged. It was ironic because during the Hoover dynasty, that and the bedroom would have been the first places taped, but with today's moralistic attitude, the bathroom was considered taboo. Odd, how things work out. Starkmore's life, private and public, had escaped five minutes of recording, and Roger didn't know how to explain that to his superiors. One would think Starkmore was the perpetrator rather than the victim.

Wainwright would ask what I proposed, but Starkmore was obviously adept at handling underlings.

In forty-eight hours things would begin happening fast. So needing think time, I wandered the streets for hours and burned off adrenaline.

The walk also gave me opportunity to observe my assigned followers. Two were first-rate, and it took me twenty minutes to spot them. As they switched off, I decided on Miller. He was just too anxious and would be my scapegoat. I almost regretted it, having already stiffed him in San Francisco when I blew his investigation of the dead girl. Such things stay on your record. Oh well, in this business one goes for the weak link.

I made a mental note—after I dodged Miller, never to be alone with him. He'd find an excuse to waste me.

The next twenty hours were horrible, because once the plan was galvanized, there was nothing to do but worry.

Wainwright had probably made a hundred calls to his superiors, but since I was still loose, everything must be okay. No doubt Buchannon had a part in that, calling in his markers from highly placed individuals.

The last night, I would have given anything for a hot bubble bath, but the room had only a shower and chattering pipes. At midnight, I prepared my departure. I had chosen my bag carefully, dark and worn from use, but with a firm handle and tight rivets holding the sides and bottom. I loaded it with my armaments, each piece carefully wrapped and taped. There were two coils on the table, one a light string, the other strong cord. I attached the ends of both to the bag handle, and played them out in opposite directions on the floor.

There are no new tricks, only modern variations of old ones. An instructor at Langley once told me to study history, and I would learn more techniques than he could ever teach.

The ancient Corinthians did not always indulge themselves with luxury and licentious behavior. They also enjoyed harassing and plundering the less fortunate locals who hid their valuables by hanging bundles from rooftops. In smuggling circles it is appropriately called a Corinth drop, although most mispronounce it as Cornith.

I tested the ordinary string for strength, secured the end to an obscure corner of the windowsill, then lowered my bag over the ledge five feet. I darkened the heavy cord with shoe polish and experimented until it dangled downward, the end just high enough to reach from the alley below.

Sitting on a rickety chair, I sipped the last of the Napoléon and mentally rehearsed what would happen next. So many things could go wrong. When other people control my destiny, it always makes me nervous.

In case Wainwright's people dropped in for an unexpected visit, I did not dare write the message until the last possible minute. Before leaving the following morning, I wrote it with a thick felt marker.

Mateo,
It was a nice plan but you blew it. Your goons in San Francisco killed the wrong girl. I have Stella Evans and she can identify you. There is a fat reward on your head. Unless you want her to call the FBI, we better talk now. I will be at the United Terminal at JFK Wednesday night at six. Have me paged through a passenger courtesy phone. I will wait only fifteen minutes.

Cantrell

Mateo would have difficulty refusing this gambit. I had connected him directly with Stella, and therefore with the murder. I suggested blackmail, a subject he understood. I had also insulted him, and anyone capable of pulling off extortion of this magnitude must possess a gigantic ego. Most important, he could contact me at the airport from literally anyplace with little fear of discovery or a trap. Naturally, that was also a prime reason I liked the arrangement; it would be impossible for his people to cover every courtesy phone in that massive building.

I clipped a carefully selected business card to the message identifying myself as a detective with the Buchannon Agency. Mateo would check, and our system was thorough. The receptionist would innocently ask for my employee number off the card, and that particular number would reflect I had been with the organization almost thirty years, and specialized in locating runaway wives and teenagers.

The last item was the coup de grace, the photo taken of Stella three days earlier. She was holding the latest *San Francisco Chronicle*, and the headlines were clear. Mateo would understand she was alive, and to add salt, I had her inscribe the picture.

Mateo,
You missed me, and now you're in deep shit! Sam loved bragging about you to impress me. I know a lot more than you think. Pay or I start talking!
Stella

I sealed the manila envelope and lined double-backed tape around the edges, then prayed Wainwright's eager beavers would not pull a quickie search when I entered the bank.

Looking around the room one last time, I mentally re-checked everything, then the Corinth drop hanging from my window. I would not be returning to the room, and depending on unforeseen events, might not be returning anyplace.

Ever.

# 11. FLUSH

FORTY MINUTES LATER, I strolled into the Chase Manhattan Bank, an enormous structure, crowded and chaotic with swarms of rushing people. I considered Mateo might have someone watching from inside, but that seemed too risky. Video cams were everywhere, recording every person.

Outside the private office on the second floor were two agents trying hard to look inconspicuous. Inside, Starkmore, Wainwright and a bevy of bank officials were probably counting, recounting and recording the million dollars.

I approached the two agents, and Miller appeared beside me. I made silly talk about weather, the elections, and last year's Super Bowl, knowing it would irritate Miller. Obviously, Wainwright had made it clear I was still hands-off material. Even though no one replied, I continued to gab nonsense. "Is everything all set with Starkmore?" I asked. No one answered so I added, "Good."

It was important the two with Miller remember me later when I made my move. I couldn't risk them getting nervous and stopping me. This way, they knew I had some association with the operation, no matter how vague, and that would buy me a few precious seconds.

Even more important, the courier had to know I was part of the group. After the warnings he would no doubt receive inside the office, I had to acquire his confidence and recognition. I would be cutting it close and timing was crucial.

A few minutes past eleven, a young, gangling uniformed courier approached, probably a night student. "Mr. Richard's office?'' he cautiously asked, being secretly photographed from a dozen angles.

Miller flipped his FBI badge and demanded identification. The poor kid almost had a hemorrhage. With shaking hands, he pointed to a card pinned to his shirt. I saw the name tag.

"Hi, Tom," I said with a friendly grin. "Relax, you haven't done anything wrong. Just rules."

"Quiet!" Miller snarled through clenched teeth.

"He's right, Tom," I confirmed. "We're not supposed to talk out here."

Agent Miller was highly agitated, but the ploy served my purpose. Tom knew this was federal business, and since I was in the group, he would not panic when I approached him in a few minutes.

Tom was ushered into the grand office and probably received the scare of his young life. Mateo's rules were explicit, allowing only three minutes for the entire transaction. I could picture the nervous kid barraged with a thousand questions. He would be handed a tiny radio transmitter on a magnetic case for attaching to his bike, and instructions for passing to the next courier. Good luck! It hadn't worked yet, but the Bureau had to do something.

The youth came out looking terrified and carrying the briefcase, followed by Roger Wainwright, who was visibly angry. Obviously, President Starkmore had just informed him I could approach Tom on the street. I looked straight at Roger but pointed to Miller. "You *will* tell *him* I have clearance."

As I trailed behind the courier, Wainwright took Miller's elbow and whispered something. "What? No!" the Fed screeched, and I knew he had just been told.

Outside, I paused until Tom had removed his bike lock, snapped the transmitter to the frame and thrown his leg over. "Wait, Tom," I shouted at the last possible second. "We forgot this."

He was stunned. "Jeez, I can't open the delivery," he protested in fear, clutching the precious cargo.

"No need," I said calmly, and peeled off the adhesive backing and pressed the envelope firmly against the case.

"Is it valuable?" He gulped.

"No, just a note, but very important, so don't lose it."

Wainwright and Miller were coming from the bank door as another agent informed them what I had done. Unprepared, the agents were caught off guard, not certain what to do. Timing was everything.

"Go now," I urged, pushing Tom on his way.

"You bastard!" Wainwright screamed. "You son of a bitch! What the fucking hell was in that letter?"

"A message."

"You've done it, Cantrell. Goddammit, this time you've gone too far. I'll burn you for this!"

Miller was standing to one side and reacted in typical cop fashion, twisting my right arm in a painful hammerlock. Other agents rushed over to assist containment of this dangerous old man. "Ask Starkmore," I offered weakly. "He gave me the okay."

"To say something to the kid. To say something! Not pass any goddamned messages!"

If I had planned and practiced their moves all day, it could not have turned out better. Wainwright turned crimson and babbled commands, thinking of the certain reprimand that would stick to him forever. The Bureau never forgets. He was furious.

"Bring him!" he snarled, and three agents cuffed my wrists from behind, tighter than I thought necessary. I struggled just enough so they had to push me a bit. Miller practically threw me to the curb, then into a waiting car.

Beautiful performance. I hoped like hell someone from Mateo's team was watching, or I had wasted it.

My only fear now, and a very realistic one, was of Wainwright's zealots and their hatred of me.

Even with many years of experience around law agencies, it is still psychologically threatening to be firmly manacled and shoved into a federal building with bystanders watching.

Miller wished I'd try something cute so he could whack me one, but I'm not that stupid. Roger screamed and ranted for fifteen minutes, with only occasional gasps of air. I was slammed down on a hard bench in a small interrogation room, cold and bare, similar to those in thousands of police stations everywhere. Ugly.

After Roger had vented and became coherent, I explained in detail what was in the envelope, but not Stella's personal notation. She was in sufficient trouble already, and with a signed admission that she knew details about the extortion, the Bureau could crucify her. I had explained this to Stella earlier, but the tough little lady insisted on helping in any way possible.

Wainwright continued to ask questions, but was constantly interrupted by the phone. "Speak," was all he would say, then hang up and scowl. Several times he left the room for a few seconds, no doubt conferring with his superiors, who at this point wanted no part of the problem. Someone had glitched, and they were quite content to let Roger hang for it. Federal agents, like good politicians, test the wind before getting involved or rendering an opinion.

Certainly, Roger was also trying to contact Buchannon, to confirm my orders and limitations. Although Wainwright was a highly competent, first-class agent, this mess was beyond his scope.

Censure of a field operative of a "friendly" agency could only come from the top down. It had to travel the management chain upward, let the top directors hack it out, then descend with pearls of wisdom and mandates. Bypassing authority for lateral directions between bipartisan agencies was unthinkable. That was Roger's problem. He didn't know what to do with me, and Buchannon probably refused to acknowledge Special Agent Roger Wainwright on the phone. A mess.

I almost felt sorry for my old buddy.

An hour passed as Miller sat like a statue, never taking his eyes from me. Roger returned, and I could tell by his attitude the money exchange had taken place, and Mateo had duped the Bureau again.

"How did they maneuver the final phase?" I asked, not really expecting a response.

He sighed twice, then reluctantly explained. "They routed through fifteen couriers and switched on the ninth. We knew it would happen but couldn't get close enough to see the action. The kid was supposed to take a particular elevator at Rockefeller Plaza, then go to an office where another courier was waiting."

"And," I continued with a degree of sympathy, "one of Mateo's people exchanged cases with the boy in the elevator?"

"Yeah." Roger grimaced. "No way to see it. The kid went on with a phony case and we tracked it across town."

"Did you grab the couriers?"

"Hell yes!" Roger snapped. "They've all been questioned. We've never learned anything from them. Next time I'm planting a transmitter on the briefcase. This is bullshit!"

"Sure, which any Boy Scout with a multifrequency scanner can spot. Then Mateo carries out his threat and blows one of Starkmore's planes. Are your shoulders broad enough to carry three hundred deaths?''

"You're not helping this botched mess with your crap. Goddammit, Cantrell, just shut up."

There was no anger in his comment this time, just frustration. I was another problem. A hip-shot decision at high level became my biggest fear. Top directors in intelligence are just like any other executives, very prone to dart board administrations. The longer it took, the better my odds.

Ergo: my fate.

Roger received another call. He listened, said "yes sir," then hung up. "In private," he said to Miller, and the young agent slowly left the room.

"Well, what am I in for? Thumbscrews or electrodes?"

He ignored my sarcasm. "Since I've been in direct contact with the entire operation, my boss feels it best to let me handle your 'involvement.' He's still trying to connect with Buchannon."

"Hah! Good luck. So, you're the stuckee?"

"Right, for now. My superior is down the hall two hundred feet, but doesn't want to get his hands dirty. Won't even come see you."

"Figures. Listen, Roger. We've crossed a few bridges together, and we know how to keep score. Your boss and mine have us both dangling. The pressure from Washington over this extortion is boiling and about to explode. Our regal leaders need scapegoats, and we're elected."

"What's new?"

"You can hold me for obstructing federal justice for how long? A week? Month? And what have you gained? Nothing! Not to mention your primary witness drops out of sight forever."

"You shithead. Cantrell, you've made fools of us all. Big points. Now, turn over the girl and get out. You've been in the service for so long, most old-timers think you're dead. This way, you can be a legend again."

"Let me play it through," I said simply. "Why not see if Mateo bites on my letter? Put a heavy tag on me, and you can name the terms. It just *might* work! And if not, no harm done."

"No harm? You mean besides losing my pension and the wife going back to chopping french fries?"

"You got to buck the wind once in a while."

He stared at me a long time, then we began a series of bartering games, back and forth, give and take, neither capitulating. He wanted Stella, and I wanted out of there. We were getting nowhere.

I jotted a note on a desk pad. TURN OFF THE LISTENERS.

Roger grinned, then pushed a button on his phone. "We're alone now."

Smiling in return, I said loudly, "Remember that time in Argentina? You were pissing razor blades for a week after a romp with two young hookers."

He chuckled. "I told you, the tapes are off."

"Okay, a trade. This is a first-class, A-1 exclusive plum, and just for you only. No one knows but me, not even Buchannon. Let me push on with my plan, unchecked, and the information is yours."

"First, I want the girl."

"Come on, Roger, you know I might need her to convince Mateo. A phone call or another photo. Without her, I'm blowing smoke."

"Okay, give me this juicy tidbit."

"Nope, sight unseen." I studied Roger and decided he was not going for it. "Okay, you're a pompous ass, but credible. I'll tell you, and it's your call. If you think it's worth it, I get a complete release."

"Only with a tight tail on you, and if Mateo bites, I monitor any kind of meeting between you two."

"Done," I agreed. "You won't regret it. We know that Mateo is taking unbelievable risks to get his payments. Every one greatly increases the odds of getting caught. Why? Why take such idiotic gambles when he could have demanded the whole twelve million in one chunk? Starkmore and TCA could afford it. Twelve mill is nothing."

"Don't you think I stay awake nights wondering about that?"

"It's because Mateo's showing off."

"Say again?"

"He wants to prove it can be done, he's capable of pulling it off, and he has the power to control and extort from a major world airline at his leisure. And right under the FBI's nose. So why? For his own ego? Or is he trying to impress someone?"

"I'm waiting for your divine answer, Cantrell."

"Because this TCA deal is just the surface. It's a trial run, so to speak. A demonstration. I believe the real show is yet to come."

"I'm still waiting."

I leaned forward. "When Mateo would meet with Avalon at Stella's house, she overheard pieces of conversation and the name, Trudeau, not once, but dozens of times, always in conjunction with planes and bombs. She thinks they're planning a snatch or hit on the former Canadian prime minister."

"Ridiculous," he scoffed.

"Of course it is, but try this. *She* thought they were saying Trudeau, but I believe it was Trudor."

Roger stared a long moment. "Holy shit," he finally whispered.

"The most-sought-after professional terrorist on earth. He's been linked to bombings in Libya, Iran, France, Syria, and a dozen other places. Think about it, Roger. Doesn't this sound like his kind of insanity?"

"Holy shit," he repeated, still staring into space.

"Trudor sets up a long-term extortion with bombs, placing them well in advance, then pops a few to show he's serious. After he gets the money, or terrorist friends out of jail, or whatever, he tells where the other bombs are hidden."

Roger was thinking. "Remember the overthrow in Chad?"

"Precisely," I agreed, grateful that Wainwright was considering the possibility. "If the Mateo extortion plot against Transcontinental works, as it seems to be doing, it's a perfect vehicle for a radical like Trudor. He loves bombs and despises Americans. A scary combination in his hands. He's been known to demolish an embassy just for simple hatred."

"Jesus, if Trudor could prove he's capable of blackmailing an entire airline for a year, he could threaten to shut down United, American, Pan Am, TWA, any of them!"

"Yep. One, or all at once."

Wainwright began pacing. "We know so damn little about him. There are Bureau reports with the theory it might even be a series of people using one name. We do know he escapes notoriety because of his dislike of the media. Most terrorists love the cameras and front page for their insane causes, but not Trudor. In the Chad incident, there is little doubt he planted bombs, extorted their government into shambles, kidnapped officials, then drifted off without his name ever making the news."

"Most terrorists are fanatic crazies, but Trudor is a simple murderer on a grand scale, to the highest bidder."

Wainwright weighed the factors. "Right, and he never bluffs."

"This extortion is Trudor's method," I pointed.

"No one's even seen Trudor for certain. Any chance he and Mateo are the same?"

"No," I said firmly. "Too many operational differences. He would never have dealt directly with triggermen like Avalon, and he would not have botched the hit on Stella. No, Mateo is running it, but I believe Trudor is in the background somewhere, commanding."

Roger shrugged. "You realize if I relay your . . . theory, it will automatically bring in the CIA ghouls. They want him for a dozen reasons."

"Yes, my alma mater will be interested, but that's your problem."

"I could sit on it." He pondered. "It's only an idea."

"Roger, my message in the envelope says to call me at Grand Central," I said, trying to plan ahead and outthink the Bureau. "I claim to know everything about the scam and want a piece of the pie. If, and I say if, Mateo bites and contacts me, I might be able to confirm or discount the Trudor theory. That's the only way we'll know for sure."

"That will be my decision point," Wainwright said, pleased he could delay for a logical period. "If it's Trudor, I have to pass it along."

Miller was invited back into the room, and we spent an hour detailing my instructions and how Wainwright's people would track me. I made numerous concessions and felt smug about it, knowing I had no intention of cooperating, but it would get me out of that place.

Knowing the Bureau, they would tell Starkmore little more than necessary, and I felt obligated, so stopped at the Transcontinental Building with Miller two paces behind.

After the stomach-grabbing express elevator, I was ushered in immediately.

"I've sent messages with the payments before," Starkmore confided. "The bastard never answered."

"He just might acknowledge this one." I explained my note and the photo from Stella.

"What will you do if he answers?"

"Make contact," I replied. "Try to shut him off."

"How?"

"Types like Mateo you don't arrest. They have too many blind spots to hide behind. No witnesses or corroboration. Even the girl can only testify he was in her house and talked about planes. That's enough for us, but not a court. All we'd bag are the peons. That's why I say this. You might be the loser."

"He could still destroy one of my planes?"

"That's always possible with a nut like him. I thought you should know, in case you want me to stop right now. There is a definite risk."

"Not to mention a definite risk to yourself."

"Also possible." I grinned. "Comes with the territory."

"I leave it entirely to you, Cantrell. The others have made no progress in three months, and I cannot continue like this."

I gazed at him. "Fine," I said softly.

Miller had waited outside the room, and I had not bothered to use the executive washroom for sound cover. Even with Starkmore's objections earlier, I knew Wainwright would have it wired. Besides, I said nothing they did not already know, and preferred not to appear devious to my escorts. After all, we were working together now, just one happy team.

The methods of ditching a trail are many, some quite creative, practically an art. Generally, the person being followed is not supposed to know he's being tagged, so he tries to make the ditch look almost accidental. In my case, Miller was a friendly, walking five to ten feet behind, making no attempt at cover. Because of that, I could pull the stops and make no pretense. It made it easier.

Posh stores in that neighborhood have rear exits, with the premises extending from one street to another through the middle of the block. After wandering aimlessly window-shopping, I entered an exclusive, outrageously priced jewelry store on Thirty-third. Putting several yards between me and my escort, I walked briskly to a pair of armed guards standing unobtrusively near the diamond displays.

"The man in the blue suit behind me is carrying a gun. I saw it. Be careful." With that, I passed between them and scurried on, but not before seeing the shocked look on their faces.

Rental cops are primarily for visual deterrent, usually working decades without unholstering a weapon. They are also amateurs and overeager. I glanced back and saw them pull on Miller. In nervous voices, they demanded he raise his hands. Very dramatic.

It would take only seconds for him to produce identification, but that was all I needed. Breaking into an open run, I hit the rear door while Miller was still yelling.

It was strictly a kindergarten exercise, but quite effective. I ran left on Thirty-fourth into a department store, and back to Thirty-third. I glanced in the jewelry store window and saw Miller racing away from me toward Thirty-fourth, so I jumped a cab and took off. I instructed him down the alley and stopped just below my hotel window. The blackened cord was difficult to spot against the filthy brick wall, but I found it and yanked hard. The weaker string above snapped, dropping the bag one floor into my arms.

I was in no mood to keep switching cabs, so the driver took me to the nearest car rental. I had to be clean. After wandering aimlessly for miles, cutting back and forth and checking my rear, I found a desolate motel in Brooklyn, ideal for my purposes.

Dumping Miller had been ridiculously simple.

I didn't know then I was being suckered.

# 12. CONTACT

ARRIVING AT KENNEDY thirty minutes early, I wondered how many of Wainwright's agents were milling around Grand Central awaiting further instructions.

It was time to check in, so I called Buchannon on his emergency transfer line. "Cantrell here."

"How's the aging boy wonder?"

"Coping."

"You're too old for this nonsense."

"I'm getting very tired of hearing that. Any citizens show recent interest in me?"

"A credit outfit wanted employment verification. The usual stuff. They claimed you applied for a charge card. The trace surfaced a cheap hotel in Queens. We followed up, and after the call, a nothing guy checked out. Zero on that. And no progress on the name Mateo connecting to the city of San Mateo. Our guess is he was passing through, or not there long enough to establish identity on any data bank. Corny says it's a wash, but he's still hacking on it."

Buchannon could immediately view the terminal screen and see I was calling from somewhere on the airport property, but he made no mention of it. "Think Mateo will come through?" he asked.

"He has nothing to risk by calling. Yeah, he will, for curiosity if no other reason."

"I assume the girl's okay. Anything to update?"

"Not yet," I answered.

Buchannon then came close to concern for my safety. "I'm not telling you to be careful, you old war-horse, but for God's sake, Cantrell, make it clean."

For a quarter hour I was suddenly very nervous. What if Mateo didn't bite? What would Wainwright do about my latest transgression? How far would Buchannon back me? And Jesus, what about Stella?

I was so preoccupied, I almost missed the public-address announcement. "Paging Mr. Cantrell. Please pick up the nearest passenger courtesy phone."

"Cantrell here," I answered into the receiver, then repeated it several times as the operator made connections.

"Hello," came the voice, gruff, uncertain.

"Mateo," I offered. "Glad you called," I responded simply, preferring him to make the initial play.

"Mr. Cantrell, I'm trying to decide if you're an idiot, or you think I am."

"Neither, I hope."

"What the hell do you want?"

"Simple. A payoff."

"And I get the girl?"

"That's negotiable. However, right now she's my insurance policy, but Stella is broke. It takes real money to disappear. She realizes that now. Look at the practical side. After what you and Sam put her through, any court would award Stella millions in damages for mental stress." I said it lightly, trying to sound relaxed and jovial. Didn't wash.

"How much?" he asked without enthusiasm.

"One of the payments. Just ask for a thirteenth instead of twelve. Won't hurt a bit."

"A million? You're fucking crazy!"

"It's a nice, tidy number. Look, Mateo, let's cut the bullshit." The light touch had failed to impress, now get serious. "If Stella Evans wanted to finger you, the FBI would have her, also your description spread across the country. All she wants is compensation. I think three months of silence have proved her worth.''

''You have nothing.''

''You must think I do, otherwise why risk a hit on her? And why call me? You damn well know Stella can burn you. Let's get on with it. I want a million, but none of this installment crap. One payment, and in ten days.''

''Impossible!'' he spit.

That was his mistake. It meant the time limit or the amount was a problem, but he was at least considering a payoff.

''How'd you know we missed the girl, and where'd you find her?''

''That's my business,'' I said, knowing he would press the issue, which was my intent. It was more effective if he wheedled the reluctant information from me.

''Bullshit! I want to know everything or kiss off right now.''

It had to be accurate for belief. I explained the eye color, and the botched-up autopsy of Cindy Cummings, and the mistaken notion it was Stella. ''I'm a private detective with a lot of years behind me. I pieced the puzzle together and found her hiding in the Midwest.''

We sparred for several minutes as Mateo quizzed me. ''Go back to the beginning,'' he demanded. ''Why'd you get involved in the first place? Huh? She was dead for three months, according to the cops. Why were you snooping?''

It was the weakest link in my pitch. Buchannon had asked me for a report to satisfy Washington, but Mateo must never learn of our association with the Feds. ''There's lots of ways to make a buck in my business. I get information others can't, and I often earn a profit from it. My specialty is locating missing people, and I have a few, let's say, underpaid friends on the police force. Whenever they turn up an unclaimed body, usually a young person, I start to dig for background. I locate family and they usually pay well. Proper burial and all that."

"And sometimes there's unclaimed inheritance, huh?"

"You have the idea."

"You're a real gem, Cantrell."

It was the kind of scam Mateo would understand. "It's a living."

"So, figuring out it was the wrong girl, you found the right one?"

"A piece of cake for me. Someone tried to kill her, so I kept the pressure on until Stella told me everything. I knew there was a buck to make someplace. And here you are."

"Then you claim to just walk up and tell Starkmore you wanted to blackmail me? Right in front of the FBI? Now who's being an idiot!"

The last fragile area, but he was still listening. "No, I merely made him an offer. I had private information known only to me, which might trap you. For a million dollars, I'd bring you in, and he's through paying."

"He bought that line of shit?"

"Why not? He has nothing to lose. No win, no pay. Besides, he's pissed that the Bureau can't grab your ass." I let Mateo think on that. Feed the ego. "You have Starkmore on the run. He's a wreck and willing to try anything."

Mateo said it very slowly. "So, either I pay you, or you come after me for a million from him?"

"You got it. Strictly business."

"Jesus, you're a real creep, you know that?"

"Yeah, but an honest creep," I mumbled. "If we're going to do business, it's best to come clean. A degree of trust, you might say."

He cleared his throat with a disgusted growl. "Why didn't you put that stupid message inside the case?"

"With the Bureau right there watching the money count?"

"How long did they hold you?"

So, he had seen them grab me. Good. "Short time, just until Starkmore explained I have permission to act independently. He's retained me privately, to investigate the problem. It's legal, and it's his money. Believe me, I didn't like sending that message, but it was the only way to contact you."

"The FBI must be all over your ass."

"Were, until this morning. I ditched them."

"You conning me now?"

"I've been around, Mateo. You've thrown those creeps three times already. It was easy."

"They know about the girl being alive?"

"*Are you kidding!* Jesus, man, you think I'd be walking around if they knew I have her? Use your head! Even Starkmore doesn't know that." It was bound to be asked and I was ready, hoping the mental jab would irritate.

"The whole damn thing stinks," Mateo mused, more to talk than anything. He was trying to assimilate all this data, looking for flaws, weak spots, logic. His extortion was planned to fastidious detail, with everything honed to a fine edge.

Mateo was extremely upset because a mistake had been made. He considered the risks, responsibility, and wondered whether to ignore me or not. Either choice was a distasteful variation of his original plan.

"Okay, okay," he responded. "Why deal with me and risk the law if you can get the same million from Starkmore?" Mateo was testing for any weakness. Desperation crept into his voice.

I replied slowly. He had to accept this part. "Because you're a sure thing. If I have to come after you, the Bureau will claim full credit, and I'll be in a pissing contest to get my reward. And don't forget, Stella would be entitled to half. Complicated. I don't like complications. That's just two reasons. Ever heard of the IRS? If Starkmore pays, I'll be lucky to keep any of it, and you know the Bureau will make sure my tax returns are filed. Mateo, friend, partner, your payment will be, let's call it, tax free."

"And if I pay this goddamned blackmail, you keep it all, and the bitch disappears?"

"Well, the police have her dead already, only you and I know the truth, and I doubt if you'll say anything."

"God, you're a beaut, a real classy guy."

"We wouldn't want her around to haunt either of us, would we? Now that we understand each other, it's a perfect setup. Neither can say anything. If you don't agree, try this. What happens if a detailed composite of you shows up in every government building and newspaper in the country? And how do you think Trudor will react?"

It was a gamble, but I needed a solid punch, and immediately knew I hit home.

"Who?" he asked weakly, without conviction.

I had him. "I hear Trudor doesn't accept mistakes, but he doesn't have to know. Let's work this out between ourselves."

Mateo answered quickly. "Okay, okay, we'll meet."

"My terms."

"I get the girl. I have to make sure this time."

"Give me the million, and she's yours."

"Okay, but I have more to risk than you, and I don't like traps. I name the meeting."

"If it's reasonable, I'll be there."

He paused a minute and covered his receiver. A good sign, because if Mateo had produced an instant location, I would have feared a prearranged trap.

After a muffled background conversation, he finally said, "The Royalton on West Forty-fourth. Hang around the lobby phones, last one on the left, five tomorrow afternoon. Sharp."

"You got it," I answered, and he clicked off without another word.

By eleven that night I was ready to take on the entire world. After too many brandies at too many places, I negotiated with several hookers, but quickly lost interest. It was something to do, any distraction to avoid conscious thought about the next phase.

At noon the following day, I had a burning stomach and throbbing head, and realized I had not eaten for two days. Great way to enter a confrontation. A real pro.

Instinctively, I called Buchannon to update him. I explained the Mateo contact and our meet, without providing time or location. He maintained strong ties to the Feds and would unquestionably snitch.

"Cantrell," he said, after hearing my news, "you have done well, and I mean that. But that's enough. Turn everything over to Wainwright and drop it. Let the Bureau send a substitute in your place. He doesn't know your voice and you haven't seen active fieldwork in over a decade. It's time to get out."

"Thanks, but my gut reaction is Mateo won't show. He'll send a proxy, testing me, so where does that leave us? Zero, that's where. I've got to do this."

"It was a damn good piece of intelligence on your part, best I've seen anywhere for a long time, but let me add this. You are no longer adept for wet action. That's why the Company turned you out. I've never told you that before, but it's true. You're not ruthless enough to survive. Let it go."

"Thanks," I replied weakly, but it was another hour before his words took meaning.

I was bloody damn scared.

Buchannon's speech gripped me, and I came close to cashing in, until a meaningless trip to Sonoma County years before with Kate flashed in my mind. She worshiped Jack London and frequently visited his museum. I was bored and weary, walking the hushed corridors beside people talking in whispers as if London had achieved sainthood with his rhetoric. But I caught one of his printed sayings that struck cold in my heart, and I have never forgotten it: "I would rather go out like a flaming star than a whimpering planet."

At five to five, standing in the Royalton lobby studying my watch, I recalled Stella's anger every time I did that, and could not help smiling. Good Lord, was it only a week ago? I wondered what she was doing.

The phone rang precisely on time. "Cantrell," I said.

"Go to the desk. Ask for a message for Simon Smith."

That was all. I followed the directions. The message read: CANTRELL: ROOM 456. NOW.

There were numerous precautions I could have taken. Instead I just knocked on the door of room 456, hoping Mateo had bought the pitch. Sink or swim.

I was disappointed. She was middle-aged, slightly overweight and adorned with cold cream and curlers, probably jazzing herself for a night out in the Big Apple. The epitome of typical touristland.

"Oh yes, you're Mr. Cantrell? The man who had this room before had to check out. He asked if I would pass this on when you called."

She handed me a sealed envelope and I felt foolish. Of course, Mateo would not trust a direct contact. His operative style reflected that. It was a simple game of using citizens to innocently relay messages, probably for his standard hundred dollars.

"Thank you." I smiled, and waited for the door to close before opening the message. I was to walk to another hotel seven blocks away and proceed to room 211. This was exactly the ploy I would have used in Mateo's place. He was taking all the precautions.

Strolling casually, I observed the many people, buildings and cars I passed, fully understanding that one or more were scanning me for transmitters, heavy metal and tracking devices. Very smooth.

Since I was completely clean, I could proceed confidently, knowing a definite meet with somebody was imminent, but he was worried about the possibility of a trap. This was becoming my game.

It was amazing the transformation that took place in me in those short blocks. He was also concerned with detection, and it cleared my mind from the earlier queasiness and fear. The irony was, they were looking for one thing, and my plan was entirely different.

Suddenly, I was in control.

No words were spoken as the door of room 211 opened. Obviously, a call from the street had confirmed I was clean.

The man who came to the door was tall and lanky with a nervous physical energy. The man sitting on the couch was short, stocky and drinking beer. A bulldog type, a tough guy straight out of Central Casting, but Lanky was the real threat. Never worry about pure strength, it's youth and speed that can kill.

Neither of these gladiators matched any description of Avalon or Mateo. This was a test case, as I expected. Time to play.

"Where's Mateo?" I asked.

"He'll be along in a minute," Bulldog said, without much effort to sound convincing.

"Kiss off, I only deal with him." I started for the door five feet away, but Lanky blocked my exit.

"What's this about?" I asked innocently, and began deep breathing. They took it as a sign of anxiety, but brief hyperventilation feeds oxygen into the muscles and central nervous system.

They witnessed my apparent terror. Bulldog came from the couch and stood beside me. "Relax," he chided. "We're supposed to make you comfortable."

"I'm leaving," I answered, weakly, humbly, pathetically.

Lanky crept behind me, and I could feel his breath. It was almost the schoolyard game where one in back drops to his knees and the second pushes you over. Cute, but this was no game.

"Where's the girl?" Bulldog asked.

"Well hidden," I told him, watching his eyes absently but concentrating on Lanky's presence behind. He would make the first move.

"Don't you understand, old man? Our friend wants the girl, and you have to cooperate. Simple, huh? Just tell us, and no one gets roughed up. You don't want that, do ya' pal?"

With left hand in the trousers pocket and right dangling loosely at my side, I offered Lanky the easy target, hoping he was part of the majority of people who are right-handed.

I was correct. He grabbed the tempting right wrist and hammerlocked it behind my back. Lanky was to hold while Bulldog applied the harm.

In close-quarters conflict, unless the attacker strikes a stupefying blow, he is seriously disadvantaged by taking the initial grip. Provided the victim knows what to do.

The instant Lanky took me with a firm hold and Bulldog approached with large, threatening fists, I knew the bastards were mine.

I fight dirty.

# 13. ROUND ONE

OF COURSE I FIGHT dirty, anyone my age has no choice. Had either fool punched me just once, I would have folded, and bye-bye Cantrell.

There is a monumental difference between those who own cutesy karate belts and people like me who just want to survive. Ten-minute struggles are very impressive on television where no one suffers more than a bloody nose or black eye, but in the real world of life and death, battles are over in five to ten seconds and all that flashy bullshit is never used.

As Lanky grabbed me, I immediately went completely limp. When attacked, the instinctive reaction of all living things is to tense up as the apprehension triggers involuntary motor reflexes. One becomes rigid, an easy target. Instead, my knees buckled, my head drooped, and I sagged like a wet rag. This does require intense practice and concentration since it contradicts all natural instincts.

When I appeared to faint, Bulldog hesitated momentarily, and Lanky had to wrap his arms around my chest to prevent me from collapsing. To keep this slumping frame erect, he then braced his body and therefore committed all four of his potential weapons, both hands and feet. Since he was totally helpless and vulnerable, I watched Bulldog. At the perfect second and with all my force, I drove the hardened leather toe of my right shoe straight into his crotch.

He screamed like a wounded animal and sank to the floor, holding his tenderized spot with both hands. Without hesitation, I continued the goju-kai move and directed the foot rearward with a vicious slam just below Lanky's kneecap, then scraped my heel torturously down his shinbone, ending with a monstrous crush on the arch, probably breaking his foot.

When his arch cracked under mine, I shifted slightly and swung my left arm in a wide circle and deposited my chopping hand between his legs.

That should have done it, but the adrenaline was flowing, my electrolytes were charged, and the anxiety sought release. Mostly, though, I was just plain pissed.

Bulldog was on his knees, still clutching painfully, and a brief thought of the harm this gorilla had intended negated any guilt I might have felt. I slammed the palms of both hands with an explosive slap on his ears. Definitely overdone, but damn, it felt good.

Using their shoelaces, I secured my new pals by tying both thumbs together behind their backs. Movies invariably show someone using miles of rope to bind, but all you need is six inches of string. While they moaned and cursed me, I rummaged the room. As expected, there was nothing of interest, so after helping myself to the beer, I leisurely scrounged through their wallets.

Confidence is one thing, but gross stupidity quite another. They obviously had had no fear that anything would go wrong this day because each carried billfolds, complete with everything from driver's licenses and credit cards to pictures of girlfriends. Mateo must have been desperate to hire these fools, or was beginning to make mistakes.

Bulldog's eardrums would take considerable time to recover, if ever, so I spoke to Lanky. His foot was broken and swelling so the initial numbness was probably wearing off. "I'm giving you a message for Mateo, then I'll call house security to cut you loose. I suggest telling them some hookers suckered you both."

They continued to whine and threaten as ego prevented their acknowledging they had been dropped. I sat on the couch and said softly, "Take all the time you want, assholes. You're the injured parties, not me."

Finally, Lanky rolled slightly toward me, grimacing as his foot touched the floor. "What do you want?" he gasped.

"Tell Mateo I'll chalk this up to ignorance. He's got one more chance. I'll be at the same number tomorrow night, same time. He'll understand. No call and the girl gets on the front page. No more hero bullshit. Think you can remember that?"

I repeated it several times, hoping it would sink into their aching skulls. Actually, the attack was precisely what I had figured Mateo would try, and it encouraged me. But only because I had won this round. I would not want to square off with Lanky or Bulldog again. One can only get away with sneaky tactics once.

Had Mateo assumed I was a nut, cop or quick scam, he would have ignored the meeting. Sending his toads to bend me was a promising sign. He was still interested. And probably worried.

At a print shop, I spent nine dollars making copies of everything in their wallets, then mailed the originals to Wainwright and copies to Buchannon, along with explanations. It was probably a dry hole but you never know. Mateo, being the cautious type, would never enter a possible trap, nor would he send key members of his group.

After crisscrossing and backtracking my path numerous times to ensure I was clean, I returned to my hotel for a few hours of fitful sleep. Boxed in by this quagmire I had created, there were only two ways out. Either charge ahead or call it off. Deciding to let fate play a round, I would leave it up to Stella and go with her decision.

During our hiatus in Sunnyvale, we had arranged for messages to be sent via the woman living in front. "I'm very sorry to bother you," I said to her, "but would you please get my daughter? It's important."

The lady talked for a minute and explained how Stella came for coffee every morning and they discussed the soaps on TV. Yes, I was very lucky to have such a sweetheart for a daughter.

"Hello, Dad," Stella finally said. "How are you?"

I first repeated the hot line number to identify myself and indicate everything was okay. We had discussed this a hundred times, and if Stella heard anything else, she was to hang up and call Buchannon immediately.

Naturally, she thought this ridiculous, and I had long ago given up explaining the number of people who wanted her dead or jailed.

"Something's happened," I said. "Can you talk?"

"Not really," she replied, indicating the woman was near.

"Okay, just listen, then give me a yes or no. This is a shitty problem to dump on you, but I've gone as far as I can alone. It's time to either call Buchannon or..."

"Or?"

"Or, come to New York and play sucker with me. Don't make up your mind now. Think on it. No kidding, things could get very hot, and the safe bet is with Buchannon."

"No, thank you."

"All I need is a quick identification. Your description of Mateo is just vague enough that I could miss. He's cagey and might throw in a ringer. I wouldn't know the difference. Ah, you will be at some risk."

"When do you want me there?" she replied without hesitation.

"Continental has an early flight to La Guardia."

"After what we know, you expect me to fly Continental?"

"Yes, Continental, not Transcontinental. There's a difference."

"Oh. Okay. What then?"

"Take an airport bus to downtown Manhattan. Get off at the New York Hilton at Rockefeller Center. Grab a cab to the RCA Building, then walk into the Channel Gardens across the street. They're very large and famous, you can't miss it. Very crowded with tourists. Got it so far?"

"I'm with you."

"At the RCA end of the gardens is a huge gilded statue of Prometheus."

"Who?" she interrupted.

"Never mind. He looks like a cherub leaping out of the fountain through a gigantic gold ring."

"Can't miss it, right?" she joked.

"Right." I sighed, feeling the irritation return. She simply did not appreciate the seriousness. "Browse around, there are shops and restaurants, the flowers are beautiful, but keep returning to that statue every fifteen minutes. Not close, just within vision. Start about seven. When you see me, that means we're clean. But don't approach me anywhere, except at the statue. Clear enough?"

"Uh-huh," she replied.

"The statue is the all-clear sign. Nothing else. Let me see you, and I'll follow. Go into any restaurant. Now, do you have enough cash?"

"Are you kidding? I'm loaded. Were could I spend it around here?"

"Bring no luggage, just a tote bag for incidentals. If all goes well, you'll leave the next evening. Got everything?"

"Consider it done," she said lightly.

After a few miserable hours trying to nap, I managed to force-feed two hot dogs and some potato salad. I had not eaten much for days, but the food was almost sickening. I was trying to pump myself up, like a football player before the crucial game. Coaches say go out and hit someone to get over the initial jitters, but they have some idea of the opposition. I had nothing more than half-assed notions and assumptions. Some way to start the big event.

I didn't even know what the enemy looked like, but there was no doubt he knew me.

The next twenty-four hours took an eternity, but I finally drove to JFK. I circled the massive airport for an hour, ensuring I was not being tagged, then parked at the Trans World section.

I wandered about the terminal, engaging in one of my favorite ploys. Even the most experienced follower can be momentarily caught off guard if you move correctly. The trick is to walk briskly and directly as if heading for a particular destination, then suddenly turn around and walk back. Very fast. Anyone trailing will probably move in close because of your speed and apparent determination, and the reversal is unnerving. For a split second indecision will falter his pattern, he is unsure what to do, and it is extremely difficult for him to obscure his movements.

I repeated the routine several times and was convinced everything looked right. I became so involved in the game, I almost missed the page. "Passenger Cantrell. White courtesy phone please." It was repeated three times before I found a phone. Damn, I should have located the phones first thing.

"Yes," I said, breathing hard. "Cantrell here."

"You play rough, Cantrell," was his reply.

"Your playmates are still alive, but not the next time, if you try that shit again."

"No big deal," he said flippantly.

"I'm a step closer to you. I can ID both of them."

"You think I'd send my first team to meet with you? Ha! They're street scum. Bought 'em for fifty bucks. Hey fella, had it been my boys, you'd be paste now."

"Well, you called so I assume it's still on?"

There was a long pause. "Okay, yeah, we might have a deal. Where's the girl?"

"Safe. This is the last chance, Mateo. Now or never. Pay me or I go to the law." It was time again to take the lead or he'd screw me around forever. "Now listen. I have you by the short hairs. I want the money and you want the girl. Simple."

"Hey, okay, okay! You can dump on my part-time help, but don't try it with me. I said we have a deal."

Pure bluff. He was scared, so I directed this time. "Waldorf. Under the canopy in front at the Fifth Avenue entrance. Noon sharp." I wanted lots of foot traffic. "I'll be reading a paper. You don't need to carry the million but have it within a five-minute walk. Notice I said walk. I won't get into a car with you or anyone else. You and I walk to the money. Clear?"

"When do I get the girl?"

"She'll be in a motel room. I'll give you the address and room key for the money."

"I don't like that."

"Too bad you didn't play it clean with me yesterday. She was right around the corner. Now, it's my way or nothing."

"Yeah, okay, okay."

"Waldorf," I repeated. "Noon sharp."

"Hey, get off my ass. We got a goddamned deal."

Driving to the city, I ran our conversation over and over in my mind. Mateo would try another wrinkle, little doubt about that. A million was a lot but his fear of disclosure had to be an even higher priority. To get Stella, and me for that matter, he had to agree on a meet. But what would he try? I tried to place myself in his place, which didn't really help. I had no idea of his influence or power.

I finally found a parking lot and took a cab to the RCA Building. After triple-checking my backside, I circled the Channel Gardens, then stood beside the statue of Prometheus, the life giver, a mythological Titan who stole fire from Olympus and gave it to mankind. It seemed an ironic symbol since we were dealing with people who preferred to take lives.

I was just beginning to worry when I spotted her. I nodded and then followed her into a small café. She was seated, but I stood by the door a minute, looking for anything outside.

Having not discussed what to wear, Stella apparently decided to be comfortable. It didn't matter because if the adverse parties were near, they'd have her regardless of disguise.

The simple, faded jeans were so tight, every inch of those long, slender legs was clearly etched. The casual moccasins, fawn vest and flat-brimmed Mexican hat were a perfect match. The hatband and rust-colored blouse, unbuttoned halfway, must have been a set. Enticing, sexy, yet revealing nothing.

Stella's long black hair dropped straight down with just the slightest wave around the shoulders. The only jewelry was a delicate gold chain around her neck and a tiny turquoise charm.

She could easily pass for an Indian princess. Careful, careful, Cantrell, an old man is one thing, a dirty old man quite another. Every male stole glances at her, and some stared openly.

As I approached, two young men were attempting to engage her in conversation. Stella lowered her magazine, glared at them with a haughty, aloof, icy gaze that quickly dissolved any misconceptions. They said something about having a nice day and slithered off.

I worried about this girl?

As I sat beside her without comment, she whispered, "Can I talk?"

"Yes, Mata Hari, we're okay."

"Jesus, you look terrible."

"Thanks, enough flattery. Flight okay?"

"Screw the flight," she said firmly. "What's happening at this end? What am I supposed to do? Do you think I should—"

"Enough! All in good time. You want something to eat?"

"No." She pouted slightly. "You said this was a risk, and now you won't talk to me. Don't I have the right?"

"Okay," I replied, "give me a chance." We ordered coffee and sat silently a minute. "I talked to Mateo a while ago. There was a possibility he wouldn't respond to my message, but he did."

"If he hadn't?"

"You'd be heading home on the next flight, and I would spend the next week with the Bureau answering questions."

"But he called."

"Yep, we're on."

"I hate to sound dumb, but why would he call you? It seems to me he's taking a big chance. What can you offer Mateo?"

"Silence, the greatest of all blackmail tools. He's afraid of identification, which is you, and I promised to give you over for a tidy sum."

"How much?"

"A million."

"Whew. That's some deal. I didn't know my butt was worth that much."

"Don't get carried away. He wants your ass dead." I watched her. "Any qualms? Ready to back out?"

"No, but I am scared all of a sudden."

"Good for you. Keep that way. Now, at twenty minutes to noon tomorrow, you walk into the Waldorf. Stand just inside the glass, out of sight if possible. Keep looking at the time, like you're waiting for a lunch date. The doorman won't bother you. I'll be just outside, so above all, don't stare at me."

"I've heard this speech before."

"I'll tell you again. Study everyone who comes near me, but don't move until it's Mateo. Be certain, then simply walk out, turn right and hail a cab, or a bus, or keep walking, but don't stay there."

"I know, then to the airport, call Buchannon and follow his instructions. I can do that without another lecture."

A chill passed, and we arrived at the motel in Brooklyn before speaking again. "I'm sorry, but I don't want anything to go wrong."

"Thanks," she said quickly, then repeated it softly. "Honest, thank you. I can be a bitch."

"Be anything you want, just don't get close to Mateo. Walk away, that's all."

I parked on the street and guided Stella across the lot. "Your room adjoins, but I haven't picked up your key. Here's mine."

The motel manager was grumpy, seemingly a prerequisite for that job. "Thought you changed your mind," he whined. "Held that room all day. Lots of people wanted it."

"Told you I'd pay. My niece was late."

"Niece, huh?" He grinned.

When in doubt, always make it seamy. People will believe a story if it's an obvious cover for a weekend tryst.

From the lobby I could see Stella standing outside my room, leaning against the wall, holding both hands to her face.

I broke into a run. "What's wrong?"

She gripped her mouth with violent intensity, holding back the retching bile. Her eyes quivered like a trapped animal's as she nodded toward the room.

Had there been danger inside, Stella would have been dead or gone, but from habit, I pulled the Walther and cautiously stepped in.

It was difficult to recognize him at first.

# 14. SECOND BLOOD

I STARED at the grisly scene for ten seconds, trying to recover my senses, then returned to Stella who was still shaking outside. I grabbed her roughly by the elbow. "Listen to me! Go to the lobby and wait for me. Don't say anything."

Her body was shaking horribly.

"Do you understand? If I'm not there in five minutes, call Buchannon—*not* the police. Got it?"

She nodded blindly. "What if...what if they come back?"

"If they were still around, we'd both be cold meat. It's okay for a few minutes. Now go!" I gave Stella a push and followed a few paces behind, holding the Walther, in range and ready, but no one approached her.

FBI Special Agent Miller had at one time carried a lot of blood in his body, but now it leaked from numerous wounds. He was propped on the bed, looking almost at ease, facing the blaring television, except his last visions must have been unspeakable horror.

The most nauseating sight was the life substance oozing from his ears down the neck on both sides. I had seen that technique used only once. It was in Nam when some Charlies captured two young marines and decided on slow, agonizing death.

I glanced quickly around the room but knew it was useless to wipe my prints. Besides, the Feds just might pick up some latent smudges from the assassins. Using new technology, a good lab can recover prints from most cloth.

Within minutes of disclosure, my photo would be flashed to every law agency in the state, but it was worth the risk if they could find anything useful.

I stood at the door a long moment. "Sorry, fella," I moaned to Agent Miller's remains. "Really I am."

After I collected a highly nervous and agitated Stella, we drove away very slowly and carefully. She didn't speak, which I was glad of, needing serious think time. Everything had gone to hell, but how? And when? And who?

I've never doubled back and cross-checked so many streets on a single operation. It seemed I was guarding the president, and right then, I felt like it. Who the hell could I trust?

"Uh, who...was...he?" Stella finally mumbled.

"A federal agent." There was no reason to be evasive any longer. If we won the game, there would be hours of endless questions. Lose, and we were dead. Some deal. I explained everything to that point, accurately and concisely.

"But how did he find your room? And how did the killer know? I don't understand."

"Neither do I, and that's what bothers me. There are a dozen possibilities but none make sense."

After cruising for another hour, I found a gamy little section in the Bronx. Many people walked the avenues, decorated with porno shows, adult bookstores, countless bars and signs promoting every possible desire.

In an alley we found a small lot, which held a dozen cars. I paid the youthful attendant ten dollars for the evening, plus another ten to park close to the one exit. While we walked to a nearby hotel, I gave Stella her instructions.

The Excelsior, it pronounced in traditional red flashing neon. The floor creaked and everything smelled of boiled cabbage and stale urine. Two pimps sat in the lobby, sharing a sacked bottle of something. Both gave Stella suggestive leers. One made a comment I didn't hear, and preferred not to. I was on their ground.

The Puerto Rican behind the desk was irritated at being disturbed. Stella looked right at him. "How much for an hour and how much for the night?"

He quickly gauged me with an experienced eye. "Twenty and seventy-five," he replied, emotionless.

I've paid less to stay at the Hilton. I tucked four twenties into his greedy fist. "No interruptions," I said firmly. "And 10:00 a.m. checkout." His nasty grin twisted into a disbelieving smirk. I handed him another bill. "Ten o'clock," I repeated.

The room was exactly as expected: dingy, torn, musty and very sad. Perfect. Stella looked horrified.

"We'll have to share the bed," I told her. "Not to worry. I can get you a separate room if you like."

"Are you kidding? In this place? Alone?"

"You could make a fortune by sunrise," I said absently, without thinking.

Stella's eyes twinkled. "Why, Cantrell, that's the closest thing to a compliment you've given me."

"I lost my head a minute," I responded quickly, then thought about the game plan, which was nonexistent at the moment. For the first time in a long career, I was completely befuddled. A dozen questions and no answers. "I have to make a call but not from around here. I'll be gone an hour."

Regardless of age, all females immediately check out a hotel room, particularly the bathroom. I'm convinced it comes with feminine genes. Stella investigated, touched things, patted the mattress and turned to me. "Can I come with you?"

"That's probably safe, but it's safer here."

"Sure," she said glumly. "Please? I have to find a rest room."

"Hey," I said jokingly, "this is a classy place. We have our own private facilities."

"You obviously haven't seen the toilet seat."

"Oh. Uh, cover it with something."

"There isn't any 'something.' "

"Haven't you ever been camping? Didn't you learn to just sort of squat? Never mind, I'll pick up *something*."

She looked crestfallen, but I could not add to her risk. Since the goons had found my motel room, they certainly had the auto license. Five bucks to the manager would have produced that, and it took only a phone call to obtain a complete description of the car. I had to dump it soon, but we were reasonably safe for a few hours.

"You stay here," I repeated. The lock was cheap and loose, but there was a chain. I deliberated a minute. We were on another planet now, and those pros in the lobby would see me depart. I gave Stella a quick lesson on the Walther.

"It's loaded, cocked and ready with the safety off. All you do is pull the trigger. Anyone tries to get in, aim at that hole in the plaster. That will scare off anybody, and for Chrissakes, don't shoot at the door. We don't need a body." I placed it on the crooked table. "If the pimps come up, they're probably just looking for another girl. Talk through the door, tell them you're busy, and agree to meet tomorrow. Say anything, but the door stays closed."

At the lobby desk, the sour-breathed attendant spotted me and was immediately subservient. "Yes sir, anything I can do?"

Money talks, and he had spotted my bills. "Yes," I answered, dropping another one and wondering how all this was going to pass Buchannon's beady-eyed accountant. Places like The Excelsior do not issue receipts.

"Take up a stack of clean towels, washcloths, sheets, pillows and toilet paper to my friend." I then remembered a nervous female upstairs with an automatic. "On second thought, leave them at the door and walk away."

He gave me directions to the nearest liquor store and I left, pausing at the corner for several minutes to observe citizens and study the area. It looked all right, but after what had happened that day I wondered about my instincts for security. Age dulls the senses. Something else to worry about.

The lot was becoming crowded, but my Ford was in the foremost slot. I gave the kid another ten to hold the space, then drove a few miles and found a lonely phone booth at a deserted filling station.

"Cantrell here," I said, and pictured Seek and Source annunciators lighting up Corny's terminal.

Buchannon's line was characteristic. "You're in deep shit."

"Thanks for the warm regards. Under the circumstances, it's nice to know somebody cares."

"I see your location is not exactly Park Avenue," he chided, always referring to his space-age technology that I was not expected to comprehend.

"I'm trying to save the department some money."

"Cantrell, you flushed Wainwright's people, and the Bureau is fuming. My backside is hurting from all the reports."

"Boss, you haven't heard anything. Agent Miller, my very own personal tail, was creamed an hour ago in my room. They ice-picked his face and ears. Not nice. So far it's unknown to the friendly party, but only for a matter of hours."

I heard him suck for a breath. Office managers in any business, legitimate or illegal, find methods to delegate shitty jobs to subordinates. After years of becoming impervious to others' dirt, they remain spotless.

I shouted louder than necessary. "I need answers now! No political crap. I'm hanging way out."

"Where's the Evans girl?"

"Safe."

"So she's with you, meaning a positive make on Mateo is needed?"

Sometimes I forget that bastards like Buchannon, with no heart and ice for blood, are frequently ingenious. He did not climb to the top by being a fool. "Yeah," I admitted.

"Turn her over," he commanded. "When they find Miller's body, the roof comes down. Use your imagination."

"Where do I stand right now?"

"Until this revelation about Miller, just in goddamned serious trouble. Now, I've no idea."

"How could Miller know where I was holed? Or Mateo's people?"

"Obviously, you were cuckolded from the beginning. How, I don't know. Certainly you are highly proficient in dusting a tail, but it appears they had you on a string. Incidentally, you are probably still connected."

The idea of a deep tag had occurred to me, particularly after seeing Miller leaking his life out, but the notion was too bizarre. It was a scam from the minute I played middleman for the money exchange. Damn! "Can you help with any information at all? Anything?"

"Besides sage advice to drop it now, sorry, nothing. You constantly forget the charter of this little family. We supply *information* to friendly agencies. We do *not* get into physical confrontations and certainly not wet operations. At this point, you know far more than I."

I asked several questions and got nowhere.

"Cantrell, if anything happens to that girl, a crucial federal witness you have illegally abducted, I mean *anything at all*, I guarantee they will find a private room for you. For life, short as that will be."

"Wrong. If anything happens to Stella, I'll already be dead."

Buchannon sighed. "What I said before is true. This is totally out of control. I assigned you because of a certain reputation for thoroughness you had. Washington demanded a detailed report examining every step all agencies had performed so far over the TCA extortion. I expected a dazzling account and nothing more. Cantrell, no one, particularly myself, thought you would actually *find* something!"

"Sorry about that."

"Now, you've opened Pandora's box, and I can't help."

"Can I expect any assistance at all?"

"Within boundaries," he offered.

"Let's go closed circuit. Internal only."

He gave that considerable thought. The implications of a senior agency director intentionally blocking a transmission were rather severe. "Okay," he finally agreed. "All recording tapes are off. Go ahead."

"I will need power backup. Someone from inside. Tell me about Barry Dirkson. I rather like the young fool."

Buchannon became the department manager, discussing a potential raise for new employees. "Intelligent, brash, competently fulfills directives, although I detect satire well entrenched in his reports. Overanxious at times, loyal, capable, quite good if a bit reckless."

"Sounds good. As I recall from his file, Dirkson is weapons qualified?"

"Certainly. All of my field people are, in case of necessity. He reminds me of you some years ago."

I knew there was a reason I liked him. "Dirkson's dying to get a gold card to the fifth floor. Have him on standby. I'll call."

"He'll have to volunteer. We have no jurisdiction."

"I want answers now before it goes any further, and so does Washington, but I'll need cover. If it goes that way, have him prepped, fully equipped and ready."

"We have nothing on Mateo other than conjecture and theory."

"I realize that. We couldn't arraign him on anything."

"So..." Buchannon paused. "Your solution is a wet sanction?"

"There is no other way."

# 15. SECRETS

THE BRANDY WAS outrageously expensive, but I still bought it. I was pleased to find my parking spot behind the hotel vacant; however, it cost me another ten for the attendant's inconvenience. The youth explained auto theft was high in that neighborhood, and he stayed all night to watch the cars. "Got to protect my regulars," he said with just a touch of sarcastic innocence.

Entering the hotel, I found a gigantic transformation had taken place, although only two hours had passed. The lobby was full, definitely the local hangout for action. Several women gathered in small groups and chatted, drinking everything from cola to cheap wine. They were probably getting ready for the big night or taking a break between tricks.

The two pimps I spotted earlier were still seated along with others, and everyone stopped to stare at me. Inspection time. An outsider. Someone sent a gesture because immediately I was ignored. The old guy's okay, it must have read.

Knocking softly on the door of our room, I repeated Stella's name several times, without standing in a direct firing line. Some people with guns get jittery.

The door opened, and she suddenly had both arms wrapped around my neck. "Oh, God, I didn't think you were coming back. I was so damn scared."

I handed her the basket that had been left outside the door. "For you," I said.

"Look at this!" she exclaimed, fondling the treasures. "Sheets! Glasses! Toilet paper! I'm in heaven. And toothbrushes!"

"We go first-class."

"This probably cost more than dinner. I'll bet you paid another semester for his kid at Yale."

"It feels like it." I poured us both one full inch of liquor.

She sniffed the glass. "Brandy, huh? It's too strong for me, unless you have fresh milk for an Alexander."

"This is not the gasoline you serve from a well. Pure Napoléon, four star. Have some."

She tried a few sips. "What's going on? You never explain anything to me."

A very long silence followed, and I stared at nothing, trying to find a crack in this bizarre puzzle.

Stella sat yoga-style on the floor in front of me and blessed the room with five minutes of silence before speaking. "You know, after all that's happened to me, since Sam wanting me dead and Cindy's murder and our insane run across the country, my biggest nightmare is I have no one to talk with. I can't share it with anyone, and that's what blixed my head. When things are the absolute pits, you have to share it or go crackers."

She leaned over and placed both palms on my left knee, then dropped her chin on top. "Since you keep telling me I'm still in danger, I can't think of anyone better to talk with. Also, I just happen to be the world's greatest listener."

I ignored her a moment. "Sorry, really, but I'm a loner by nature. I've spent twice your lifetime thinking alone, figuring the possibilities, analyzing, trying to survive. Nothing personal."

She looked disappointed but remained there. "Well, can't you think out loud?"

My eyes burned painfully, and I felt the creeping rush of surrender beginning to haunt me. I was so damn tired. Ironically, she kept me going. Why, I was not sure. Had this been a paper chase, I would have canceled long ago.

After a while I said, "The only thing that figures is Miller let me ditch him on purpose." I explained my maneuver through the jewelry store. "Then, with relay teams, they kept me on track."

"So they followed you the whole time?"

"Don't rub salt in my wounds. Yes, that's the logical explanation. I was suckered and didn't know it. Thinking back, I used that wrinkle more than once, and it's something Wainwright would know. He was expecting a dodge and had his people covering. I should have realized it was too easy. I fell right into it. I'll wager even the cabbie who drove by so damn conveniently at that moment was a plant."

I gulped the brandy and felt foolish. "Jesus, the driver was one of them. No wonder I didn't spot anyone, he was in the car with me!"

"It's not your fault," she weakly suggested.

"The hell it's not!" I screamed, suddenly outraged and wanting to lash out at anyone. "I'm supposed to be a pro. Christ, I played this game before you were in diapers. And now a good man has been chopped because of my screwups. Don't patronize me. You haven't earned the right!"

She stared at me defiantly. "Now, is it time for your over-the-hill act? Jesus, I am so tired of that shit! What are you, middle fifties? That's nothing!"

"Girl, in this business I'm ten times that."

"Poor me, poor me," she teased.

I shouted, "Damn right! There's not a single agent alive today who I worked with just a decade ago. Yeah, I am a dinosaur!"

The silence was deafening. I could hear rattling pipes from a dozen toilets. I gave a passing thought to what was being flushed. The outside fluorescent bulbs were buzzing bright red, and I vaguely recalled science lectures. "Ionization occurs when residual voltage drops across the capacitor, resulting in flux electronic flow...."

She tugged at my trousers, demanding attention. "Your precious goddamn watch is the greatest thing since popcorn, you've convinced me of that, so it must have an alarm." Stella burned me with those angry dark eyes. "Set it to ring when you're through feeling sorry for yourself. Then we can talk."

If Mateo, or Wainwright, or Trudor, or Buchannon did not kill this little shit, I probably would. "You don't even know what's going on, do you?"

"No, I don't. But I do understand this. The older people get, the more they enjoy carrying guilt. Self-pity keeps you people occupied. Something to complain about. Please God, don't let me reach forty."

"Quite the philosopher, aren't we?"

"I can still think. I've had enough nightmares in the past month for a lifetime, and seeing Miller tonight will always stay with me, but there is no way I'll believe it was your fault."

"Thanks," I mused.

"Was Cindy's death my fault?"

"That was different."

"Oh sure, it's always different. Mateo wanted me dead, but his friends got Cindy instead. Tonight he wanted you dead, but they got Miller. Yeah, really different."

She paced the floor, walking in circles, carefully dodging the furniture. "If you want to indulge in self-pity, then go ahead. Meanwhile, some people want us both dead, so we do share something in common. I would like to discuss this. I've earned that much.''

She was right. Everyone was playing games, and we were the dumping ground. "Okay, tomorrow I meet with Mateo, assuming he'll show. The odds are stacked against me, so I need every edge. Anything. I must know what the hell is going on. There are questions, all vital. How did Miller track me to the motel? Answer, the cabbie did it somehow. Next, how did Mateo's people find it? And last, why the hell did they kill Miller?''

"One at a time," Stella offered. "Miller tricked you and had you followed."

"I believe that, I have to, but how? I changed cabs, rented a car and dodged for an hour. I always know when I'm tracked. Always. After a few years it becomes instinct.''

"But don't you guys go to the same schools? Hiding and following and such? Maybe they knew the same techniques?''

"Not likely," I disagreed. "Anyway, if the Feds were on me the whole time, why not grab you at the café?''

"I don't know. Maybe they just waited at the motel," Stella suggested.

"Doesn't wash.''

"Okay, your second question. How did Mateo know?''

"Beats the hell out of me. And why torture Miller? Jesus, not a federal agent! The killers will be hounded forever. No one's that dumb.''

Stella began pacing again. Imprinting between humans in high stress is rapid. She moved about the room, her eyes almost glazed, oblivious to everything. She was becoming me.

"Let me brainstorm a minute," she said suddenly. "Be patient. What are the ways Mateo could find you? A leak in the department?''

"Not possible. Security is beyond belief. Besides, nobody knew where I was going, including me. It was a random motel I picked at the last minute."

"Okay, so he just spotted you?"

"In New York? The odds are a billion to one."

She stopped and looked at me. "But obviously *Miller* knew, so Mateo's people followed him right to your door!"

It made sense. Occam's Law: the simplest explanation of the facts is probably correct. The easiest person to tag is a cop on duty because he's supposed to be the follower, not the target, and never considers someone behind. "So, my ditch worked on Mateo, but they'd seen Miller at the bank and stayed on him."

"And Mateo follows Miller to the motel."

"Another hurry-up job botched. Miller's there, probably tossing my room while I'm at the airport. Mateo's goons are told to waste me, no, bend me to reveal your location. He tried that before."

"They were hired to get the information from a guy in a room. Just like the mistake with Cindy in San Francisco. They assumed it was you."

"And Miller was hard as steel. He'd never crack, so they killed him. But why didn't the Feds grab you at Rockefeller Center, assuming they were still on me?"

"Waiting for instructions?"

"That figures, too. Miller was in charge. They wouldn't act without his direction."

"And Miller was already dead."

"Questions two and three fall nicely into place. But I'd still love to know how Miller tagged me."

"Two out of three isn't bad. Uh, knowing Mateo had Miller killed, do you still meet with him tomorrow?"

"No choice. I checked for Miller's wallet. It was gone, so Mateo knows his goons screwed up again. Yeah, he'll be there."

"I think you're nuts. Why don't we just split back to California and leave this to the police?"

"I don't like running. There's no future in that."

"Okay, hero, I'll do my part." Stella yawned. "And now, jet lag has caught up. I'm bushed."

I kissed her lightly on the cheek. "I'll be in the bathroom five minutes. Go to bed."

It was exactly as she described, filthy, stained and ugly. Stella had layered several towels on the toilet seat. I sat on the makeshift barrier and tried to sort out the details. Mateo had the money, but I had Stella. He had wasted a government agent, and I was blackmailing him. Wainwright's people would come apart when they found the bloody motel scene. And how did Trudor fit into the scheme of things? Was he calling the moves from a safe distance or was Mateo ad-libbing on his own? Would Wainwright report that an international terrorist was involved, thus bringing in the CIA?

Since 1970 when Hoover's FBI severed relations with the Company, the agencies had become jealous, distrusting relatives under the same roof. I could easily get pinched between those two giants.

Damn, with Miller's death, Stella's circumstances became worse. A no-win situation. I considered shipping her to Canada.

The mind is a remarkable organ, capable of receiving, sifting and storing billions of thoughts and sensations, but when overloaded, it simply shuts off. The doctors explained that to me years before when I lost two friends. The brain secretes effrons to numb the senses so we can continue, function and control, but with excessive anxiety, it drops over the edge and takes a rest.

I experienced similar feelings of anxiety and fought the notion I was about to crack.

Quietly returning to the bedside, I stared at this beauty in all her lovely innocence. Stella's long hair cascaded over the blankets, and she slept with the peaceful softness of childhood. I wondered if she believed the television image, good people never get hurt.

Her shoulders were bare, and I recalled she'd brought no luggage, no nightwear. It's not the monumental events that trigger emotions but rather trivial, insignificant, meaningless gestures that spark the imagination.

Thrown carelessly over the dresser were Stella's clothes, stacked in order of removal, jacket, blouse and jeans on the bottom, underwear on top. A flood of painful memories rushed through me.

That had been Kate's signal a thousand years ago. Man cannot move mountains or a woman if she's not in the mood. Being a late-night person myself, we never retired at the same time.

Couples develop signals and that was hers. It was never discussed, but a secret gesture to me. If her panties were neatly folded away it was no go, but if they were thrown casually on the nightstand, it meant she wanted me to wake her for playtime.

I knew Stella had no such thought, but the coincidence struck me. Was I becoming lecherous or just experiencing simple lust? Stella was incredibly magnetic, but Jesus, I had suits older than her.

Staring at her underwear, I could not dissolve the thought. The panties were Kate's signal.

Signal . . . signal . . . *signal*!

"Stupid goddamn idiot!" I screamed.

"What?" Stella moaned, suddenly awake.

"I'm going out. Chain the door and don't shoot when I knock."

I left before her questions began. The street was filled with girls parading in shorts and hawkers buying and selling every possible commodity. When I turned the corner, the back alley was dark and grimy. The boy in the parking lot was half-asleep, wearing earphones and grasping a gigantic portable radio. He came alert and studied me.

"That's my Ford up front," I told him.

"Hey man, you paid for all night. I can't give refunds."

"No problem. What time do you get off in the morning?"

"About eight."

The youth was maybe eighteen, tall, black, with quick watchful eyes. "How would you like to earn an easy hundred?"

He stared suspiciously. "Go down the street for a deal, man. I don't know you."

"Nothing like that. You saw the lady I came with? She has a jealous boyfriend with redneck friends. They don't approve of me. He doesn't know this car but found out where I rented it. They're going to be waiting for me at Hertz in the morning."

"So?"

"So it's worth a hundred to me if you return the car. I have to get it back. Look here." I displayed my driver's license and rental forms. "See, it's paid in advance. Call Hertz and check if you want. Nothing illegal. Just give us a ride until I spot a cab, then you drop the Ford in their lot. You don't even go inside. I'll let them know."

"I dunno. It looks spooky to me. What about the boyfriend?"

"He's not looking for you. Just park it and leave." I handed him fifty before he refused. "Half now, half in the morning."

We discussed the arrangements, a definite gamble on my part but worth the risk. Besides, I was desperate.

Minutes later I knocked on her door. Stella had a dozen questions, but I had to plan beyond the morning. "Not now," I shushed her.

"We're back on that kick again? Trust you, sight unseen?"

She had dressed while I was gone. As I lay on the bed, Stella angrily yanked off a blanket and snuggled in a chair, moaned discomfort and sulked.

I paid little attention as I plotted the details.

Everyone was either screwing us around or just plain screwing up. A botched mess if I ever saw one. But something was certain. No way could anyone follow me without my noticing. Only one way could the Feds manage the track, and it explained everything.

While I had been filling out the rental forms at Hertz, the planted cabdriver had dropped a signaling device on the Ford.

No wonder they didn't have to get close. The car was wired.

# 16. SCATTER

AFTER A HORRIBLE, fitful night, my watch alarm finally ended the agony. I was amused to find Stella on the bed beside me, snuggled tightly in her blanket.

"Let's go," I said. "Twenty minutes."

"I'm not going," she announced defiantly.

"Okay," I responded very slowly. "That was the original deal. You cancel any time you want. Call Buchannon when I leave and follow his instructions."

"You bastard! I want to stay, but give me some damn answers."

"Deal, but you can still call it quits. Get dressed and just listen from the bathroom. No comments. I made a call to Mateo last night," I explained. "He's finally convinced I'm okay and that I will exchange you for the million dollars. I'll arrange it with Wainwright, so the Feds can be there to catch him with the money. Otherwise, we have nothing concrete. Your testimony is almost worthless."

"What do you mean, worthless?" She leaped from the bathroom wrapped in a towel. "I can identify him!"

"Sure, as what? A man who visited with your boyfriend? And discussed things you couldn't hear? Or understand? Snatches of conversation that could mean anything?"

"But he had Miller killed!"

"We know that. Prove it. He delegates dirty work."

"Then why does he want me dead?"

"Because he let you slip through and you can identify him. Mateo is a pawn for terrorists and more afraid of his associates than of the law."

"Jesus, why is it so complicated?"

"You are valuable property, as I've said all along. But not because of legal testimony. You're here to identify Mateo for me and the Feds."

I continued to prattle things we had discussed earlier as I scratched a note and hushed her to silence.

Stella,
Trust me *now* and *say nothing*! Will explain later. The car and this room are wired to the FBI! This conversation is for their benefit.

I made frantic gestures for quiet as I repeated nonsense. In the lobby I grabbed her arm. "We're clean here. I have no intention of calling the Feds, but maybe it will give us some slack. Now, I've hired a boy to take over the car. Say nothing. They expect us to drive away, and they're watching us. At the right time, I'll make a break and drop you near a store. I'll stop only a second. Get out quickly and go inside. Then wait for me."

"How will I know when?"

"Oh, you'll know. But get out without a word! Got that?"

In the back alley I motioned the young attendant, who had told me his name was Harry, to a spot several feet out of transmitter range, as Stella waited by the car.

"Ready, good." I motioned toward Stella. "Ah, Harry, we had a battle this morning, and she's pissed at me. Understand?"

"Yeah, man, I dig it."

"She sulks, you know? So let's have no talking in the car. Okay? Not a single word. We'll ignore her, and she'll get over it that way." I gave him the other fifty.

Harry looked at me suspiciously, but then took the money, and I maneuvered him between us on the front seat. I cranked the radio on loud, convinced a sound mike was planted inside, then pulled into the morning traffic. There was no chance of spotting our trackers. They were using triangulation and could play us very loose.

My two riders were faithfully quiet. I was tempted to make idle conversation for appearance's sake to our followers but decided against it. Harry might say something.

The morning commuter traffic was heavier than I'd hoped for, which worked in our favor. The thoroughfare was two-way and divided, with three lanes in both directions. Altering our pace through several intersections, I managed to stop as the lead car in the center lane. I had timed the amber lights at six seconds.

When the amber for cross traffic flashed on, I counted five and punched the Ford, grinding into a hard U-turn, cutting off a very angry driver on the left who hit his brakes and swerved into the divider. Oncoming traffic was rolling on their green light, blasting horns, squealing tires and shouting insults.

"Why didn't you warn us?" Stella screamed. "Jesus Christ!"

"I said, you'd know." We headed in the opposite direction, and with the accelerator floored passed sixty in seconds, approaching the next cluster of traffic ahead. The group we'd escaped numbered over a hundred cars, and the primary trackers should be caught in the middle.

In theory, two other trackers would be pacing a few blocks to the left and right, maintaining the transmitted triangle. Instantly, they would know we were running, but it would take a minute to reestablish, and that was all I needed.

"Hey man! I want outta here!" Harry was moaning.

"It's just the boyfriend. I'll give you another hundred."

Speed and timing were critical. The unseen car on the left would maintain a parallel course, seeing we were coming their way, while the right car would double back and follow the signal. The primary track would be gridlocked in traffic for a half minute. Once regrouped, they could monitor us across the country.

I sliced through an intersection and rocketed down a cross street. "No talking!" I shouted above the blaring radio.

This could only last momentarily while our followers caught their balance. We approached a neighborhood hardware store, and I pointed as Stella understood and nodded. I hit the brakes without squealing, and she leaped out, looked back at me, then gave the door a hardy shove. I should have warned her about the noise but leaned over and caught it before the slam.

Easing forward, I punched it without screaming the tires, turned right and right, and handed Harry a previously written note, with a quick shudder at the thought that he might be one of the functionally illiterate.

Don't talk. This car is bugged. Drive it anywhere you want and dump it. Keep Moving!

I slowed quickly, hurled another bill to him and got out, grabbing my case from the floor. Harry sat there, puzzled, as I wildly gestured for him to go!

Finally, the realization struck home, and he leaned out to shout above the radio. "Cops, huh? Why the fuck didn't you say so!"

Harry and the Ford were down the street in seconds, and I could still hear the punished tires. It was a class-three neighborhood, mostly brown fronts with occasional mom-and-pop stores. I walked briskly around the corner and into a produce market.

They possibly could grab Harry in minutes and back-track to me, so there was no time to waste. I placed my case in a large shopping bag, with some lettuce to take up space. I paid, and at the door stuffed my jacket and tie into the sack. Walking away, I rolled up my sleeves, then partially covered my face with the bag while listening for approaching cars.

At the hardware store, I found Stella looking at hammers.

"Sorry I'm late," I said, the clerk listening, "but the car broke down again."

We took a cab, swapped twice, then rented a car from Avis, making certain this time no one went near it. I was rapidly running out of usable identification.

"I'm starved," Stella said simply, not yet asking the million questions I knew she had.

I started for a doughnut shop but she remarked confidently, "I want real food, not hypoglycemia."

In the next block was a greasy spoon. Stella shuddered but did not complain. She asked for bacon, eggs, toast, juice and tea while I ordered coffee.

"That's a great start for a big day," she cautioned.

"Thanks, Mom. After the abuse this body has endured, missing breakfast is not fatal. You eat, I'll talk."

"About time."

I ignored that. "Everything fell into place last night, the two cabbies, motel room, Miller's action and murder. When I rented the Ford, the second cabbie dropped a magnetic transmitter on the bumper. Takes two seconds. After that, we were a shining beacon.''

"And we stayed in that sleazy hotel? After driving all over town?''

"They were right with us. Probably next door with a wall amplifier.''

"Damn, and I agreed to that rat hole to avoid them. Wait! That means they heard everything we said.''

"One of our few lucky breaks, due to Bureau policy etched in granite. Chain of command and authority. They were told to monitor and relay through their commander, Miller. When he was dropped, panic must have set in and they called Wainwright. Cooler heads prevailed.''

"Why did they leave us alone?'' Stella asked, wiping her plate clean with toast, a practice I consider repulsive.

"Would you forgo that?'' I demanded, moving her plate away. "You're a blackjack player, do you know high-low poker?''

"Sure, the best and worst hands split the pot.''

"Right, but in this game, Wainwright is stuck in the middle with no win either way. If he grabs you, he risks losing his string to Mateo. If he loses you, he's back to square one with nothing. The man is hurting, so he'd prefer standing off and letting us take the blows and lead him to Mateo. He knows I've set a meet and can't risk screwing it up. So his Feds watch and wait.''

"But now we've lost them.''

"Yeah.'' I snickered, feeling a bit cocky but dangerously alone. "One thing, now Wainwright knows that *we know*, so he'll pick us up. Guaranteed. He's got a dead agent to explain, an extortionist plot linked to worldwide terrorists and two people who slipped his net. Yeah, he's pissed.''

"So what now?''

"We go shopping for clothes. Both of us.''

She beamed. "Just once, I'd like to see Bloomingdale's."

Since Buchannon was footing the bill, we parked in the lot and entered the magic kingdom. "Dress, shoes, hat, everything."

"Don't tell me I have four minutes, or I'll scream." She grinned.

I gave her a roll of hundreds. "No, but ninety minutes, tops."

"Tell you what," Stella suggested. "I've seen your taste. Let me get you started. It'll come off my time."

The clerk in Bloomingdale's menswear had never seen a hurricane sweep through his department before. Without pausing, Stella quickly grabbed a dozen expensive dress shirts and carried them to the suits. She yanked several jackets from the rack and arranged them on a counter with the shirts carefully positioned.

She said to the clerk, "Don't ask him anything. He hasn't bought clothes since the Great War. Any of these combinations will do," she continued, "but in his size. The shirts, probably thirty-six with a sixteen neck, and we'll need tacks in the cuffs. He'll wear them today. I'd say he's at least six foot and about 190. Wouldn't you agree? Oh, and put this back, it's too drab. Takes away from his salt-and-pepper hair. Here, this is perfect."

She stood back for one last appraisal. "Yeah, that should do it."

Stella left in a flash, and the clerk stared wide-eyed at me. "Makes it easy, doesn't she?" he said.

Forty minutes later I sat in the car, admiring Stella's selection. I had never owned a pure wool suit before, and the sensation was rather heady.

It was time to check the firepower. I wiped down the shotgun and racked it several times, loaded with six rounds of double-ought buck, then checked the single, chopped pistol grip. At short range, such an illegal weapon is awesome, and with New York having the strongest gun control laws in the country, I could do three to five there for just carrying this monster.

Carefully laying the Ithaca on the back seat and covering it with my old clothes, I checked over the Walther. I removed the standard ammo and popped in a clip with 158-grain, .38 specials, SPD loads with hollow points. Every edge might help. I had become unaccustomed to wearing the automatic in the past decade. But it felt good now.

Stella approached, and I openly stared at her. The old cliché was appropriate. She was a vision.

The knee-length dress was a light powder blue, so soft and wispy it resembled cotton candy. The hat, gloves, coat and shoes matched with delicate blue stitching. Her shiny long hair caressed the shoulders, and Stella's dark eyes glistened.

"Well?" she asked, doing a pirouette.

"Not bad," I mumbled.

"Let's see how you did," she said eagerly, opening the door and pulling me out. "Not bad," she parroted, judging this self-conscious statue. "See? The wine flecks in the jacket highlight the shirt and the— Dammit, Cantrell!" She threw her arms in despair. "Look at your shoes! They came from a barnyard. Why didn't you buy new ones?"

"This is no time to break in new kicks," I defended.

"I thought this was going to be a class act." She shrugged. "At least get a shave."

"Promise. Let's go."

As Stella tossed her bags into the back seat, my sack was shoved aside revealing the scattergun's barrel. She stared at it a long minute, then slowly pulled everything away until the Ithaca was in full view.

"Funny," she whimpered. "For a little while, I forgot what we were doing." Stella sat back in a daze. "The past hour has been like a kid's game, blowing her savings account in a toy store. I really lost track of what's happening."

"It'll be over soon," I responded with a forced enthusiasm I didn't feel. "You walk out of the hotel, go home, keep the clothes."

"Is that necessary?" she asked, nodding to the back seat.

"Probably not. Insurance, that's all."

"Bull," she said with a grimace. "I saw what they did to Miller."

We drove for several minutes. "It could be so easy," she offered. "Call Wainwright now. He'll thank you, and arrest Mateo. We can go home together."

"It's not that simple," I said carefully, controlling my anger. "You and I both have been bloody *pawns*! Sacrificial lambs! Everyone is screwing us over, and I'm tired of it. The Feds can't grab Mateo on what they have because they have nothing! Mateo would be on the street in ten minutes, Starkmore and his precious Transcontinental Airline would be raped on the news, probably bankrupt, and if Wainwright survived the bureaucratic purge, he'd sharpen pencils in Alaska until pension time. The terrorists win again! Okay? *End of conversation!*"

"So, you're going to play shoot-out at the OK Corral? Can I sell tickets and make some money? Cantrell, you are challenging them, comparing macho bullshit, and so who's the idiot? My dad can whip your dad? My John Wayne act is better than yours? Christ, you are your own worst pawn!"

"You don't understand," I repeated.

"Balls," she whispered. "You're just like any other jerk I've known. Go ahead, be a fucking dead hero. See if I light a candle." She crossed her arms and sulked.

As usual, I should have listened to Stella.

# 17. MATEO

A FEW MINUTES past eleven, we pulled around the corner from the Park Avenue entrance of the Waldorf, and I repeated instructions to a nervous, upset, fidgety Stella Evans. "Almost an hour," I told her, "Stay in the lobby until 11:45. Mateo will have people scouting the scene."

"Will you do me one favor?" she asked, her first words in a long time. "I don't want to know what happens. If you make it back to San Francisco, promise not to contact me. In any way. Ever."

That caught me unprepared. "Why?"

"Because if I expect your call, and it doesn't come, I'll know what happened. This way, I can pretend you're okay, no matter what, and I'll never know for sure. It's better."

"Okay," I agreed, trying to fathom this child.

Stella leaned over and smacked a quick sisterly kiss on my cheek, then said two words repeated in every movie and millions of homes, a universal message when nothing else can be said. "Be careful."

Watching her leave, I placed a mental bet Stella would turn around at the last minute and smile, or something, but she didn't, and I felt a peculiar rush of intense loneliness. It suddenly occurred to me I would never see her again. Odd, I had been trying to unload her from the beginning, but I truly would miss that sassy little vixen.

I took my time finding an open lot some blocks away and strolled back casually on Fifth Avenue. The Walther provided a comfortable bulge against my back.

Stopping a hundred feet away, I studied the scene but saw nothing, nor did I expect to. At five to the hour, I sincerely regretted not saying something clever, witty or charming to Stella as she left.

I cursed myself for the emotional barrier surrounding my feelings, which had taken years to perfect, and now isolated me from uttering the simplest comment. That's why I was best suited to field operations. To survive, you become a nonperson.

At the door of the hotel, I stepped to one side near the hedge and glimpsed Stella just inside, beyond the glass. It was a bittersweet, gentle smile, confused and lonely, and maybe she, too, just realized we would not meet again.

Control, dammit, I told myself. Business. Concentrate.

A dark Buick pulled to the curb and stopped in the No Parking zone, blocking the valet's precious territory, but a generous tip from a fiftyish man satisfied the doorman.

"Cantrell, I'm Mateo," he said. He fit the vague description. Age, height, swarthy, slightly over two hundred pounds, dark unruly hair with scattered smudges of gray, and his harsh eastern clipped voice resembled the phone conversations.

But Stella did not move.

"Tell Mateo he has sixty seconds to show," I said, looking straight at him, then my watch. "Fifty-nine, fifty-eight..."

The ringer quickly scurried away, entered the Buick and drove off. It took several seconds for me to realize another man stood behind me. I wondered how long he had been watching, waiting, judging.

He must have approached from the hotel, meaning he walked right by Stella. "Cantrell, welcome to Big Town," he chided.

Stella stepped outside and walked away.

"Where's the girl?" he asked.

This was definitely Mateo. His expression displayed survival at any cost. Jungle instincts. "Where's the money?" I responded.

"Five minutes. Walking. You know what? I don't like terms from anyone! 'Specially worthless ol' snoops. Not at all."

"You better get used to it," I threatened. "Ever been inside a federal house? Real fun, hundreds of little punks telling you when to sit, where to stand, when to bend over and how to crap. You'll love it."

"Where is she?" he repeated.

"Close. When I see the money, one of your fools can get her. I'll even stand hostage until you're sure."

"Damn nice of you. What makes you think I'd pass a million until I have her? Huh? Huh? Use your head! It's your move."

I sensed something was wrong. We sparred again, the words and threats becoming trite, and I realized Mateo was increasingly nervous. I did not like that. Tension leads to unpredictable behavior.

"What the hell is it?" I demanded. "Still worried about me?"

He was waiting for something.

The Buick returned to the curb, honked three times, then twice, and Mateo became a changed man.

"Savino did his job but liked bragging to the fluff. Stupid jerk. Always showing off. So he's gone. *Finito*."

His grin exposed an ugly, dark bicuspid, probably a dead tooth he refused to have pulled. Surrounded by gold caps, it displayed a bizarre, vicious look.

"Gotcha, asshole," he snarled. "I gotcha by the short hairs."

At that second, I still had no idea of the impending calamity and little understanding of his sudden behavioral shift. When in doubt, shut up. I said nothing.

Mateo began poking me in the chest like a redneck picking a fight in a sleazy bar. I allowed it and listened, still trying to comprehend the aggressive transformation.

"I don't like being pushed, asshole," he repeated several times.

"What do you want?" I finally asked.

"I don't tell you what I want. I just take it! Understand, asshole?" He handed me a scrap of paper. "Call me at three today, and I'll tell you about another meet. My terms, this time."

"Why should I?"

"Because I said so, that's why." He poked and grinned again. "It's an answering service. Straight arrow. Can't be traced. I call from anywhere and they connect us. Just call and wait."

I stared at the paper, confused and trying to think.

"Technology today, ain't it fuckin' great?" He jabbed. "I never understood why them Japs lost the war. Everything we use comes from them clever bastards. I call that number and get connected to anyplace on earth."

"Amazing," I mused.

"And be on time or you get nuthin'."

He took several steps as I watched, completely baffled, having lost all control of the situation.

Mateo turned. "Oh, did I forget to mention? I'm only paying you a finder's fee because I'm such a nice guy. Know why? Because we got the bitch already. My boys picked her up right down the street. I don't owe you shit, but I'm willing to pay for your troubles. Better call if you want it."

He began strolling away as my head was spinning. Did he have her? If so, why not burn me then and there? I looked around at the foot traffic. Too crowded. He wanted me in a secluded place. That was his reason for the offer.

Mateo took several more steps, then shouted over his shoulder. "Hey, Cantrell? You think you're fuckin' with kids? Huh?"

Welcome to the Big Apple.

# 18. SNOOKERED

OCCASIONALLY THE MIND enters a time warp. It was impossible to figure how long I stood there. Finally, the doorman asked if I wanted a cab.

"What?" I mumbled, trying to think yet completely overwhelmed. Confused, I walked away still in shock.

Was Mateo bluffing? Did his goons have Stella? Could he have spotted her inside the Waldorf? Was he expecting that?

An image of Miller's hideously ripped face haunted me. The vision of that happening to Stella made me physically ill. I could taste the bile in my throat. Lord, what had I done now?

At the first phone booth I called Buchannon and confessed my shame. "If she followed my instructions," I said, trying to be calm and professional, although my insides were in turmoil, "Stella should easily reach JFK by two and call you. If she fails to make contact by then, we can assume Mateo grabbed her."

I expected loud tirades and accusations of my gross stupidity and ineptness, but they were temporarily set aside until the problem was resolved. Buchannon was an unfeeling bastard, but he always took the long view. "Sounds reasonable," he finally agreed, coldly evaluating the situation like a surgeon about to slice. The chastisements would come later. "Since that seems the case," he pondered coolly, "what are your intentions?"

I didn't want to admit how foolish and inept I felt at that minute. "I'm not sure," I finally said.

"Should you follow my continual advice and alert Mr. Wainwright, please let me know." He said it clearly, knowing our link was taped and provided further evidence he was innocent of my recklessness.

"Will do."

"Do you still want Dirkson?"

"Definitely. Have him check into the Statler. I'll contact."

Buchannon paused only slightly. "Cantrell, you are bleeding a dangerously anemic contingency fund. Is the Statler really necessary for a merc contact?"

"It's necessary," I said firmly.

He sighed. "Very well." He suggested numerous tactics, all quite useless, but I had to listen. He was feeling the typical armchair warrior, moving pins on a field map, loving the battle, and marshaling his troops through the horrors of death. But we both knew watching the Super Bowl was the closest he came to real physical harm.

Why had I called? Desperation, I told myself. "Later," I said, and hung up.

Street noise melts everything into insignificance. I walked for several blocks, then found a newsstand on Fifty-fourth, operated by an abrasive, loud, aging man of unknown extraction.

"Whatcha want?" he demanded.

I grabbed a paper, pulled the lopsided stool toward me and stuffed a ten in his hand. "To sit here a few minutes."

"You got it, friend."

It was a perfect escape, and I didn't read a line. The surrounding avalanche of street sounds engulfed me as the roar invaded my brain and allowed me to purge. I ate hot dogs drenched in onions and mustard, several warm beers and pretzels, then began to think.

I scribbled some notes, depicting possibles and probables. Things were churning rapidly and beginning to clear. As a trained observer with a few connections, I was a far greater threat to Mateo than Stella. He had to realize that, so now I became his critical phase. He wanted me on quiet ground. I had bluffed and fooled him earlier, but the game was still on. Mateo wanted my bacon. He would deal.

I found a phone booth in a coffee shop and called Buchannon just after two. "She contact you yet?"

"No," he answered calmly.

"We need a three-way. Will you patch Cornwall into this line?"

No serious, sane or creative field director ever refuses an agent's request. The experienced operator never, *never* calls for assistance unless his butt is dangling over the edge. Buchannon knew that, and being deadly serious, occasionally sane and wholeheartedly creative, he patched me through without comment.

Corny answered the buzz, and seeing the blinking lights, knew it was top priority. "Yes, sir," he answered.

I gave him two numbers, mine at the phone booth and Mateo's service. "He wants me to call and hold for a relay. Can you tap it? Trace the original source?"

"Sure," Corny replied with obvious pride.

"Okay, in fifty minutes. Three, Eastern time."

"Wait a minute!" he screeched. "I thought you meant in theory. Or with plenty of time. There's no way it can be done that fast!"

"You hear that, boss?" I said. "You are about to have the greatest coup of your career laid on a platter, and Mr. Cornwall has a minor wiring problem."

"A minor wiring problem? Cantrell, you don't have any idea of the complications!" Corny gasped. "The goddamned phone system is the toughest of all. They make

NASA look like witch doctors. And New York from here? You're asking for the impossible."

"Can't do it?" I probed, touching his ego.

His reply was quick. "Of course I can! But I need things."

"What do you need?" Buchannon finally interjected.

"Entry codes, multiplexer keys, data segregations, module dephasers for substations, not to mention—"

"Enough," Buchannon interrupted. "I have juice in New York. Get your requirements to me in five minutes."

"Corny," I said. "I owe you again. I'll need coordinates."

"You'll have what I get," he replied, a testy note in his voice.

I hesitated before asking Buchannon the next question, but wanted to know. "What are the friendlies doing about Miller's death?"

"Nothing yet, but they found your prints all over the room, along with a thousand others. Was the girl there?"

It was an innocent-sounding question but heavily loaded. A wanted federal witness, on scene at the murder of an FBI agent, would complicate the mess to disastrous proportions. "No," I answered, recalling that Stella had stood at the door and had not entered, thus had left no latent prints.

We confirmed a few details, then clicked off, leaving me with wasting time, the most difficult of conditions. They never teach that at Langley. It took a few minutes to prepare logistically, and the remainder was mental. Wait and think.

At a nearby shop, I recalled Stella's admonishment and splurged for a shave and shine. They would not harm her, I kept telling myself, until Mateo had me. I had used Stella to sucker him into my web, and now he was returning the gesture. Poor kid, we all used her.

No amount of training can numb the anticipation. It's not the actual contact that horrifies, but rather the imagination preceding the physical event. The thought of dying is always present, but like my unique compatriots, I never had a fear of death. We live with that constant possibility, but it carries definite finality. Once snuffed, there is nothing to worry about.

But pain is quite another matter. Permanent agony is a death worse than anything. Knowing that, my plan was simple. A clean loss or win with no middle ground.

I placed an Out of Order sign on a phone booth to avoid its being used by others. There were several minutes to go, which became pure hell. For some reason, I still kept thinking about Stella in that ridiculous Western outfit. At three o'clock sharp, I removed the sign and dialed. It took several rings.

"Mr Cantrell here. A Mr. Mateo has made arrangements with your office for a relayed conversation."

"Stand by, please," said the voice. "Mr. Mateo is on the line."

There were several crackling sounds as the service made connections. "Cantrell?" he said.

"I'm waiting," I answered, and pictured Cornwall three thousand miles away, feverishly pushing buttons and tracing displays on his magic screens. Buchannon was no doubt leaning over, his hawklike and stooped features observing every move.

I had no idea how Corny was doing it, but he tapped into all lines of the answering service and tried to match my encoding with their callers. Corny could not hear the conversation, just harmonize the connections and back-trace Mateo's to its source. If it worked.

My only fear was that Mateo might use an innocent phone booth like me, but he had bragged about this system, and I believed he felt confident to use his working domicile.

"We'll meet at nine tonight," Mateo said without wasting time. "If you still want your finder's fee."

"How much?"

"Ten thousand."

I tried to sound amused. "There was no mention of a discount. That's quite a reduction from a million."

"Yeah, but ten thou more than you deserve. Our deal was you deliver the goods. I have it now, so why pay anything?"

Mateo knew that answer as I did. He wanted me on secluded ground. Hopefully, he didn't realize that I understood his motives. He was cautious not to mention Stella by name, or anything incriminating. He probably thought I was taping. "How do I know you have the package?"

"It's wrapped in this pretty blue bag with white stuff around the edges. Looks good enough to eat." Mateo laughed. "I might just do that, huh?"

My stomach tightened into knots.

"Since you've already been inside the package—" he chuckled "—you already seen the little pieces underneath are blue, too. We had to look, you know, can't have damaged merchandise."

Waves of nausea and outrage swept over me. They still needed her to get me. "One hundred thousand," I countered, steadying my voice. "You wouldn't have the package without me."

We dickered price a while, a useless exercise since he was not going to pay. Mateo wanted me burned. We negotiated like fishwives and his performance was actually impressive. He had the girl and did not have to pay anything. Technically, Stella only represented theories and surmises. My testimony was even lower scaled, third-level hearsay and legally useless.

But Mateo did not fear the law. No, it was Trudor who kept him awake nights. Trudor would hit anyone who posed a threat, and Mateo had screwed up, leaving two eyewitnesses alive.

We were more than a nuisance, Mateo desperately needed us out.

"Look, Cantrell," he spit, "I've had you checked out. You've got two hundred in checking, a couple thousand in savings and a pension that ain't worth piss. You been chasing down missing wives and husbands 'cause you got some weird gift for finding people that don't want to be found. Okay, I respect talent. But I also found out if the missing person has any bucks, you get a payoff and never seem to find them. Then bleed them a while. Huh? Right?"

I remained silent, my guilt speaking for me.

"I thought so, you friggin' bloodsucker. I got the shit on you. You're nobody." Mateo huffed a moment. "Okay, you understand. But I always pay my debts, and I owe ya. Fifty big ones, and that's it. Take it or shove it."

He offered just enough to pique my greed, yet not so much to indicate his desperation and frighten me off. I was impressed. Mateo was a superb con. After hesitating a few seconds, I accepted. "Okay," I told him, with the right touch of forced thankfulness.

He gave me an address in Queens. "Nine tonight," he commanded.

Ten seconds later I dialed Buchannon and held my breath. "Get it?" I asked, recalling a long-forgotten prayer.

"Corny has the switching signals. Just a minute to match coordinates. Cantrell, this better pay. I cashed a lot of favors to enter New York's phone system."

"You'll have a hero's badge," I said, suddenly irritated, thinking of what that maniac could do to Stella, and Buchannon was concerned with bureaucratic favors.

After summarizing my conversation with Mateo, Buchannon critiqued it with typical grunts. "Nothing surprising," he commented. "Mateo bought the material in your unsavory file, otherwise he would never agree."

"Did you ever trace who requested my file?"

"There were telex inquiries posing as minor government agencies. We supplied accordingly, but nothing traceable."

"Anything new on Miller?"

"The Bureau has it nailed to a pair of local cowboys. Dime shooters. Wainwright's covering the streets with full force, along with NYPD."

This was another reason I hated the rotten business. An average citizen gets offed, and if a quick solution is not obtained, the investigation is filed away for a low-crime day. But harm any government watchdog, and they assign entire departments.

It was the ultimate form of discrimination by stature. God, this was my last. No matter which way it turned, this was my last.

Corny finally clicked on and breathlessly explained the monumental difficulties he had surmounted.

"Please," I interrupted. "Just the address."

His pride was tweaked. "Listed as Huxley Computer Repair Service. The locale is lower East Side, hardly the spot for an electronic business."

"Then again, perfect," I added. "Few customers. Buchannon?"

"Yes," he answered, cool, miles ahead and interpreting his many options. Each decision was critical, and he mentally projected the outcomes, assumed their impact and how each would ultimately affect him and the department.

I understood his position, and he knew that. "We've gone this far," I said patiently. "Another step is little gamble. All I'm asking is you hold transmission of that address to the Feds until five o'clock, my time."

"Cantrell," he scoffed, "why is it you believe yourself the only person to comprehend the situation? I'm supposed to violate every rule, so you can play James Bond?"

"Five," I repeated. "If Wainwright's redcoats show too early, we all lose, and everything was for nothing."

He pondered the chaos. One call to Wainwright, and Mateo would be grabbed, but Buchannon would achieve only a footnote on the official report for supplying some minor information.

"Done," he finally said. "Five sharp. But Cantrell, if you screw the pooch, don't come home."

A sensitive, caring employer. "One more thing. Minor stuff. If this jells, tell Wainwright that Stella Evans will turn herself in with full cooperation. No charges against her, and nothing public."

"He'll buy that," Buchannon said, knowing Wainwright would accept any compromise to remove the smudge without a messy explanation.

It took an hour to locate the Huxley Computer Repair Service, buried in the long row of dilapidated buildings. There was some street activity from apartments and small businesses, several liquor stores and two neighborhood churches.

I had noted a pet store some distance back and returned for a special purchase.

Parking several feet from Huxley's I checked my equipment while observing the repair shop. As expected, no one entered or left, but there were four cars parked directly in front.

At four-fifteen I stood beside the rented Chevy and prepared. The shotgun went on the left side, barrel down, and pistol grip firmly into my armpit. A long band of Velcro tape around my waist and through the trigger guard held the weapon tight against my body. The Walther was at home on my spine.

It would take exactly two seconds to unband the scattergun, but I had no idea what to expect in there. Speed and surprise were my primary allies.

I carried the small metal case from the pet store in my left hand, leaving the right free. After taking several large breaths, I entered the Huxley repair shop at 4:22.

That gave me thirty-eight minutes. Either way, plenty of time.

# 19. BANG

THE STOREFRONT WAS narrow, consisting mostly of glass protected by heavy grillwork. I studied the alarm system, a standard Ni-Tech that I knew well. It's an excellent system, with door and window switches, glass sensors, weight and floor devices, infrared and motion detectors.

The tiny green LED signal on the outside panel was illuminated, but not the red, meaning the system was not armed. Good.

The outer reception area was fifteen feet deep and loaded with a hodgepodge of electronic and mechanical junk, totally disheveled and stacked haphazardly. The counter was littered with paper and empty coffee cups, and a crudely printed sign: Ring Bell for Service.

I wondered when was the last time the bell was used. A wall behind the counter had a curtained opening to the left. I peered through the gap and studied the shop, which was four times larger and in greater disarray than the front.

Halfway down the right was a man working on something. I wondered about the bombs. They could easily be constructed here, and the electronic paraphernalia was a perfect cover. Only an M.I.T. graduate could determine if this stuff was dangerous.

The man was soldering, and I approached him silently, my hand on the Walther. He nodded, I nodded, and he continued to work. Even a front needs a few legitimate employees. Either that, or he did not recognize me.

The last dozen steps brought be to the aft wall and the one single door. I stood there listening, not wanting to charge in and discover I'd raided the toilet.

I heard a muffled male voice, then another. I hyperventilated a few seconds and gave it one last thought.

The element of surprise can take many forms, the most disarming being sincerity and calmness. Then, you plunge. I opened the door and walked in like I belonged there, showing a friendly smile.

In a fraction of a second I surveyed the scene. The office was tiny, bedroom size, with another door on the right wall. Mateo sat in the second room behind a glass partition.

The man before me looked up, so I gave him a congenial smile. "I'll only be a minute," I said quickly, and stepped into Mateo's office. There was no time to reconsider. *Go, Cantrell,* my mind screamed.

He was talking with another man across the desk I had not seen at first. That made three. I dropped the metal box and quickly unbanded the Ithaca, then fired a shell into the wall.

The sound of a scattergun at close range is deafening. When unexpected, inside a small room it becomes a stupefying explosion.

It happened so fast, Mateo was dumbfounded. I instantly racked the shotgun, and before the shock waves subsided, pulled the Walther and rammed it against his throat. The chopped Ithaca pistol grip in my left hand covered the two sitting men, both in stunned silence. "Freeze!" I shouted, a ridiculous command because they were already frozen.

Mateo recovered first. "What the fuck are you doing? Get this maniac off me! Jerry, get him!"

"That wall will be your belly, Jerry. Don't move." I looked to the outer room and motioned the man to me. I had forced Mateo back in his chair with the handgun, so I could detect any motion.

The technician ran in, looking startled, and I directed all three to the floor. "Facedown, arms outstretched, fingers locked together. That's it, just like a steeple."

Mateo was continually babbling, swearing, threatening, which I ignored until the others were secure.

I felt the move. Mateo was leaning slightly, reaching for the drawer, so I cracked him one with the barrel across his nose. "Bring it out slowly," I warned.

He produced a mean-looking .45 and placed it gingerly on the desk. I tossed it into a corner, then positioned myself in front of Mateo.

"Game's over," I seethed, and quickly shoved the shotgun's barrel straight in his mouth. It was still hot, and the pungent odor of burned cordite was powerful.

"Don't move," I commanded, and waited for the reaction. I was not surprised. Mateo was tough and probably grew up with guns, street gangs and battles. He had no fear of this old man.

His voice was distorted by the barrel, but still recognizable. "I'll give you a hundred thousand. Two hundred!"

"Too late. I want the girl. Now."

"She's not here."

"Get her here. Five minutes."

His bulging eyes displayed fear, but not enough. This would not crack him. I had dropped the metal box close enough to reach it. I opened the lid so Mateo could see inside. Under a steel screen were several brown rats.

"These are babies," I explained, and his eyes trembled. "Real hungry. I saw this done once and never believed I could do it. I was wrong."

I could feel his face quiver. "It was in China, and no man ever suffered worse. Do you have any idea how long it takes to die from the inside? With starving rats eating out your guts? The poor bastard was begging to be shot.''

"You can't make me,'' he mouthed.

"Oh, but I can, and very easily. The Chinese had thousands of years to perfect the method. When the gun comes out, in goes the first. Know what he does? Smells all that wonderful garbage in your gut. Crawls straight to it, like a sewer.''

Mateo was shaking his head, not certain if I could really do it.

"After a few minutes and you start to scream, the next few go in real easy. You can't keep your mouth closed for the yelling. No way to get them out. I'll leave and you can die alone. You deserve that much. A little privacy.''

"I'll gag. You can't make me swallow.''

"I don't have to. When they smell that beautiful lunch you had, they'll chew their way down your throat. Ever tried to keep hungry rats from food?''

That was the magic phrase. He believed me. "Get the girl here now,'' I commanded, and repositioned the gun into his neck, very firmly. "One man only. And don't say anything stupid.''

"One man can't handle that bitch.''

"All right, two, but no more. Make that clear.'' I mentally agreed. Her keepers would be suspicious if they were told just one man.

Mateo was on the phone, and I nudged the barrel. "Tony?'' he demanded. "You and Joboy bring the girl to me. Yes, now. Yes, just you two. Goddammit, just do it!''

The three on the floor were quite motionless, wanting no part of this crazy old fart, or the scattergun. The cordite was still strong.

"We chat now,'' I said. "How'd you find my room?'' It took prodding, but the truth came out, basically as Stella and I had theorized. They lost me and followed Miller, who was not looking behind.

"Why kill Miller?"

Mateo was anxious to talk about that, eager to explain he had no part. "A giant fiasco," he said. "Hired two jerks to rough you up. Scare you off, you know? Gave them your room number. Stupid assholes. The guy finally convinced them he was a Fed. They panicked."

"So they iced him?"

"Yeah, but hey, hey! Not my fault! I refused to pay the jerks."

Mateo said it as if that made everything even. "Okay, now Trudor. How do you contact?"

Mateo stared at me with murderous eyes.

"Part of the deal," I said firmly. "I want the girl and Trudor's location."

This was too much. Mateo would risk exchanging Stella for his life; after all, he'd put a hit contract on us minutes later. But fingering a merciless killer like Trudor was quite fatal. "You know, I think it's a bluff. In fact, you couldn't get one of those friggin' things in my mouth."

I had been waiting for that. Mateo's hand was flat on the desk, and I quickly slammed the shotgun grip on his fingers, cracking some bones. He screamed and jumped, and I whacked him again on the shoulder.

"I could have dropped a baseball in that fat mouth. I told you, the Chinese are masters at torture. There are a hundred ways to get your mouth open. Now, Trudor. How do you contact?"

"Messages," he whined, holding his bloody fingers. "We exchange cablegrams. In code."

"Give them to me."

"I burn them."

"You better have saved some. The rats are getting hungrier."

"In that cabinet."

I followed with the gun never leaving his neck, a most distracting and uncomfortable persuader. He unlocked a drawer and produced a manila file.

With·my free hand I thumbed through the sheets, all a series of meaningless numbers. Corny could probably crack them, but I had no interest in the words. They were all marked Heraklion, Crete. "This his base?"

"How the hell would I know? That's where they come from."

"And you reply to the same place?"

He nodded. "Cantrell, we can still deal. Let's make it three hundred thousand right now. Leave the girl with me. You don't need her."

"Tony and Joboy better hurry," I replied. "I'm getting nervous, and you don't want me nervous."

At ten minutes past five, I heard commotion from the shop. "You three on the floor. Don't move, and you'll live through this." I quickly swapped weapons, leveled the scattergun toward the door, and pushed the Walther deep into Mateo's fleshy neck. "I hope you have control over your goons. You'll get it first." My fear was having to shoot the big gun and needing the second hand to pump. Mateo certainly knew that.

I heard weak feminine protest, garbled and lethargic. She was probably drugged. Great, that's all I needed.

The first man entered the outer office and stared through the glass at the partially destroyed wall. "Hey, you guys have a par—"

He saw me and froze. I motioned with the scattergun to the corner, but he was dumbstruck and didn't move.

A second voice came from behind him. "Where you want little Miss Bitch?" He was half supporting Stella as she slumped, and things happened fast when Mateo screamed.

"Kill this fucking maniac!"

The first soldier reached, pulled a shoulder gun, and I didn't wait. The salvo took out the glass and most of the partition, and blasted him straight back into a pile.

Mateo jumped up, shouting like a lunatic. "Kill him! Get him!"

I was tempted to end it right there, straight through that fat slobby neck. It would be so damn easy, but I had already decided that was my last resort. If his info about Trudor was wrong, the Feds would need him.

Mateo grabbed for my handgun and twisted it away from his face. I brought the shotgun around with full force and cracked him across the mouth, spewing teeth and blood everywhere.

He instantly sagged, and I turned to the second man, glancing at the three on the floor. They were trying to disappear. No threat.

The Walther dropped to the desk as I racked the monster and stared at a very frightened young man. He had released Stella, and thank God, she fell, out of the way.

A small-bore revolver was pointing at me from a trembling hand. I was aiming right at his midsection. "Don't do it," I said softly. "I'm squeezing slightly. No matter how good you shoot with that popgun, I'll cut you in half."

"Don't shoot," he moaned.

"Point it to the floor. Good. Now bend over and lay it down gently."

Mateo was gaining stability and shouting again through busted teeth and split lips. "One hundred thousand to anyone who gets him!"

"Sure, guys," I said loudly. "You'll get an expensive funeral." I picked up the Walther, kicked the other two handguns well into the shop, then commanded the shaking gunman to the floor.

Mateo was yelling incoherent orders, which everyone ignored. Stella was barely conscious of her surroundings. They had doped her enough to avoid trouble, but not too much. They didn't want to carry her.

I took her wrist and pulled. "Go outside, Stella. Walk out the front door."

She looked confused, babbled something and shook her head trying to clear the fog. Stella took a few crooked steps and dropped to her knees. I raised her with my forearm and aimed the scattergun with the free hand. They already knew I would use it.

I positioned Stella with my left arm around her waist, so she was stumbling forward as I walked backward, holding the Ithaca. It was the only way to support her and protect our exit.

Two of them stood at the office door while Mateo yelled from behind. He was still offering ludicrous sums to burn me.

"Come on, baby," I insisted. "I'll get us out of here, but you have to walk now." She was shuffling so slow, it took all my strength to keep her upright.

We had managed about half the distance through the shop with forty paces to go when one of Mateo's people slowly ventured toward us. "That door is the boundary," I shouted. "First man through gets creamed."

Stella was scuffling one foot in front of the other. They must have zapped her with another jolt just before arriving, and it was taking effect.

Mateo voiced encouragement to his fools, and I suddenly thought of the .45 in the corner. I had kicked away the two guns but in the excitement had overlooked that one.

"Mateo," I shouted. "Why don't *you* try it?"

My fear was the curtained opening separating the shop and entry office. Once through it, my vision would be zero, and they could charge to within five feet. We would be defenseless.

At ten feet from the curtain, I distinctly heard noises from the entry area behind me, and I realized Mateo's phone was in his office. He had been out of sight long enough to call for help, probably from the same room that Stella was held.

A cross fire would be deadly, and we had no chance if they moved first. I whipped Stella around, so her back was against my chest, giving me leverage to quickly operate the shotgun. At this point, it was the only way. We would live or die together.

I fired toward Mateo and company, racked it, backpedaled quickly to the flimsy barrier, dropped Stella to the floor, fired and racked again, then burst through the curtain crouching low.

They might have been citizens or even Feds, but the street clothes and drawn guns dispelled that notion. Expecting us to be running, the two were aiming high, and I did not let the closest one correct. I took him away as he fired, but the second was quick and shot twice as I pumped, then he flew partially through the window from my blast, twisting wrought iron and scattering glass to the street.

Shotgun empty, I threw it aside and blindly fired three times to the rear office with the Walther automatic as I grabbed Stella by the wrist and yanked her like a sack of potatoes.

"Get up and run!" I screamed. "Run!"

Dragging her, I felt the searing pain torch into my right arm and realized I bought one. At that precise moment, I briefly thought about ruining my new coat. Crazy.

Stella tried to get erect, and I gripped her dress collar like that of an errant child. Mateo or someone was shooting with that huge .45 from the rear, but we had cleared the curtain and were slightly off angle.

Struggling through the outer lobby onto the street, we stepped around the spread-eagled form lying on the window ledge. From the street, I put four timed shots through the curtain as we finally managed the car.

This had taken too much time. I emptied the clip with dispersed rounds into the store, just before jumping into the driver's seat.

I had tested the car's ability to quick-start before renting it, but still I held my breath. I kept waiting for the crack of return fire, but was fifty feet away before the first thumps hit the rear deck. Pulling Stella down viciously by the hair, I held her face on the seat when the next two came through the rear window and out the front.

On her side.

# 20. SHELTER

LUCKILY, STELLA WAS doped enough to keep her head down.

I held the throttle hard and zigzagged down the street as the shooters tried to find their range. It would take them a few seconds to reach their cars, but by then, we had turned a few corners and lost them. Hopefully, Wainwright's people were on time.

Grinding out lefts and rights, we finally blended with traffic in case Wainwright's redcoats were late and Mateo's people followed us. I had cut it quite thin but knew Buchannon's alert to Wainwright would be relayed to the local NYPD for a net around Huxley's store until the Feds arrived.

"Oh my God!" Stella suddenly screeched, waking from her dreamworld. She was staring at my arm. "Are you all right?"

"Yes, you awake now?"

She nodded, horrified.

I asked her several questions, clearing the mind, bringing her back from a semicomatose state. They had really zapped her. She applied a tourniquet to my arm with her belt, a feeble attempt, but it kept her mind functioning.

Stella insisted on driving, but I refused, knowing she would pile us into the first wall. She was still not back on earth.

A citizen directed us to an emergency clinic, and we circled the area ten times before spotting the neighborhood trauma center. In the small dingy waiting room was every form of human misery: beaten wives, broken and confused elders, busted faces from street battles and the noise I've heard around the world, a sound that accompanies all anguish and violence—the crying and whimpering of helpless children.

A nurse eyed us carefully, having no doubt witnessed this scene hundreds of times each day. "I have to report all gunshot wounds to the proper authorities," she announced coolly.

"I understand. My daughter's a junkie, and I caught her shooting up. She panicked and shot me. It's okay, we've forgiven each other, but I need this patched."

The nurse looked sympathetic. It was a credible story, and one she could relate with, looking at Stella's spaced-out appearance. Also, if I'd been mugged or attacked, I would have been screaming for the law.

"I still have to report it," she apologized.

"No problem. I won't press charges," I confided, and displayed the Wade identification.

I returned to Stella. We held each other for a while, quietly coaxing and squeezing, touching and sighing, both glad to be alive. She was coming down and soon passed out. After bundling her on a hard bench, I told the nurse to call me if Stella woke. Applying a proper tourniquet to my arm, she said it would be a twenty-minute wait. I found the one pay phone.

I dialed Buchannon and briefly summarized the Mateo situation. "Details later. I've been hit and may need cover."

"Bad?"

"Ruined a five-hundred-dollar suit. Heard from Wainwright?"

"Not through channels, but he called unofficially minutes ago."

"Am I listed in his plus or minus column?"

"I would describe it as a love-hate relationship at this point. He loves you for leading him to Mateo. With the guns, drugs, unaccounted-for cash and illegal explosives they found, Wainwright can hold them almost indefinitely. But he would also like to hang your ass for the bloody mess you left behind."

"He'll get over it. Everyone's off the hook."

"Cantrell, you continually forget this is an age of un-paralleled individual rights. Meaning, Wainwright will be completing reports for months and answering to review boards for a year. Remember, the FBI is our friend, they are nice people, and never, *never* shoot anyone. They are still rebuilding PR over butchering Dillinger."

Shock was affecting me, and I felt lighthearted and silly. "Does this mean my raise is out?"

He ignored me. "Mr. Wainwright would like to know the meaning of a little box of baby mice found on Mateo's desk. Are they related to anything important?"

I ignored him. "I have Trudor pegged. I think. At least, a damn good probable."

"It better be more than a probable. Cantrell, you have been allowed unprecedented latitude in this affair from the beginning. Trudor has been the ultimate target since his name surfaced, and certain key people are convinced you can reach him. Please score one for the Gipper, and don't let us down."

"Us?" I responded, sarcastically. "Okay, but I need things. Have Wainwright clear me. I'll be going through JFK and do not want entanglements. Wire more money to Dirkson. We'll need grease."

"There goes your raise. Pity."

"Next, when Stella gets there, lay off. She'll come to you. Give her five thousand as a reward, and if the department can't cut that, take it from my savings. I'm certain Corny can tap into my account.''

"Please don't attempt moralistic indignation. It does not fit you. Yes, the department can arrange something for our heroine. Ah, before Sir Lancelot charges off, what about your reports? I assume you taped everything?''

"From the moment I entered Mateo's little playpen. And my personal comments will be included. First thing.''

"Excellent. Ah, Cantrell, you did a superb job. Really. I do not approve of your actions and prefer you to cease immediately, but it is equally obvious you have become obsessed with this situation. So, since you appear unstoppable, well, you know what I am trying to say, good luck and all that.''

"Thanks,'' I managed to say, suddenly feeling very tired.

The attending physician was young but experienced. In that neighborhood, he probably treated more gunshot wounds than Army medics do. He probed some, and the X rays showed only a few fragments, which he retrieved. The slug had passed through, nicking a chunk of the ulna bone. Painful, but not serious.

Conversation was nil, the doctor preferring not to know anything of his street patients. "Keep the bandages tight,'' he finally said, and explained when and how to change them. He handed me a small packet of Darvon with a prescription for more.

The arm was burning, so I decided to gamble and produced my old CIA identification. "Doc, you do fine work,'' I commented, "but I'm facing some really tough days ahead. Could you rewrite this for Demerol? I know how to handle it.''

He shrugged and wrote another one. "You spooks frighten me.''

"Me, too,'' I replied, without sarcasm.

I called a cab from the pay phone, not wanting to drive a bullet-holed car through New York, inviting the attention of a curious police officer.

Stella was out cold and had no desire to leave the comfy womb of the hospital. We struggled to the emergency entrance and waited for our chariot. I chuckled, thinking about Buchannon's wrath when Avis sent that bill.

Arriving at the Statler was an event—one grimy, bandaged old man wearing ripped and bloody clothes, helping a young female doped to oblivion, with a blue dress splattered red. I explained to the desk clerk about the auto accident. "In fifteen minutes could you send someone to collect this suit and her dress? And have them stitched and cleaned by morning?" I gave him a bill. "Appreciate it."

The bellboy helped me deposit Stella in the bedroom, and it took me some time to remove the dress. Mateo was right. Her delicate undies were matching blue, and I vowed not to ask her what had happened. Stella would tell me if she wanted. I tucked the unconscious woman under a thick comforter.

The cognac arrived and I sipped away, relating the events of our brutal day into the recorder. My body throbbed, screaming for sleep. Strange things can happen after a severe physiological crash, and I did not want Stella to wake in a panic, so I left a note on the dresser.

Everything is okay. You're safe. Call room service for dinner. I'm sleeping in the next room.

CANTRELL

When Stella tugged my good arm to waken me, my entire being hurt. "Time to get up," she insisted quietly. "Dinner is served."

Stretching away the cobwebs and mental fog, I wobbled to the table and stared at the smorgasbord of delight. The huge cart was covered with a dozen dishes, from shaved beef Wellington to chilled shrimp on skewers and hot lobster chunks, surrounded by pâté, dips, three steaming fresh vegetables, hollandaise and a variety of desserts. Two bottles of champagne caught my eye, and I opened one.

Stella stood near, waiting my reaction. "I didn't know what you wanted, so here's a bit of everything."

"Perfect." I smiled, seeing she was pleased. That touched me.

"You deserve the best," she cooed, trying not to look embarrassed. "If it's too much, I'll pay."

"Buchannon likes his people to go first-class." She had wrapped a sheet around her body, and somehow it stayed in place. I always wondered how women could do that. "There's enough here for six people. It's time you met my assistant."

I called the desk for Dirkson's room number and was about to ring him when Stella began giggling.

"Does Mr. Dirkson enjoy his meals early or late?" she asked, continuing to laugh. "It's five in the morning!"

For some reason, that broke me up. Everything seemed so silly. Here I was, a grown man, tired and hurting, wounded and with no appetite and laughing insanely at three-hundred-dollars'-worth of fantastic dinner.

Calming my giggles, I asked her, "How did you manage room service at this hour?"

"Easy, I tipped the breakfast crew to microwave the dinner entrées. It's all frozen anyway."

"You are remarkable."

"No, just hungry. Given proper motivation, I can do anything." She guided me into a chair and began massaging my neck. "I want to hear the complete story, every detail, but first this. My Lord, you're all knotted up. Here," she coaxed, and stood behind, squeezing the aching, stiffened muscles. "You're too tight. Come on, you need a sizzling hot shower. The warming dishes have candles. Everything will stay hot."

Stella adjusted the jet spray to needle-fine, then cranked it full blast. "Hot as you can stand," she instructed. "Over the neck and shoulders. Don't worry if the bandage gets wet. I'll change it."

For several minutes, luxurious pulsating darts of steaming water drove into this weary frame. Pure heaven.

There was no pretentious teasing or posing. Stella merely opened the shower door and stepped inside without a word. She took the heavily scented soap and began scrubbing my body.

I looked upward, distant, enjoying the professional touch, like receiving an overdue sponge bath from a gifted nurse. But it became impossible to keep my eyes off her incredible body, svelte, streamlined, slender and perfectly firm in all places.

We must have been there a long time, never saying a word, because the candles burned out, and our food turned cold.

# 21. DIRKSON

OUR CLOTHES ARRIVED at eight-fifteen, so I buzzed Dirkson and quickly regretted it. The anxious bastard was at the door in two minutes. He must have been dressed and waiting by the phone. I was never that gung ho.

We were quite a trio. Dirkson wore his three-piece Brooks Brothers. I sat on the couch nibbling cheesecake with a towel around my waist, and Stella was dressed in only my silk shirt, looking bizarre with one sleeve missing. She insisted, and I did not ask why. Women are strange.

The back side almost reached the bottom of those lovely curved cheeks. She was fussing about, arranging things, and careful to turn her fanny away when bending over.

Dirkson could not take his eyes off her. "Like shrimp?" I asked, offering a plate.

"I prefer coffee and toast in the morning," he responded.

"The coffee is cold," Stella said, "but we have champagne."

"I'll try that," I said, and we both stared as Stella poured. Quite a sight. "Talk to Buchannon?" I asked him.

"Huh? Oh yeah. He called last night and updated me."

"I'll fill in details later. How are things at the center?"

"Chaotic, but all things considered, Mr. Buchannon seemed calm enough. He's been smoothing things with, uh, other parties," Dirkson said, cautiously glancing at Stella. "Mr. Buchannon has last-minute instructions for you, but he was concerned we'd leave early, so he relayed them to me."

Dirkson made that pointedly clear, knowing it was highly inappropriate for the director to bypass the senior operative. "Please don't give me the old fight song," I snapped. "No company cheers, I get nauseated."

"It's not that."

"Look, I'm out of touch and far from a hundred percent, but I don't need a desk general to update me on field operations. I wrote the book on half that shit." I said too much but felt surprisingly offended. This pup was going to brief me! My ego is usually well barricaded, mentally, but he had struck a sensitive nerve.

"It's involved," he said quietly, and glanced at Stella.

I retrieved the tapes. "Stella, get dressed. Here, these are valuable. Take a cab to the nearest stereo store and make two copies of everything. Ask for a demonstration. Buy the tape deck if you have to but refuse payment until you have the copies. Got that? If the clerk stands there, turn the volume to zero so he can't hear."

"If I have to buy the tape deck, what do I do with it?"

"Call it a gift from a grateful Starkmore." I handed her my card. "Keep the originals and mail the copies to this address. Send one set air mail, the second group special delivery."

She looked confused so I clarified the instructions. "I'll mail the originals from the airport," I told her. "The odds are astronomical against our faithful postal system losing all three sets. It's just insurance. And get my prescription filled."

While Stella dressed, Dirkson and I phoned several airlines to make our arrangements along with Stella's return to San Francisco.

She came from the bedroom wearing the cotton-candy dress, only the image was distorted where it had been ripped and torn. The repairs were hasty and crude, and blood-stains do not disappear easily in such material.

"You look like hell," I said with a smile. "The dress is ruined."

"Not to worry." She smiled back. "All that wrestling on the floor."

"Get a new outfit, something comfortable. We have time."

"Okay, but I'm keeping the dress," she exclaimed. "May I?"

I nodded, and she brushed a quick sisterly kiss on my cheek but held it a split second too long. Dirkson looked away.

"The tapes? Isn't that risky?" he asked, after she left. "I know protocol and shouldn't question, but in the hands of a citizen?"

"Stella lived through it. She could make her own recording," I responded, irritated at his challenge.

I stared at Barry Dirkson. "Okay," I said, helping myself to the bubbly. "So, what's Captain America want?"

Dirkson cleared his throat. "Mr. Buchannon says our top priority is to ensure that our actions and presence cannot be traced back to the agency. *That* is our top priority, *not* Trudor. He comes second. Mr. Buchannon feels the security of the department is more important than any terrorist who can be erased with a simple contract."

"Sure," I fumed, "when no one's ever got close to him before."

"Anyway," Dirkson continued, "at the slightest setback or risk of discovery, before or during the engagement, we are to break off and cancel."

"That's standard," I commented, noting Dirkson had it memorized.

"Yes, but with a new wrinkle. If you uh, go down, I am to ensure your, uh, remains cannot be identified. Naturally, the same goes for me. Then the survivor is to make certain he cannot be associated in any way with the fallen operative."

"Jesus, Buchannon is becoming bloody damn ruthless! How are we supposed to accomplish that?"

"He suggested dismemberment, mutilation or fire."

"Christ," I mused, watching his expressionless face. "Could you do that to me?"

"Mr. Buchannon asked the same thing. I had to admit, I didn't know. A stranger, probably, but not to a partner. Since I had reservations, he ordered an alternate option. Your body or mine is never to be found."

"Much smarter. If Interpol finds so much as a tooth, they have the resources and patience to track it back to the agency. It would be embarrassing."

We looked away momentarily, both horrified at this monstrous policy, yet neither admitting nor questioning the necessity, knowing there are often good reasons for seemingly insane commands.

I shrugged. "Let's think this out. Figuring a simple matrix, there are only four possibilities. One, we both get out clean. Two and three, either you or I go down. And four, we both buy the farm. How do we handle the last one? Does he expect one of us will hang on long enough to hide his own body?"

"I've thought of nothing else for hours." Dirkson sighed. "If Mr. Buchannon is really that concerned about a back trace, it's not like him to leave that door open."

"Agreed, and stop calling him mister!" I snapped. "Now, how could he avoid a contingency plan for the last condition? Incidentally, both of us going under is a distinct possibility. I'd hate to see Corny's probability study on that, but bet your ass Buchannon has. So—'' I grinned ''—what is your conclusion?''

"There's a backup in the field. Someone who will cover our tracks if we strike out."

"Right. Like who?" I asked, letting my young charge work it out.

"With Mist . . . ah, Buchannon's connections, it could be anyone."

"Wrong. No one from our section. That would put Buchannon in double jeopardy. His people would both lead and smoke the operation."

"Outsiders? The Bureau?"

"Believe it or not, they are a righteous bunch of bastards and don't like messy involvements. Particularly outside our national borders. Boy Scouts don't get dirty, especially on foreign turf."

"Well," Dirkson added cautiously, "I don't think it could be military, state department or DIA, certainly not counterinsurgence, and Buchannon wouldn't trade with Interpol without getting a fat prize in return. Would he?" Dirkson asked, uncertain.

"No, he wouldn't. That only leaves the ghouls."

"The CIA? I can't believe it."

"Think, man, think! Consider the circumstances. Starkmore with Transcontinental has clout. That's obvious. He knows senators, congressmen and Lord knows who else. As far as we know, Trudor has committed no crime against this country, until his extortion from TCA."

"So, the ghouls are involved?"

"Probably have been since Wainwright passed the Trudor connection through channels. The Company would love to put the skids to Trudor, but he's holed in a country that doesn't like outside intervention, particularly American. I'll bet Trudor hasn't even broken a Greek traffic law."

"So jurisdictional dispute, international constraints and complications are protecting Trudor."

"Right. Now, the Company can sit back and watch us without direct involvement. If we foul out, they haven't gambled or lost anything."

"And our agency is clean, no matter what. That's why Buchannon cannot risk any connection to the source." Dirkson wrung his hands, not believing our own department would play us at both ends.

"Welcome to the real world," I said. "You're catching on. We are to be used or discarded as needs dictate, and nobody gets their hands or reputations soiled."

"Cute," was all Dirkson could manage. He bit into some sliced beef from the silver tray.

"Dirkson, you don't have to go any farther."

"Neither do you," he countered.

"In my own way, I do."

"Then so do I."

After a thoughtful silence, I told him to bring the equipment from his room. While waiting, I considered calling Wainwright. There was something that needed to be said. I chose not.

Dirkson returned with the gear and proudly displayed his arrangement. Agencies always prepack and recommend certain techniques but allow operatives the right to redistribute hardware to their individual preferences. Dirkson had done a fine job.

He unwrapped the distorting foil. "I prefer the Colt AR-15 Assault but decided to match yours. Makes the ammo simpler."

Broken down and lying at oblique angles to confuse X-ray detection were two German MP5-Ks, sustained automatic submachine guns. They fired 9 mm slugs at 840 rounds per minute and could empty the 30-shell clips in a blazing two seconds. Assembled, the awesome weapon weighed under five pounds and measured fractionally more than twelve inches.

"How many clips?"

"Fifty. Lined in rows like steel reinforcement for the suitcase walls."

"Clever. That's fifteen hundred rounds. Going to war?"

"I read Trudor's file, what there is. During the past two embassy takeovers, his people used SPAS-12s. I thought we needed the firepower."

"Good," I mumbled, knowing what could be done by a SPAS-12, basically a small, hand-held automatic cannon, holding eight rounds of three-inch shells in the circular magazine, plus one in the chamber. Each shell could be filled with buckshot, incendiaries, explosives or a combination. One man could hold off a squad or attack a building.

"Any bangs?" I asked.

"Five standard chunks of C-4 with acid-to-brass firing mechanisms."

I noticed his nunchaku, a deadly combat weapon, one chain with two wood handles. "Get rid of that."

"I'm good with it," Dirkson defended.

"If you get close enough to use it, we're already dead. Take everything out and rough up the suitcase to look well used. New suitcases mean new clothes. It's a theft target. And for Crissakes, get rid of that!" I pointed to a large sticker on the side: Handle with Care. Photo Equipment.

"That explains the weird shapes under security X ray. My own idea," he said proudly.

"Don't try new ideas on me. Get killed on your own mission. That's an open invitation to be robbed. Photo gear means cameras, the easiest thing on earth to peddle."

He was peeling off the label when Stella returned. She could see I was in a foul mood. I didn't know why Dirkson got under my skin. He was competent and tried hard enough.

After he left with the empty bag, I sat near her. "You look nice. Some women wear jeans for convenience, but you're born to them."

"I'm not certain if that's a compliment or not."

"Your flight leaves an hour before ours. No one will meet you in San Francisco. Call that number. Be prepared for two or three days of questioning. Nothing rough, but they'll know everything before you leave."

"Everything?" she cooed, with that wispy touch of vixen.

"There's no way to predict how they'll play it," I continued, ignoring her innuendo, "but probably a trade-off. You'll have to sign a dozen papers admitting guilt in the murder cover-up of Cindy Cummings, plus the knowledge of Savino Avalon's complicity in the extortion plot, your interstate flight to avoid prosecution and anything else they can think of. That will be their stranglehold. If you ever go public with any part of the true story, your butt is grass. Promise."

"I understand. If I stay quiet, I'm out of jail."

"You got it. Make damn certain you get papers to that effect. They'll probably say something about public gratitude, and thank you for the efforts that prevented a major crime. In exchange for that, all charges are dismissed, nothing on the record, and if you committed any crime, it was through fear and intimidation."

"Meaning shut up and be free?"

"Exactly. And have Buchannon square the credit card things you charged in San Francisco before running to Denver."

I lectured Stella for an hour, like a daughter on her first date. She began doing the bored act, which pissed me, but I continued. "Since it's an unsolved homicide, your things have been stored at the sheriff's department. Buchannon will get them back."

"So," she asked softly, "is this it? I won't see you again?"

"I thought you decided that already."

"It was different then. I knew what you were doing. This new thing, I don't understand at all."

"Me neither. Uh, if you want, you can reach me through the office. Maybe I'll call when I get home."

"Just maybe, huh?" Stella began folding her dress into a shopping bag. "Nothing happened," she said suddenly.

"What?"

"You haven't asked about it, but I want you to know. When those people held me in that apartment nothing happened."

"That's your business, but Buchannon will demand details. It adds to the charges against Mateo."

"There was a lot of grab-ass but not anything I haven't endured in bars."

"Were you scared?"

"Damn right!" she exclaimed, and gave me a hug. "Thanks isn't enough, but that's all I can think of."

"It's enough," I said awkwardly, and offered her several hundred dollars. "This will get you started. Buchannon has a fund for helpful, displaced witnesses. He'll arrange more."

"I don't need it," she said in a huff, and we briefly played the money-back-and-forth game, both of us insisting.

"Dammit!" I commanded. "Take it for my sake. Make an old man happy."

Stella looked suddenly chilled, her dark eyes brooding. "Funny, I thought I did that this morning."

# 22. GOODBYE

THE SILENCE WAS THICK until Dirkson returned with the scarred and battered suitcase. It looked like a refugee's survival bag from a death march. I thought he overdid it but said nothing. Never hold back eager players who follow instructions.

He had covered the firepower with towels and managed to carry the arms to the bedroom, so Stella could not see them. Before he packed, I retrieved one morphine syrette from the medical kit and gave myself a subcutaneous injection. The wound was beginning to throb badly. Stella watched from a distance, and if I'd expected any sympathy, I was disappointed.

The three of us silently watched inane television, each with our own thoughts, until leaving for the airport.

The cab dropped us, and I instructed Dirkson to check in, cash the money order sent from Buchannon and mail the original tape recordings. I would meet him later in the waiting lounge.

Dirkson seemed surprised I had carried a passport. "Do you leave the house without your goddamn wallet?" I snapped. "In this business you take a passport to the toilet! You never know when it's needed."

I was unusually harsh, but everything pissed me.

Stella was given her ticket, and after the preliminaries were complete, we sat in awkward, sustained silence.

She finally coughed self-consciously. "Seems like we're always at airports, but it's a little different this time. We're not hiding, or running, or wearing ridiculous costumes. God, I'll never forget that first outfit."

"You were great," I offered.

"It's almost boring this way, being a normal traveler. Well, Cantrell, if nothing else, you brought some spark into my life."

"Thanks, I think."

Stella hesitated. "Sorry about being a bitch. You know me."

"Forget it," I said sharply, wanting to leave.

"That was a cheap shot at the hotel. Sorry," she mumbled, and toyed with loose threads on her new blouse. "You must really miss her."

"Who?"

"Kate. You said her name several times. Maybe I was jealous."

"That's ridiculous."

"Of course, but women don't always make sense." She had rolled the thread into a tiny ball and rubbed it nervously between her fingers.

"Not much to tell," I began, surprising Stella when I spoke. "Usual story. We were married several years but I don't recall how many. Bad sign, right?" I tried to joke. "Doesn't matter. It was a long time ago. The funny thing was she probably didn't realize how much I loved her. Kate was my rock, my Gibraltar. The thoughts of her pulled me through some very nasty times."

Stella broke the melancholy. "So, now you're off to Greece to play hero again and catch this Trudor terrorist."

I stared harshly. "I'm almost afraid to ask how you know that."

"Knowing me as you do, did you honestly think I wouldn't listen to those tapes while I made copies? I heard everything."

"For God's sake, don't tell Buchannon what you did. If this thing in Greece goes badly, you are a witness again, and in serious shit."

"I didn't learn survival being a fool. The secrets are safe with Mata Hari." She paused a minute. "Ah... promise you'll come back?"

"I told you. When you're settled, and it's over, I'll call."

"I didn't ask if you'd call. I asked if you're going to make it back! There is a difference. Or is this another suicidal trip? Self-destruct?"

"Goddammit, child!" I roared, suddenly furious. "I just happen to be goddamn good! I haven't been in the field for a decade, but let me tell you, I was one of the best! The years of experience are still there, and those fuckers never faced a pro!"

I was breathing deeply, and felt silly and foolish after my juvenile outburst, but did not apologize.

We did not speak until they announced her flight. Stella turned to me and whispered, "You don't have to prove anything to me, old man. I was at Mateo's, remember? All I'm asking is you be certain why you're doing this. And it's worth it. That's all."

Without looking at her, I answered. "Doesn't matter right now."

At the gate she gave me a quick, empty kiss, mumbled something, then scurried to the plane. I watched it taxi away and felt ancient.

I located Dirkson in the Trans World lounge, feeding his face with tepid hot dogs. "They serve first-class food on this flight," I reminded him.

"I'm always hungry. The wife says it's glands."

With an hour to kill, I submerged myself in the paper, couldn't finish the crossword, decided new cars cost too much in New York and generally felt like hell.

Still angry and wanting to vent, I elbowed Dirkson. "You wanted to know if I could disfigure your corpse to prevent identification?"

He nodded.

"You better not find out."

# 23. EAST

At twenty minutes to boarding time, I swallowed hard and made one last call, which I dreaded immensely but had to face.

The secretary claimed Wainwright was not there; however, when I gave my name, he mysteriously appeared.

His greeting was typical. "Cantrell! You son of a bitch!"

"Greetings to you, Mr. Special Agent."

"You left one hell of a mess."

"Don't con this old bird. You're getting all the credit. You Boy Scouts have saved Starkmore and his airline. Free passes for life, right? Come on, fess up."

He grunted. "Listen hero, I'm not really pissed because this whole fiasco had become my Achilles' heel. In a way I'm grateful, but I'll never admit that to anyone."

He lowered his voice, a ridiculous effort because we both knew all calls to the Bureau are automatically recorded. However, he had the power to "lose" certain tapes. "My only question is, why didn't you burn Mateo? Now, I'm stuck with a story. What am I supposed to do with him? He's a leper. Taboo. One grand jury, and the whole mess is exposed."

"Consider it a challenge," I offered. "I'm looking forward to reading your official report. I want to see how you nimbly-foot around the issue."

"Hell, since you'll read it anyway, we're going to launder the raid specifics with a planted agent story. Someone who is so valuable, he and the details must remain covert.

You'll probably become a goddamn myth. Christ, we're even assigning a code name to cover you and the mess, so now you're part of us. Hoover must be rolling over in his grave."

"Anything for the glory of the Bureau."

"Screw off."

"Roger," I said, trying to find the right words and knowing they did not exist. "Actually, I just called for one reason. It might be my only chance. I'm really sorry about Miller. Honest, I didn't know. They suckered me. Sorry," I repeated.

He sighed long and painfully. "Don't take the blame. It was our fault. We were all suckered. Miller was a friend, and I had to tell his family. That was tough."

"It always is," I said quietly, not wanting to count the number of times I had suffered that agony. You feel guilty for being alive and he's dead, and his wife feels the same, but never says it.

"Wainwright?" I asked, wanting to know. "Why didn't you tell me Miller was on deep tag? I could have watched for him."

"Cantrell, you sanctimonious bastard! You crossed my people all the way. Talk about personal wars! You charged out like a vigilante and never talked to anyone!"

I gave that long and careful thought. "You're probably right. I guess the point has been reached when ... I don't trust anyone."

He sighed. "Well, you taught me that, a long time back. For an old fart, you're still kicking hard."

"And still learning. Do me a favor, if I have the right to ask. Stella Evans is en route to San Francisco. Give her an edge, okay? Anything you can do?"

"That's a promise."

"One more. When we jumped from that rented car, the kid drove away as a dodge. I conned him. Take off the heat. He's clean."

Wainwright paused. "Sure, glad to, if we ever find him. We never caught the little bastard."

"You're kidding! With a three-legged radio tag on him?"

"The shit found the bug and stuck it on a Greyhound bus. He's probably in Mexico by now, selling the car."

We chatted for a minute, goading each other, playing old games, then Wainwright dropped his voice to a bare whisper. "Officially, I don't know what you're doing, but you taught me how to piece things together, so unofficially..."

"Yeah?"

"Don't play Trudor like Mateo. It won't work. This freak makes Attila the Hun into a choirboy. Erase the fucker."

Dirkson and I were three hours out of Kennedy, sometime between a lavish meal and the movie before Dirkson said much. I had been silent, and as I've been told before, I am not the easiest person to work with.

"Uh..." he struggled, "I'm still curious about the passport. Buchannon said I should bring yours, which I checked out from security, but you already had one. That's not standard procedure."

"Screw the SOP, you'll live longer. Actually I have several, one from the agency, another issued to a cover, and a few no one knows about. Cantrell's law, part one: design new wrinkles and tell nobody. If you do, they'll appear in some goddamn training manual and thereafter be useless. Depend only on yourself." I looked straight at him. "That's why I've buried so many partners. They forgot the rules of survival."

"I'll remember," he promised.

"And forget the academy. That was kindergarten. This is real."

"Yes, sir," he chimed, and I was instantly pissed again at this upstart jerk.

I ordered the most expensive cognac on the plane. "I read your qual sheet but refresh me anyway."

"Uh, I graduated summa cum laude from Stanford, law major with—"

"Please, skip the blue ribbons. Tell me something."

"Uh, sure. I have considerable field training but very little field experience. I did a hitch with the 101st Airborne, Paratroop Commandos. No live action. I requalify on the range every month, and can handle myself both armed and by hand." He glanced at me. "Plus, I'm not afraid."

"Then you're a fool. What have you done with the agency?"

"Buchannon said in time I would move up, so for the past year I've worked with Edwards."

"Good man," I commented. Edwards was a dinosaur like me, too old and slow for hard times, but with remarkable experience to pass along to newcomers. I thought to myself, Buchannon was no fool and would never risk an agency glitch because of operator incompetence or ineptness. "Why did you want this assignment?"

"I'm tired of rehearsals. That is not why I was recruited."

It was a dumb answer, predictable and logical, but I let it pass. Lord keep me from glory hounds, but the kid had impressed me with the murder investigation in California.

"This will be a strictly wet operation," I explained. "It will violate every international law, meaning no medals or recognition. Totally hush. Only a punched hole in certain key cards will indicate you even took part, and the computer will read ambiguous terms, like 'mission completed,' or 'agent negated.' That's it. No glory, gold stars, raises, accommodations or attaboys. If you survive, which is highly doubtful, walk down the agency hall and not even the director or the janitor will realize you're a big friggin' hero. I assume you've given this considerable thought?''

He nodded without comment.

"Which tells you what?" I demanded.

"We are totally expendable."

"Could not have said it better myself. Now, tell me about Trudor. Summarize what you know."

He took a breath. "Basically, a terrorist for hire. Assassin, smuggler and killer, who specializes in kidnapping, extortion, riots, insurgence, takeovers, anything for a profit. No known political or religious convictions, no causes or preferences, loyal to anyone who pays the bill. A marked hatred of Americans. Reason, unknown. He is usually contacted through a series of middlemen, demands and receives payments in advance, uses intricate plans and storm trooper tactics, getting him in and out quickly, usually hires local grunts for dirty work and eliminates them later. He maintains a well-trained and loyal group of fanatics as his personal team of bodyguards."

I interrupted Dirkson with a wave. "Which is our biggest problem. We'll discuss that in detail later. Stay on the man."

Dirkson sighed, as if taking a test. "There are no known pictures or descriptions of Trudor, but it's rumored he has Hispanic features, could pass for any of a dozen nationalities and speaks several languages. He's glorified by the militant underground and leftist groups, particularly terrorist movements with fanatic sympathies. Trudor has been linked to four government shake-ups and numerous coups, and has been paid in the millions. On the psychological side, he is a sadistic killer who enjoys his power, is treacherous, ingenious, and recognizes no law but his own."

"Ergo," I prompted, "a nut."

"But a dangerous one."

"So how do we get the bastard?"

Dirkson looked pained. "I'm, uh, not sure."

"A straight sanction," I said. "Nothing fancy and no middle ground. We have to use his own tactics of hit and run like hell. We can never establish ourselves on Crete, so we'll have to float at all times. Like we're not there. No trace possible."

"I understand that much."

Dirkson was silent as we gorged ourselves on airline treats. Every few minutes, another tray of first-class delicacies arrived, and I studied the dessert platter of brandy, candy, fruit and mints.

"Okay, hero," I said as I poked at the food. "The first two phases are relatively straightforward. One, we find Trudor and two, we eliminate him. The Company will certainly not interfere because that is their prime objective. They'll let us do the dirty deed, take the fall and only watch. Assuming we make it that far, how do we get off Crete alive?"

Dirkson sighed. "I don't have the slightest idea."

My sigh was far deeper, knowing the pitfalls. "Neither do I."

# 24. ATHENS

I PURPOSELY CHOSE our route through international airports with the poorest security. We were carrying arms in the baggage department and preferred to avoid airports that X-rayed checked luggage.

The connection through Madrid was routine and simple, but Rome is the world's worst airport. The passenger systems are not run by airline employees, but rather by city officials who enjoy harassing confused and exhausted travelers. Once in Rome, they like to keep you there.

My primary concern was the armaments. Without underground connections in Greece, obtaining firepower would have been time-consuming if not impossible. Dirkson had done a noteworthy job of camouflaging our bags from nosy X rays, but no one could anticipate what might happen at Rome's Da Vinci Airport. Quickie strikes occur there every day, from cabbies to bus drivers, baggage loaders and concessionaires. Our fear was a sudden stoppage, when the bored attendants would curiously begin opening suitcases. It happens.

Using forged diplomatic passports, one can slither through the bureaucratic customs hodgepodge, but we were winging it, with no connection to the agency. The type of arms we carried meant very serious trouble, and Buchannon would not recognize us.

An eternity after landing, we cleared and finally boarded the continuation to Athens. With bags in the cargo hold, intact and untouched, I began to relax.

From a smuggler's viewpoint, Tel Aviv and London's Heathrow are the most difficult, with security systems far superior to Moscow or Washington. In that regard, Athens is a joke. One could carry a hydrogen bomb through the gate and porters would assist.

After the grueling flight, jet lag had its effect. I craved another morphine zap but decided against it. The mind was already soupish.

"Syntagma," I told the cabbie. The English name is Constitution Square, but saying that often doubles the price for tourists.

The square borders a small, lush green park, surrounded by the famous King George Hotel, numerous shops of every description and several sidewalk cafés, specializing in girl watching and tourists. I instructed the cabbie to drop us a block from the George, beyond the range of overhelpful porters.

"What now?" Dirkson asked, struggling with the bags.

"Carry those and check in. I'm going across the street for retsina wine and to see if anyone's interested. Stay in the room."

In any organization, there are a few pros mixed with countless amateurs. Whoever tagged us at the airport had decided nothing of value would happen the first day, so assigned the office fool. Since they had our photos and identification, and well understood the eventual goal, they relaxed until we took a firm direction. Then the big boys would take over.

It took me fifteen seconds to spot the watcher.

Undoubtedly, they expected Dirkson and me to stay together, at least in the beginning, and had assigned a single monitor. When we split, the young idiot with frayed hair was confused, standing there looking back and forth from Dirkson to me, wondering what to do.

Dirkson was entering a hotel with our belongings, so the fool assumed that was our base, and that I would return. Therefore, he stayed on Dirkson. But I was much older and sitting on my ass while the other hauled heavy bags. Obviously, I was in charge, and he missed that. Amateur night.

Needing to confront him, but on my terms, I did the only logical thing. I called a cop.

A uniform was strolling by the park. I screamed in the universal language, *"Polizia! Polizia!"* and frantically gestured him into the prestigious King George.

I pointed to the trailer and continued a loud barrage. "Thief!"

As customs and rules dictate worldwide, the first thing the blue demanded was the man's identification. He was startled, babbling innocence, fumbled and dropped his wallet twice. He spoke in English and emphatically denied my accusations. "I don't know what the hell he's talking about!"

Like mine, his ID was probably false, and I had no interest in checking it. His reaction to this unorthodox public embarrassment was all I wanted.

Had he been Greek police, undercover narcotics or customs, even Interpol, a quick badge would have made the cop disappear. But that did not happen. The soft, twangy drawl indicated Kentucky or farther south, and my suspicions were confirmed. Good ol' boys were attracted to the Company, dedicated rednecks, blindly loyal Americans to the core. I had valued that commodity many times in the past, it had saved my bacon more than once, but not now.

I had no fear of this child—hell, he was fresh from the senior prom and the academy—but he represented the big kids, and they don't play games. I know.

Seconds later, I produced my wallet, looked surprised, expressed apologies all around and walked away from the two.

The thought of the CIA ghouls already on our ass was no real shock, their tentacles reach everywhere, but it still made me uneasy.

It was late afternoon, and I was zonked but hyped by the Company's presence. It forced so many questions that had to be resolved. I knew Dirkson was napping in his room after being told to hold for the evening.

Greek retsina leaves a horrible aftertaste, similar to sucking the resin from a dead tree, which is how the name originated. I returned to the sidewalk café and had several more glasses. The price was right, and I enjoyed being watched, wondering how many ghouls were on the job.

In a room somewhere across the square was a young man sleeping soundly, and the silly bastard was counting on me. I was decades out of shape, operating on bluff and wit, but he had faith.

I really needed Dirkson to finish this. His file displayed pictures of a pixie blond wife, all smiles and bubbly personality, two precocious brats, and two grungy dogs roaming around a neatly trimmed lawn. Suburbia. God, a picket fence, two-car garage, station wagon and cable TV. I just knew they mailed Christmas pictures of the family.

Damn!

I wandered back to the George and sat in the lobby, watching unintelligible Greek television, and contemplating why I hated Dirkson. After careful consideration, I realized it was not because he had every corny, dumb, silly thing I wanted and would never possess, nor because he was sleeping and I would forever be a hopeless insomniac. The simple fact was that Dirkson did not truly comprehend the situation.

Just like that idiot child Stella, the overanxious fool was under my wing. I was responsible! Or was I honestly suicidal and afraid to face it alone?

When I finally dropped on my own bed fully dressed and exhausted, my last conscious thoughts were of Mrs. Dirkson, those brats, the cutesy house and why I hated him.

If anything happened to Dirkson, I would have to tell her.

# 25. CRETE

I MET DIRKSON at the magnificent bar of the King George the following morning. The palatial, deeply burnished wood reeked of history and past adventures. Statesmen, poets, Pulitzers and international gangsters called it home. Hemingway's signature was on a dozen photos, and it was long the unofficial meeting grounds for newspapermen from around the globe. Gossip said William Hearst started and ended more small wars over cocktails in that room than generals of major governments.

I was aching, hung over, mentally numb, and my arm throbbed while Dirkson looked fresh and energetic. A Cub Scout at his first overnighter. Jesus, I hate young people.

"Let's go for a walk," I said, gladly interrupting his disgusting breakfast of eggplant and pastry.

We strolled the winding streets, while I updated him on our trailing friend. "He was nothing. A scout. But now they'll come in two teams, the lights and darks. The names change, but that's their mode. The lights watch and report and nothing else. No sweat. The darks are the heavies. They stay hidden, organizing info from the lights and deciding when and where to hit. At any given minute, they'll have a dozen contingency plans to cover every situation."

"How do we beat them?"

I ignored his stupid question. "They used to be called white-and-black teams, but for obvious cultural reasons, gave that up."

"On us now?"

"Of course. They have Athens sewed up. My report to Buchannon, which you can bet was forwarded, said only Greece."

"So they have no idea where we're going?"

"Not yet, but once we hit the dock, their prayers are answered. If we took a car inland, they would have to follow, but the boat is perfect for them. They'll simply chopper ahead to every port and wait for us. Can't miss."

"What can we do?" Dirkson asked helplessly.

"Nothing, but if you want to entertain yourself and give the lights something to think about, visit the travel bureaus around Syntagma and get boat schedules to everyplace. Greece has about two thousand islands, and Trudor could be anywhere. It'll give them a few worries. Might as well have some fun."

"Some fun," he mumbled.

"We'll split at the George. Make your way to the port of Piraeus about five. The ferry leaves at six tonight. You get the stateroom. First-class for two. I'll meet you in the main deck bar."

"Anything I should do?"

"Yeah, expand your education. Shop for the family at the bazaars. See how many ghouls you identify. After I humiliated their spotter, you can bet they'll bring in the first team."

"That's it? Play tag?" Dirkson was disappointed.

"These are not classroom exercises. And if you're really bored, try to figure how the hell we're going to get off Crete."

I killed the day wandering through the national museum and various other tourist sights. It soon became apparent I had touched some ego the day before, because the lights made it subtly clear they knew, and I knew, and they knew

I knew, ad infinitum. I would have given anything to read
our file. It might have helped.

At four, I took a cab to Piraeus, the great Athens port.
Fishing boats, world-class liners, thousands of sailboats and
plush yachts lined the docks. Miles out in deep water nestled the Greek navy: gunboats, destroyers, frigates and occasional full cruisers.

Dozens of ships were boarding passengers, baggage and
cargo bound for every port in the Mediterranean and points
beyond. A scurry of pandemonium surrounded every pier,
for ships preferred to sail on the evening tide, gaining momentum to clear the harbor without sacrificing precious fuel
for extra power.

The ship to Crete is called a ferry, which by American
standards means a scow to Staten Island or Sausalito on an
hourly basis. This was a seventy-thousand-ton liner, capable of carrying the population of a small town. Weight and
bulk helps, and with good reason, because the Aegean is
most treacherous in winter. Horrendous winds and thirty-
foot waves appear from nowhere.

That thought plagued me when I found Dirkson in the
ship's main bar. I ordered a double brandy. "Did your
summa cum bullshit from Stanford teach you anything
about Mediterranean history?"

"A bit," he defended, without much enthusiasm.

I took a long sip and shuddered. Bar stock. "Alexander
the Great, Cleopatra, a few Caesars, several Egyptian
pharaohs and even the Nazis with their giant war machines
prolonged attack plans, feared what the Aegean could do
with troop carriers. Unbelievable. One minute glass, the
next maelstrom."

"So?" he asked cautiously.

"So, in many ways, the history of civilization was written around the weather of the Aegean."

"And?" he tried again.

"And this sea is our only possible escape off Crete. The one airport will be under full monitor, along with choppers." I toasted him with my glass. "There is only the sea."

It was a fourteen-hour cruise, and after a mediocre meal, family style, we nestled back in the bar. I insisted Dirkson keep the firepower bag with him at all times. He had reserved a cabin for four and paid for all berths, but I did not trust leaving that suitcase alone.

We stared at a map of Crete and theorized the situation. "Trudor picked a tough place," I commented. "The logistics problems are immense, as the Nazis learned during the occupation. The locals are fiercely proud of their heritage and do not welcome outsiders. They enjoy tourists and the money but recognize a distinct barrier. It's a conglomerate of ancient Mediterranean nationalities, but the core civilization stems from the Minoans. Did you know they had flush toilets and public libraries two thousand years before Christ?"

"Fascinating," Dirkson remarked sarcastically. "Meaning?"

"Meaning, you pompous asshole! I am trying to teach you something! What the hell did you learn for Chrissakes?" I looked away briefly, then wondered if the adverse party witnessed my outburst. Definitely not good.

"Look, Barry," I said calmly and quietly. "You've known about Greece for forty-eight hours and Crete for over a day. Why didn't you study the situation? By now, you should be a goddamned authority. Research your terrain! It might save your ass."

"Sorry, uh, I didn't think of that. Looking at travel brochures and all. It didn't seem important."

"Jesus," I moaned. "Okay, I will explain our dilemma. We do not speak the language, the roads are slow, and once outside coastal towns, you can forget any kind of movement without detection. The people will not help us, so there is no chance of cover or going to ground. They have an underground intelligence system that dates back a thousand years. Even school kids and farmers are utilized. Loyalty is fierce and not cooperative to our side. During the war, women and children hid in mountain caves and came down every night to kill German soldiers with pitchforks and clubs."

"I have read a bit," he said. "I know that Crete is the only place the Germans failed to take a commanding hold. They deployed an entire division to control the locals."

"And still failed. Remember, Trudor is hiding among these people. Pleasant dreams."

It was a gentle crossing. As we approached the island a porter rapped on our door. "One hour to docking."

Standing on the quarterdeck, we watched the approach of Heraklion, a mixture of a dozen cultures from centuries of warring nations. Close to the port was the beginning of the commercial district, similar to any other, except for the many factions of integrated societies and foreign influence. Arabic and Muslim steeples stood beside Roman towers and Turkish buildings, all mixed with Greek Orthodox.

At the dock were several tour buses, anxious to capture tourists. "Take one of those," I told Dirkson. "Learn everything you can about roads, buses, anything. Tip the driver in private and find where you can get a woman for the night."

We agreed to meet at a hotel mentioned in travel books. It was early, so I wandered the streets, barely dodging motor scooters and insane taxis. This was the largest city on Crete, contrasting modern buildings with fish sold on the curb.

I located the cablegram office and watched it from a taverna, learning nothing, but studying the traffic. I found a detailed map of Crete, far superior to the version purchased in Athens.

The island is a geographical oddity, cigar shaped, one hundred miles long and twenty across at the widest. Through millenia of evolutionary upheaval near mankind's birthplace, Crete was left a twisted, gnarled, jagged wreck of tortuous cliffs, hills sprinkled with thousands of caves, interspersed with splotches of beautiful white beaches and damp green forests.

Rolling hills of wet, lush foliage plus thousands of acres with olives and grapes are bordered by massive rocks with hundred-foot sheer sides. Tiny villages dot the land, although most border the coast. Small, often unimproved roads connect one village to another with a few principal roads in cobweb fashion.

I studied the map and shuddered again. A logistic nightmare.

At noon, I began my search.

From Johnny's Place in Hong Kong to Elly's Bar in Nairobi, gay hangouts exist in every large city. Gays are the most cautious of people for obvious fear of exposure, and nowhere is that paranoia more prevalent than in Mediterranean countries, especially Greece and Italy, the pseudo-macho capitals of the world.

Ironically, or perhaps *because* of that machismo, Greek towns, like all others, possess definite homosexual communities, and that secret society maintains an effective underground information system within a country that prides itself on subterfuge as a national heritage.

It took me five hours and several minor bribes to locate the right club.

The bar was called Knossos's Palace, a typical watering hole with more grandeur in name than decor. The mirrored wall behind the bar was adorned with trinkets, messages, holy crosses, hundreds of photos in helter-skelter fashion, all held by thumbtacks or yellowed tape.

Most of the twenty-odd stools were occupied by foreigners of all ages and nationalities.

At the bar, I conversed with a German dentist, who made references to his wife on tour that day, adding he had other interests.

After several rounds, I confidentially asked if he knew of a local "businessman" with "access" to things not advertised in the travel guides. We kidded each other with the expected playful elbow jabs and "ahas!"

We eventually walked to another taverna where an hour later he introduced me to Michael. We chatted about nonsense until the dentist became bored and left.

I laid five twenties on the table, hidden from others by our glasses. "I am looking for a special man," I said clearly, "a policeman who arranges things. Not too young, an older fellow with two or three stripes but not an officer." Another twenty on the table. "And he must have many contacts and gets things done without mistake."

"There is always a possibility of mistake," Michael said.

Another twenty. "That is why I need a special policeman. I'm looking for a simple arrangement that involves no drugs or danger, or even breaking the law. But this must be done quietly, and if not exactly right, it will leave me in difficulty."

I placed another bill on top, leaned back and tasted seven-star gold Metaxa, a marvelously smooth liqueur unavailable in the States. The gesture indicated my limit was reached.

He sipped his watered ouzo, a weak milky concoction the Greeks love. "Michael might know such a man," he said, taking the third-person role, "but sometimes supplying information to strangers comes back to haunt Michael."

"I wouldn't know about that," I said emphatically. "I don't know anyone named Michael."

It was the correct response. He wrote a name in surprisingly neat script, which I memorized. I thanked him and left, never mentioning the money on the table.

The police station resembled a million others the world over, a flat, nondescript stone building with traditional black-and-white cars, and uniforms strolling in and out.

Sergeant Panos sat at a desk in one corner covered with mounds of paper and a month of dust. He was a broad-shouldered, thick-chested man, characteristics definitely not acquired from desk patrol. The rough callused hands and protruding knuckles indicated a farm boy. His dark, unruly dandruffy hair was askew and windblown.

"What can I do for you?" he politely asked in his "another-tourist-with-a-problem" tone.

"My name is Cantrell," I greeted him, and showed him a badge. Buchannon was convinced people are impressed with fancy official baubles, so we carry solid gold replicas of police badges. Panos gazed at it briefly, then took the offered business card. The ident number, if checked at the agency, would result in a laudatory commentary on my detective reputation. Panos would not bother now but might call later.

"I'd like to rent a car, but my international driver's license is outdated," I told him. "Can you issue one or update mine?"

Panos said no and explained my options, so I thanked him and left. That was enough for now.

Dirkson was at the restaurant feeding his face. He had learned the Greek word for *hot* and ordered by pointing to each dish on display under glass, similar to a meat market. *"Zesto,"* he said, and the waiter dutifully heated the meal, which Cretans found amusing since they prefer food, including fish, lukewarm or cold.

We exchanged information, both taking several notes. "Tomorrow," I instructed, "rent a car from a small dealer without using your passport. Tip someone or say it's at the hotel. Use phony ID. Where are the whorehouses?"

Dirkson had the location of six, all protected by the mandatory police bribes. We took a cab to the first four, which did not satisfy me. Greece is a puritanical country; nude sunbathing means a five-hundred-dollar fine and jail. I didn't want to risk a cheap operation that might be raided before we finished.

The next appeared long established, judging by faded and torn signs in the window offering "travel for the sophisticated connoisseur."

We walked casually toward the entrance of the ordinary old stone structure, similar to those surrounding it, except for the modern second story obviously added recently. Business must be good.

"I didn't know you like game ladies," Dirkson said, snickering.

"Don't be an idiot!" I snapped. "Girlie houses do not ask for passports, and I don't want us listed at any hotel."

Dirkson looked sheepish. "I know that. Just making a joke."

Perhaps I was too harsh. "I never can tell with you."

Inside, a proper young lady acted as receptionist, sitting behind a bare counter, the walls covered with travel posters. "Yes?"

Dirkson mentioned a man who referred us, and then gave her three hundred drachmas, about ten dollars, to register as members of the club. We were ushered to a small cocktail lounge, twenty by forty feet, with a circular bar in the middle upholstered with gaudy red vinyl held by huge brass tacks.

An Oriental girl was pouring outrageously priced drinks for two European men. The house did not need night ladies; the liquor profit alone must have been staggering. There were four or five pretty girls calmly reading in the corner, facing toward us and looking mildly flirtatious. Two more talked to a man near the door.

It was all very proper, but I noticed a distinct absence of Greek females. The locals would never allow Greek whores, regardless of bribery.

A tall, casually attired middle-aged Englishwoman approached. "Good evening, I am Monica. What brings you to my little paradise?"

She had clearly established herself as boss. I smiled and dropped the name Dirkson had acquired. "He said we could find a room tonight with two beds."

"That is true." She nodded. "Would you like to take a trip with anyone?"

"Perhaps," I answered. "Right now, we're interested in a room."

"Very well. I have several hostesses who can describe our tours. In private. They speak many languages. I should explain there is a single fee for the night, with or without company."

"Sounds fine," I told her. "Right now, the bar will do. We'll be on Crete several days, so if the accommodations are satisfactory, we'll probably return every night."

"That can be arranged." She smiled warmly. In a country where a large bottle of ouzo sells for thirty cents, she then announced the hundred-dollar tab each, without blinking an eye.

Dirkson paid, but she spoke to me. "If there's anything you want, just point."

After several drinks, we were directed to the second floor. The room was amazingly clean and tastefully decorated. I suspected it belonged to one of the girls, probably the Oriental, judging by the imitation jade statues and woven mats. Two small beds were placed against opposite walls.

"Christ," Dirkson said, squirming, "what if a girl shows up?"

I was busy studying the maps. "You're bright. Use your imagination. Call it a contribution to God and country."

# 26. SEARCH

SOMETIME DURING THE NIGHT, a soft rapping woke me, and Dirkson responded by talking at the door with the Oriental girl. She entered the room, apologized and removed things from her dresser. I dozed off, and she left. I think.

In the morning a tray was on the nightstand, with grape juice, dates and sugarless pastry. I looked at Dirkson. "You want mine?" I asked. "Or would you prefer a shot of penicillin?"

My sarcasm escaped him. "Nicki says there's breakfast downstairs. Comes with the room."

"Tell Nicki thanks, but I'll pass. Coffee's enough. Rent the car and meet me opposite the cable office."

There has long been a theory that countries with strong, thick coffee make it tenfold more powerful to see if American tourists will politely drink it. Two cups of Greek coffee will wake the dead.

Settling for cola after my caffeine buzz, I sat with visiting Canadians at an outdoor café until Dirkson appeared. He drove up in a battered old Mercedes, covered with dents and replaced fenders of various colors. It ran like a fine watch with a powerful, smooth purr, but I would have canceled my pension rather than admit to Dirkson it was perfect. I grunted a token approval.

We walked to the cable office when it cleared of customers and approached the one clerk.

Dirkson dropped the stack of cables from Trudor to Mateo on the counter, then I added the great American equalizer, twenty-dollar bills. "We would like to know who sent these."

The elderly man looked away, totally uninterested.

Such information was confidential, and we all knew that, so I continued to add more money. The man ignored us.

Then I noticed several ancient scars on his hands and arms. I recognized my faux pas and sent Dirkson to the car.

"I apologize for the insult," I told him, pulling away the money, "but we are new here. The people who sent these cables murder men, women and children, just for money. I want to find them. The police cannot help."

The man looked both ways, paused a minute, then glanced at me. "I could lose my job."

"Anything you say will die with me. My promise. My word."

He hesitated only slightly. "I do not know a name or where he comes from, but there is a messenger. He comes to pick up the cables. If there is one, he takes it and comes back with an answer to be sent."

"How long before returning with an answer?"

He thought on that. "Three or four hours or the next morning. There are none for him now."

"And the last time?"

"Yesterday, but no cables. He could be back anytime."

"Are they always in number code like these?" I asked.

"Yes, long rows of numbers. The young man checks my work before I transmit, to make certain they are perfect."

"One last thing, and most important. Will you signal me when he comes? That's all I ask."

The feeble man grabbed my wrist with surprising strength. "Are they Nazis?"

"No, friend, but they work with Nazis and people like Nazis. They kill people on any side for money. They have no honor." I paused a minute. "Will you help us?"

He waited a long time. "Of course. Be outside. I will signal at the window when he arrives."

Nothing happened that day, and by evening Dirkson and I began digging on each other's nerves. Hours spent waiting in cars is the true mark of partnership, as every cop understands.

Things went well at the cathouse. We were just a pair of nutsy Americans with plenty of cash, so no one asked questions. It was getting late, and I watched with some amusement as a bored girl taught Dirkson backgammon.

Monica sent a drink to me, imported cognac, and I nodded thanks.

"No," she said, shaking her head. "It is not from me."

Sergeant Panos, dressed in civvies, stood behind me, and I twitched slightly. Not from his presence, but it's rare someone can get that close without my sensing it.

"Good evening, Mr. Cantrell," he said, without expecting a response. "Have you solved your driver's license problem?"

I was pleased he recalled my name. "Actually, I misread the date. It's still good for another month."

"Excellent. Violating our traffic laws can be serious." A large Scotch arrived for him without his asking. "Particularly driving that rental car. It is well-known in Heraklion."

"Should we worry?"

"No, no, the owner takes incredible care of the engine and gear train but allows the body to rot. It is quite distinguishable."

The sergeant's English was very good, and I said so.

"Here, everyone in school must take a second language. Most prefer French because that is the chosen tongue of the elite who live in Athens. A rich man's language. Many there can speak English but never do because it means they are low class. Working people.''

"But you chose English.''

"It is a practical language, that's all. This is a strange and unusual empire all by itself. We owe technical allegiance to Athens and Greek law, but we are also very independent. We surrendered that independence, but only on paper. Many of us still believe this is our own country, and act accordingly. Do you understand?''

"I think so.''

"That is why I knew you had rented the Mercedes. I know everything that happens in my home. Good night, Mr. Cantrell.''

Later, I recounted the conversation to Dirkson, who was upset. "What if the ghouls have this Panos fellow in their pocket? Didn't he give you a warning, of sorts?''

"Yes, but I'm not certain what.''

"I don't trust him,'' Dirkson said firmly. "You?''

"Too soon to tell, but we're sure going to find out.''

After an hour outside the cable office the following morning, Dirkson decided he was still hungry. Recalling my warning never to eat breakfast in front of me, he excused himself and left for a café.

Minutes later, the clerk appeared at the office window and feigned making adjustments to the shade. A young Hispanic soon left and mounted a motorcycle.

I put the Mercedes in gear and began a casual pursuit. There was no time to roust Dirkson in the opposite direction. It was an easy tag because there were few turnoffs from the main road along the coast highway. It would appear normal to see my car behind for miles.

Three hours later I returned and found Dirkson at the taverna. "Get in,'' I said, feeling depressed and worried.

We had lunch at Monica's establishment, a place that understood privacy. "Trudor could not have chosen a better spot if he planned for years, which he probably did."

I spread the map of Crete on the bar. Dirkson looked at the cigar-shaped island. I pointed to Heraklion at the top, slightly right of center. "The highway hugs the coast along the north, then because of high cliffs, it turns inward a few miles following the western curves of the island. About midway around the extreme end is a tiny village called Sitia, high in the hills. Right there."

I leaned back and sipped a Greek beer. "The road goes through the center of Sitia and continues. The village has a tavern or two, a combination café and market, a few small churches and several dozen old houses. I suspect the locals tend the olive fields around the area. Maybe a hundred inhabitants."

"Trudor's there?"

"Don't I wish. Dead center from town is a road that winds down steep hills to the beach below. It has a name. Arvi. See here? At the bottom are three cottages, two of which seem empty, an old church, unused for decades by the looks, and a large villa, a half mile up the beach."

"Aha. Our man likes seclusion."

"And he certainly has it. My map showed no side roads, so I waited a few minutes for the motorcycle to get ahead, then started down. It's a mother of a road. When I got close I used the glasses and spotted four cars at the villa, plus the cycle. There are long, empty beaches on both sides, and that road is the only access. He's totally and completely isolated."

"See anyone?"

"Didn't get that close. I stopped at the church, saw an old couple from the one cottage tending fruit trees, and drove back up. When I got to the village on the hill, there were people at the taverna watching me. Either I was an oddity for driving down there, or had broken some rule.''

"Sounds great." He sighed.

"Wait till you see it. By the way, can you fish?" I told Dirkson what to get.

Tourists are notorious camera enthusiasts and most cities boast remarkable equipment. I purchased a 1,000 mm Oneida scope, a powerful little telescope with nine-inch reflecting lens, yet barely a foot long. I experimented with the window of an apartment across the street, and looked directly at a man's ear while he shaved.

I met Dirkson with his gear, and we drove to Sitia. An hour later we sat in the café, ordering beer and *geero*, a local taco filled with meat and cheese. A dozen older men sat and watched us. The town offered no attraction for tourists, so we were unique. Two minutes, and we had already attracted attention.

Directly across from us, the road began down the twisting hills. "It winds constantly," I said softly. "From the scale on the map, I'd say about eight miles, but with hairpins and switchbacks, probably double that."

"Shhhiiit," Dirkson moaned, thinking ahead of the difficulty.

"Most intelligent thing you've said. The Mercedes hugs well, but it's a slow road. I'd say thirty minutes down and forty-five back up."

Dirkson shuddered. That road was our only route to the villa, and most important, our only escape.

"Eight miles," he mumbled. "So from here, they'll see the fireworks on the horizon, and with any onshore breeze, hear the explosions. We have to return a half mile in the sand on foot, then drive up the hill. Jesus!" he moaned again.

It was late afternoon and time for the next phase. "Go get the fishing gear from the car," I instructed. "Bring the line and load up the reels. Make a big deal of it."

I soon witnessed the universal brotherhood of fishermen. Dirkson sat calmly knotting the new line, beginning the slow process of winding it on the reels. Several of the locals stared openly and jabbered in Greek. All the gear was new, modern and expensive, and most of these fellows probably used the same poles as their fathers.

One senior could stand it no longer. A crouching, thickly mustached, leathery skinned man grabbed the supply spool and held it with thumb and fingers as Barry continued winding.

Another man stepped forward and explained. "The tension is all wrong. It must be just right."

Suddenly everyone was an expert, and a dozen men jabbered at once. I spoke to the interpreter. "I promised a friend we'd try our luck down there." I pointed. "He said they were difficult to catch but worth the effort." I feared he might say no fish had been caught there in this century.

Instead, he nodded. "Wade out during the ebbing tide and cast far," he suggested. "Use heavy weights and let the backwash carry your line."

After a few rounds of ouzo, we were all buddies. I even let the bartender water mine, to fit into the crowd.

I asked about pensions or nearby hostels, and they directed us to a home engulfed with lush greenery, bright flowers and trestles of berries almost covering the stone house. He explained the farmers often rented out rooms during festivals, and this family would be happy to have us.

We offered twenty dollars, which embarrassed them. The interpreter insisted five was more than enough. We met the father, who spoke little English but gestured in a friendly manner, and the mother, who quickly disappeared in the kitchen, followed by three children.

Greeks do not drink alcohol without something to snack on, so after sipping ouzo and making friends, we were not hungry, but the wife insisted. We were served by a grandmother, dressed totally in black from shoes to shawl.

Dirkson and I said very little that night. I set the alarm early, hoping to leave before the family awoke, but the children were leaving for school when we got up, and Papa was already in the olive orchards.

The car was loaded so we left immediately, turned off by the café and began the slow, perilous journey down the hills. Dirkson kept the Mercedes in low and cursed the whole time.

We drove by the church and up the beach, seeing how far we dared maneuver on the sand. Not far. Wearing shorts and rubber boots, we waded into the gentle surf and began casting. Dirkson was very good; I looked like an idiot.

After four hours, we inched our way along, similar to all fishermen who fail to score yet believe the big ones are just a few feet farther.

Terrorists like Trudor incorporate complex and thorough security systems. That was what I needed to observe. I dropped behind a clump of thick coastal grass and cautiously scanned the building with the 12x50 Zeiss Icon field glasses. There was no visible activity and windows were out of range for clarity.

From the large fishing chest, I inserted the 18-mm ocular eyepiece into the Oneida, giving me a fifty-five-power view, an easy scan from window to window.

The man was on the second floor with binoculars, idly watching Dirkson, fifty feet from me. He was undoubtedly part of a permanent team that watched the beach twenty-four hours a day. The opposite direction led eventually into a sheer cliff. Almost foolproof.

Almost.

Dirkson took the next few minutes, and we alternated all day, each taking notes.

He caught a few fish, nothing spectacular by any standard, but it provided us a logical excuse to return the following morning. We gave the catch to the farm wife who was thrilled and baked three for dinner.

We observed for two boring days, then sat at a taverna in the next village, unable to find privacy in Sitia among the regulars.

"We're not going to learn any more," I said. "Trudor ordered Mateo to smoke me, and he might be getting worried with no cables coming." We had seen the messenger leaving every day.

"Do we agree on seven men and the old couple next door?" Dirkson asked, comparing notes.

"So far," I confirmed, "but it's a large place, and perhaps more are on the other side. Including Trudor, since neither of us have seen him. You have sleeping stuff in the medical kit, right? Okay, we say good-night to the old couple. Something to keep them out for hours."

"Right," Dirkson continued. "I've studied the villa. I say plant the C-4 at these points," He indicated our crude drawing. "Flush them out front."

"Uh-uh," I disagreed. "Blowing the back wall means we're fully exposed and looking into the flames. Torch the sides."

"Then the plastique isn't enough."

"What do you need?"

"Quartz crystal oscillating chips, aluminum powder and ammonium nitrate, but finding that material is a problem."

"Dammit, don't waste time telling me what we can't do!"

Dirkson felt slighted. "Okay, modified Molotovs. I can find potassium nitrate, sulfur and powder coal. I'll place jugs of gas on top. Except somehow they'll need to be ignited."

"We'll plant them near the C-4. What else?"

"I'd feel better with another night peek," Dirkson admitted.

"Me, too, but we increase the risk of being spotted. No, this is a one-shot deal. One thing going for us," I said, wanting to rebuild our diminishing confidence, "so far, we've seen no evidence of sonic, infrared or trip systems. They feel secure with a commanding view of the beach and three miles of hillside."

"Let's hope so," he said.

I stared at him, my patience exhausted and frustration sinking in. It was preop jitters for us both, and nerves scraped raw. We should have sprung that first day, armed with enthusiasm, spirit, adrenaline and motor senses peaked.

Now we suffered uncertainty, apprehension, normal fear and, worst of all, a growing dissent between us. Any suggestion one made, the other refused to accept. Technically, I was Control, but he had the right to comment. We quarreled frequently, and that was taboo. In a short time, we would literally depend on each other for life.

Dirkson had several ideas about hiding on the island after the deed until the pressure dropped, but I nixed them all. We'd have both police and the ghouls looking for us. No go.

We argued for another hour, each becoming more irritated.

I tried to reason one last time. "The only problem, assuming we're successful, is that damn road up to the village. In an hour, you know goddamn well the locals will be there waiting, curious, maybe armed. Hell, they might even start down in those olive trucks and block our exit!''

"So?'' he asked.

"So, are you prepared to fire on those people? Maybe crash through to reach the dock? Run them over the cliff? There won't be time to discuss it.''

"You know damn well I wouldn't.'' Dirkson sighed. "Okay, we go your way. One question, Cantrell. Can you swim that far?''

"We'll find out, won't we?''

# 27. STRATEGY

---

WE EXCHANGED few words the next morning, both mentally committed.

En route to Heraklion, I stopped in Khania, the second largest city in Crete and the industrial center of the island. Dirkson felt confident he could charter a car and driver for the day and locate the necessary chemicals without attracting notice. We agreed on a meeting site, and I continued on.

Monica appeared quickly at the round bar, confirming my suspicions of a peephole.

"Good morning," she greeted me warmly. "We missed you these past two days. Find another diversion?"

"Not really. Just touring."

"And where is your friend?"

"Shopping for those famous Greek bargains."

"There is only one bargain on Crete," she cooed, "and you already found us."

"Perhaps later," I replied. "Tell me, you know that man who bought me a drink the other day? A Greek."

"Better not say that around him. Monsieur Panos is Cretan. Yes, I know the gentleman."

Monica had not called him sergeant. "I am trying to locate him," I said. "Perhaps you can invite him over for a private drink?"

She looked disappointed. "Whenever a man mentions a private drink, I am assured it is business and nothing to do with me."

"It's important," I said, and walked away from the bar to a table, leaving considerable change.

Monica disappeared behind a door. There was little doubt she had strong connections with Panos. In her business, mutual dealings were common and essential. I had noticed Panos did not pay for his drinks the other day, a sign of comfortable rapport and understanding.

After an hour, I was becoming worried. Being shunned would have been awkward, indicating Panos had no interest in meeting with me.

"Good day," he said loudly in English, ignoring the traditional Greek phrases spoken by everyone, including tourists. "I hope your morning was better than mine."

A Scotch arrived without mention, and he explained his adventures with confused, irritated, angry American tourists. "No offense, my friend," he said, laughing heartily. "I love Americans, but ohhhh."

We exchanged tourist stories, fulfilling the perfunctory chat.

"Look, I was told you can arrange just about anything, so I'd like to ask an important favor."

He sipped away the Scotch, and it was quickly replaced. "To refuse a simple courtesy would be difficult," Panos said, choosing his words carefully. "But understand, I am a policeman first and friend second. Before asking, please recognize that."

I was equally cautious. "I believe you are a Cretan first, policeman second and friend third."

"Perhaps. At any rate, I can listen briefly, as you say on American television, 'off the record.'"

"We would like to charter a fishing boat for two or three days. Maybe take a trip to another island."

"That is no problem, but ferry service is much cheaper. However, if you prefer the privacy of a fishing boat, the catch is slow right now, and many would be eager to earn extra money.''

"This is a very special trip, so I need a special crew. Not ordinary. Someone who can be trusted completely and not ask questions.''

His policeman expression grew wary. "Meaning what?''

The light in the bar was poor, so I opened the map and slid a candle near. "Instead of the dock, I want to be picked up right here.'' I drew a thick red dot where Trudor's beach villa was located. "At Arvi,'' I added. "Near the old church.''

He studied it a moment. "I know that area well. There are no docks, not even a private launch for small boats.''

"I realize that. There is a large villa up the beach. Tomorrow morning it will be lit, very well lit, and we want the boat lying just offshore as close as possible. Between four and four-thirty, my friend and I will swim out to the boat.''

Panos leaned back and gazed at nothing, considering all he'd heard, in a manner I have done a thousand times. My intentions were obviously illegal, which probably did not bother him. After all, clandestine activities were a way of life, but the degree was another matter.

"I'm told boats can be chartered for a hundred a day,'' I added. "I'll pay triple that for the right boat and dependable crew.''

"You place me in an awkward position.'' He shrugged.

"Not really,'' I answered. "There is nothing wrong or illegal, just unusual. Travelers are free to move between Greek islands without passports. You have time to check on me, if you haven't already.''

I waited a long moment before continuing. "I can promise you two things. It has nothing to do with smuggling or drugs. On my mother's eyes, I give you my word. In fact, your friends on the fishing boat will be welcome to search us thoroughly. We merely want to get off the island at that time, in that manner."

"It's intriguing you mention no drugs or smuggling, the two areas I could not help with."

"No, this is a matter of honor."

"So, what is the crime?" he asked. "Or, excuse me, the reason?"

"I am quite certain no harm will come to any Cretan citizen, and no crime will be committed against Cretan people. It's a private affair, outsiders only. I cannot say more than that."

I placed an envelope on the table. "That's three days' charter, plus minor expenses." I knew Panos quickly calculated a thousand dollars and a generous slice would be for himself. Business.

He studied it for several minutes, and I did not interrupt his thoughts.

"A matter of honor, you say?" he finally asked. "Outsiders only?"

I nodded. Everything had been said.

Panos picked up the envelope and placed it in his pocket.

Leaving, I said one last thing. "The lights at the villa I mentioned will be very bright and impossible to miss. Have them navigate on that. And noise. Lots of noise. Tell your friends not to be afraid."

"The men I know are very good. They will do their best."

"I hope so," I added to emphasize the importance. "If they fail, we will be dead."

"Then, my friend, you had better be on time."

Driving back to Khania, I thought of a thousand things that could go wrong. There were so many ifs, and the implications frightened me.

I found Dirkson on the pier. He had had the material delivered there, claiming it was destined for another island. We loaded the Mercedes with several boxes and a dozen large glass jugs.

After I recounted my conversation with Panos, Dirkson asked the obvious. "Trust him?"

"As they say, do we have a choice?"

"Ch-christ," he stammered.

I opened a bottle of expensive cognac, took a healthy gulp and passed it to him as we negotiated the twisting highway back to Sitia.

"Good Lord," he said with a laugh. "I can't believe you'd drink your precious stuff without a heated brandy snifter. We must be desperate."

"No, thirsty." I watched him wipe the bottle neck. I tried to joke. "Jesus, we'll probably be wasted by those slime-balls, and you're worried about germs."

We stopped at the taverna and greeted the locals, then moved to a veranda and watched the bleeding sun die a silent death.

Surprisingly, there were three new people dining at the café and looking for rooms, two young men and a girl, supposedly American college students. We introduced ourselves all around, drank a few toasts, exchanged stories and left them.

Dirkson and I had the same thoughts. How often did this village get a single overnight tourist, and now five in a few days?

In private we discussed strategies and the individuals we had spotted around the villa. English, so nicknamed because of his pasty skin and ruddy cheeks, was short and broad. Cuban was the messenger, not considered an overpowering threat. One pair we dubbed Couple because they seemed inseparable, never one man without the other.

There were three more, whom we judged the most dangerous. Stretch, with his towering yet graceful height, was athletic and quick. Muscles had monstrous biceps and exercised vigorously every day. A zealot. And Boris, the ugly one. His description was mentioned in several Trudor dossiers, where he was noted as a fanatic killer.

Still, no sign of Trudor. If absent, he would go to deep ground, probably for years. Nothing could be done about that, I told myself. We were gambling that he kept to the far side of the villa.

Dirkson finally asked the question that had been bothering him for so long. "So, once we're off Crete, will the ghouls assume we're out clean and ignore us?"

"That is my sincere hope."

Around midnight the panic took over. In a cold sweat, I tried all the meditation, biofeedback and psychological tricks I knew in an attempt to quell the rising nausea.

Then I looked toward Dirkson, calmly sleeping in his cot. There was little moon, but reflections from the taverna lights outlined his form.

I shook him violently. "What's wrong?" he shouted, jumping up.

"Nothing," I said sternly. "I'll take you to the next village. Grab a bus to the dock, and the first ship away."

"Bullshit! You're nuts! You don't have a chance without me."

"Don't you understand, you stupid jerk! We don't have a chance at all, with or without you. I can wreak havoc in that villa, take some terrorists with me, maybe even Trudor himself, and feel good about it. That's enough!"

"Cantrell, we started this mission together, and we'll finish the same way. I knew the risks coming in." He turned to the table.

"I said you're out and that's it!"

Dirkson picked up the empty cognac bottle. "Cheap bastard, didn't leave me anything. Look...boss, I don' know what the hell is happening. I've asked you a dozen times why you're in this. Even Buchannon said it was probably suicide and left me a dozen outs. He said you believe you're the only person on earth with a personal vendetta. A private war. You've elected yourself to carry the Holy Grail alone."

"You damn punk," I said softly. "You've got a wife and kids and payments and dogs and all that crap. Stay alive and enjoy it. What can you possibly win, huh? A raise? Gold stars?"

Dirkson sat on his cot and spoke into the darkness. "I'll try to explain something. Not even Barbara would understand this. The files attribute over six hundred deaths to Trudor, and that's only the known ones. God knows how many can be added from mercenary actions and government coups. Thousands. Trudor is a maggot. He must be stopped. I'd like to take one crack at this slime. Trudor cannot be negotiated or jailed. He must be exterminated."

I snuffed the horrible cigarette and wished there was more cognac. "Okay, hero," I said toward Dirkson. "See you in two hours."

# 28. TRUDOR

FINALLY, IT BEGAN.

No more sweat, no time for mental indulgence.

We dressed quietly in thinly knit white jerseys and light khaki pants. Our approach to the villa was over sand, and the colors would blend, plus hopefully appear more visible to the rescue crew.

A background check on field operatives would produce altered data and distorted files, including fingerprints. Therefore, it was unnecessary to attempt the impossible task of wiping everything we had touched these past days. However, in order to appear as hired professionals and leave no prints, we had oiled clean the firepower that would be left behind, while wearing surgical gloves.

Having left our car earlier at the café near the downhill road, we now walked the deserted few hundred yards from the farmhouse. I nervously glanced around, searching for the minute red laser streak of somebody scanning us. The Company was out there someplace, I knew that.

To avoid waking the villagers, Dirkson and I pushed the heavy car and jumped in at the last second. The steep slope quickly provided momentum and I coasted some distance before starting the engine.

With headlights on and braking, we carefully monitored the odometer and stopped at 22.6 kilometers, switching off the lights. The wires to all other illumination from the vehicle had been cut. A small incline was before us, and beyond that, a long, continual descent to the beach. Any light would easily be visible from the villa.

Dirkson got out and led me on foot with a tiny purse flash held behind his back. There was no moon and the severe turns were impossible for me to see. The road was barely wide enough for one car, and numerous times I felt gravel slipping over the cliffs.

We stopped near the church and exchanged positions. Dirkson drove on packed sand toward the villa. The gentle surf was enough to cover the sound of the engine, and he would continue on foot when the tires bogged down. The villa occupants used an old cracked and potted tarmac road, located just above the beach on solid ground, but we feared it, figuring the one access to the villa would most likely be wired for detection.

I dreaded my task. During the day, I had studied the old folks' house enough times to determine the layout. My flash was a modified Russian Loti, similar to an ordinary light, but emitting a variable and incredibly sharp one-inch beam of remarkable intensity.

The simple rotary latch was easy to pop. I moved silently through the small house, noticing they were Orthodox with a mantel covered with religious mementos. I was feeling guilty about this, and feared I might see a picture of Jesus with eyes that would follow me across the room.

At the bedroom door, I removed the saturated cloth from a tube. Playing the flash on the floor, I held the material above the quietly sleeping woman and squeezed the perforated liner. Administering the anesthetic requires practice, for chloroform is distasteful, and the first whiff often causes panic. She went under very gently as I slowly eased the cloth closer.

I repeated the process with the elderly man, then slipped each a Syrette of Thorazine, carefully measured by their approximate body weight. They would sleep soundly and peacefully and wake with no knowledge of the intrusion. Also, it very likely would save their lives. No doubt, they would otherwise have come running when the fires hit.

The second floor light at the villa provided a beacon. I walked directly at it, watching for flickering movements. The Mercedes was abandoned three hundred yards from the building. The trunk was open and empty. Dirkson had already hauled the equipment forward. Although we had agreed to rendezvous two hundred feet in a straight line from the south wall, it still took minutes to find him.

"How we doing?" I whispered in almost total darkness.

"C-4s in place," Dirkson replied, "and so're the nitrite bombs. I'm placing the gas jugs now. Almost done." He grabbed two and moved away quietly.

The villa was large and square, and according to men at the café, it had once been a famous restaurant. The bottom floor was one massive room with a full-width kitchen on the ocean side. During the occupation, the Germans had converted it to an officers' dance hall and party house, and added two levels above for private entertainment. An open staircase stood in the center with beamed balconies on both floors.

Since then, it had been owned by a reputable British firm that leased it for five-year periods to recluses, although it had been vacant for long periods until the current lessee. A perfect hole for Trudor.

Dirkson found me. "All set," he said. "Those are thick stone walls. We'll get some damage but not much. Mostly flame and noise. The back kitchen is wood. Lots of fire there."

"That's what we need. Are they timed correctly?"

His voice seemed offended. "Just like you wanted."

"I don't like surprises. Tell me again."

He sighed. "They go off front right, front left, front door, followed later by two in back. Spaced like you said."

"And the first?"

I could dimly see him look at the illuminated watch. "Six minutes. Ah, any last-minute pearls of wisdom?"

"Yeah, don't get killed."

"Cantrell," he whispered fiercely, grabbing my arm, "if I do buy the farm, can you really waste my body?"

I did not answer.

The front door was massive, ten feet across and probably reinforced, but windows extended on both sides to the outer walls. I took the right, ducked below the concrete sash, knowing the first blast would occur around the protecting corner, ten yards away. It was dark inside on the ground level, but I knew Dirkson was poised near the left window, holding a large piece of driftwood.

My field skills were rusty and slow, but one does accumulate operative techniques to give an edge. The MP5-K empties a clip in two seconds, so it's not aimed, but rather sprayed. The trick is to reload with all possible speed. Experienced jungle fighters listen to the firing rhythm of their opponents, then shoot during that critical reload time.

A Special Forces veteran taught me how to reclip a subgun with incredible dexterity and speed, by holding the next one in my bracing hand, dropping and grabbing a full one while firing. I'd never forgotten.

Sweat trickled on my chest as I glanced at the Seiko, and it reminded me of Stella. I almost smiled but the blast knocked me numb. Even when expected, the shock is staggering.

I recovered quickly and avoided looking at the blaze, not wanting to lose night vision. Everything depended on surprise and speed.

Opening fire through the shattered window, I sprayed left, right and up, but not down, as Dirkson smashed his window and was crawling across left to right under my fire. He would get close to the flame and cover my entrance, knowing the adverse parties would be forced to look into that blazing light.

The C-4 and nitrite bombs took out only part of the wall, but the splattered gasoline produced a monstrous fire. I reclipped and emptied three times and waited. They were keeping heads down.

The second explosion to the left was not as terrifying because I was partially deafened. I leaped through and crossed left as Dirkson covered with strafing fire from the right. I moved until the heat was too much, then crept forward.

The tactic was simple. We remained on opposite sides, one firing while the other advanced a few feet, alternating, driving them back where the last two charges were waiting. We had to command the bottom floor quickly. Anyone upstairs would be trapped in cross fire.

So far, there had been no return. We had either caught them unprepared, dumbfounded, or were being suckered in. I spotted the staircase and sprayed it, along with the balcony above. I also broke a cardinal rule by staying in one spot too long because someone opened with the unmistakable thunder of an Uzi subgun.

As all hell exploded around me, I wanted to claw my way through the tile floor. Chunks of glass, wood, pottery and stone flew everywhere, and I thought I took it on the face. Several gashes on the cheek instantly burned, and blood from my forehead ran into my eyes.

Dirkson saw the flash and fired in that direction until the Uzi was silenced and someone screamed.

We were halfway through the building when return fire commenced from two directions, pinning us, forcing our bodies to the floor. Someone else moved into position and three guns were shredding with brutal fire.

Luckily, Greeks love very thick, heavy oak tables, which protected me, and I prayed Dirkson had found similar cover. I could not even raise my head as those bastards began alternating fire and reload.

I was beginning to have great doubts about Dirkson's timing abilities when the third bang turned the huge room into a blazing inferno. The stupefying explosion had been set against the massive front door, and huge chunks of flaming wood roared inside.

Dirkson and I were prepared and expecting it, so we jumped up and charged forward, spraying 9 mm slugs in every direction—a blitzkrieg tactic they did not expect.

Leaving their backside open, thinking the storm troopers were coming, they retreated quickly. We unleashed combined firepower in that direction toward shadows, yells, reflections, movements, anything.

The Couple had been standing in the middle and were caught by the blast. English was to the right, bent over a table and not moving. I saw a flicker and emptied into Stretch as he attempted to return fire but not quickly enough. He spun around and briefly left the floor.

From the eerie light, I saw Dirkson had downed Muscles. That left Boris, Cuban and Trudor, at least. Dirkson appeared okay, from what I could see, but he was clutching his firing hand and slow to reload.

We had forced them toward the kitchen at the rear. If they decided to rabbit to the beach, all the better. The villa had lit the sky, and the beach offered no protection. Dirkson had already slashed their tires.

The last two explosions ripped the kitchen apart. It was too dangerous to charge in, but suddenly there was no choice. A SPAS-12 unleashed a fury of lead pellets from overhead. I was whacked several times, and hurled through the swinging doors into the kitchen.

I hit the floor mainly because of the SPAS blast, and that saved me. Uzi slugs from the far corner chewed the wall above. They would have sliced me in half.

Dirkson came through the right doors seconds after me, subgun blazing, and he caught Boris trying to reposition. I breathed heavily a minute, and saw Cuban lying a few feet away. He was right beside the C-4 explosives.

Five-six-seven. That was all we'd seen, but outside the kitchen wall, somebody was tearing up the place with that SPAS, alternating shot and explosive shells. The long room was becoming an inferno, but I could not move.

I had been hit by numerous heavy lead pellets from the right shoulder to knee, then realized my leg was throbbing just below the hip. Someone had nailed me with a big one, and the instant I realized that, the pain tripled and my leg would not move. Blood soaked my pants.

Dozens of crackling fires produced a strange, haunted-house effect.

Crouching, Dirkson approached me, blood dripping from his hands and arm. "You okay?" he asked.

I wanted to say something witty, but couldn't. "No," I answered.

"The whole back wall is gone," he shouted above the roar. "The breeze is feeding the flames, but it's taking the smoke out."

We moved into a relatively untouched corner, away from the heat. "That's Trudor firing," I said, the logic suddenly becoming clear. "I just realized he's alone up there. There's no sleeping room on this floor, so the guards would use the second, leaving the top for him. I say he's a loner, not the type to mix with peons."

"What do we do?"

"He's using the SPAS to keep us pinned or drive us out. The village knows by now. We've got twenty minutes, tops."

Dirkson was becoming a blur to me. "I'll take him," he said.

"Wait for me."

"Can't. We don't know what the villagers will do. Now or never." He turned about for the right door, which was almost burned away, but still smoldering.

I bellied my way through when a voice came from the balcony above.

"Gentlemen. How many are you?" I did not respond, and he continued, as if addressing the Rotary Club. "I ask only to ascertain the price. I assume you have one in mind?"

The gasoline had burned down, leaving only spots of scattered tables and wood flaming, but not much light. The kitchen was burning violently, but with the partition still standing, it produced only refracted illumination in the main hall. The voice echoed slightly in the large space, and the balcony extended all around the main room. He could have been anywhere.

Dirkson was moving along the far side, and I continued my struggle for position.

"Come, come, you are only two or three," Trudor continued. "What are they paying you? I will triple it. Immediate cash."

"Show yourself," Dirkson said from the shadows, and I cursed my young charge for such stupidity. Trudor had firing command of the main floor below him and was locating us by sound. He could easily fire explosives and burn Dirkson.

But he didn't. Trudor knew there was at least one more. He wanted us all before committing.

"Don't be foolish, my friend," Trudor answered, his voice ringing up and down the open floors. "I will offer more than a generous reward. I can stay here indefinitely, and you must realize that. My friends will soon be here to rescue me. How many can you kill?''

My ears were still ringing from the explosions and fire-fight, so I shook my head to clear the throbbing. Sound plays tricks on wounded eardrums.

"Too bad you did not submit résumés," the goading continued. "It's obvious you could do a superior job of protecting my fortress. Perhaps you are for hire? My salary package is quite superior."

All firing had ceased, and each man jockeyed for position without giving his own away. A standoff. Given time, we could maneuver him into the open, but there was no time, and he knew it. Trudor stalled.

Positions reversed, I would have been lying prone, the SPAS barely extended through the wood slats of the balcony, keeping my face and body well back. I knew the technique. He would be scanning for any noise or movement. The instant he located me, he would quickly fire on us both.

I was stretched out fully, the subgun across my wrists as I pulled myself forward in fractional increments. My leg was useless, and I dared not push with the other, fearing a scraping sound.

My hand touched a bottle on the floor. It was half full of liquor. My pants were shredded from the pellets, and I found a large piece of material about to come loose. It seemed forever as I slowly and quietly pulled the torn cloth apart, wishing Trudor would talk so I could rip the damn thing.

"Well, friends?" he teased. "I can hear vehicles. You have little time. The money is still yours. As compatriots, we can explain how these traitors tried to kill me, and you came to the rescue. I believe that deserves an additional bonus.

Say, a quarter million each, just for confirmation? American cash, of course."

Trudor was desperate. Surrounded by bodies, he could invent any story and, with his connections, get away with it.

His offer gave me the chance at last to yank the frayed cloth free. I poked all but two inches inside the bottle and swirled the liquid so the material was saturated. A very short fuse. I had managed to crawl a quarter way into the main room and hoped Dirkson was ready.

Being under the balcony, I could only throw to the opposite side. I had to reach the second floor. I touched the wick to a piece of burning wood, it flashed, and I lobbed away.

Compared to the other bombs, it was a puny explosion, but after the long minutes of silenced gunfire, it produced considerable shock.

A loud bang was followed by flames spewed in all directions. Dirkson apparently had a bead and took quick advantage of the distraction. He fired a burst directly above me, and I added a spray to the floor over my head, shooting blindly, racking back and forth, hoping it would penetrate the wood.

Trudor had the SPAS charged with heavy shot, lethal stuff with a wide dispersion, and he put two loads at Dirkson, then rolled away, trying to regain firing posture.

While firing, I had pulled myself upright on the staircase, reclipped, and from the blaze, saw the SPAS swing toward me, so I poured all thirty rounds into the target.

Other than a distinct pounding in my ears, everything was suddenly very still.

Vehicle lights were bouncing off the walls, and I recalled the road dips. They were very close. Maybe two minutes.

"You okay?" I tried to shout, but gagged and coughed several times. I had seen Dirkson flung backward in that brief second. "You there?" I repeated, dreading the silence.

I heard strange scuffing sounds and thought Trudor was still alive. I could not believe it, but rammed another clip.

"Got to see him," Dirkson moaned, crawling up the stairs. "Got to. Came this far."

"Save it," I suggested. "For the swim."

"Ha," he replied without humor, and finally reached his feet.

If we were going to spend eternity in a horrendous Greek jail, he at least deserved a peek at what it was for. Buchannon and the agency could do nothing. After diplomatic screaming and pretense, all would be forgotten, and we'd rot on some dank island.

For one insane infinitesimal second, I considered putting one into Dirkson's head. He was a young man, and not emotionally adaptable to forty years in a stone cellar. But the impulse passed.

Dirkson spoke with a gasp. "The bastard's nothing! Looks like a goddamned insurance salesman."

"What'd you expect?" I spoke to the balcony above, barely able to move.

"I don't know. Maybe a superman or something. But he's just like anybody on the street."

"No," I disagreed. "Trudor was very different."

I rolled over and the pain electrified my entire body. At that moment, I would have sold my country for morphine. "I can't make the boat," I announced. "Go ahead if you can. Take a chance."

"You got to be kidding," he wheezed from above. "They're here," he said a minute later. "They'll separate us, you know. Maybe this is it. Tell me why, asshole. I deserve to know."

Light beams cut across the room from outside. They were coming slow, checking for ambush. "During the Nuremberg trials," I groaned, "they learned it was easier to prosecute Nazis for murdering one person than thousands. Judges couldn't conceive mass slaughter."

"Cantrell, you son of a bitch! Just once, just once could you say something without a fucking history lesson?" His gasping was uncontrollable, and I recognized the sound of chest wounds.

"I'm trying. I didn't really care about all of Trudor's killings. That's the way of things. Not my problem."

"You mean the Evans girl? You did this for her?"

"No, for a nothing kid named Cindy something. An innocent fool caught in the wrong place and buried in the wrong grave." I tried to piece logic from the mayhem around me. "I guess it was my little revenge for all the Cindys in this world."

I then remained quiet, motionless, hoping to join the angels in private. I tried to picture Kate.

Spoken by one person, the Greek language is difficult enough, but when a dozen all yell at once, the blare is unintelligible.

A light beam split into my skull, and I smelled garlic.

"You missed the boat," he said softly.

In spite of the pain, I laughed at the cliché, which Sergeant Panos did not understand. "Interested in fishing?" I asked him.

"It seems I've already caught my limit," he replied.

"My friend's upstairs on the balcony. Please tend—"

"Someone is there now." Panos rattled some Greek and was answered from above. He relayed to me, "Your friend is serious, but not fatal."

I realized two men had sliced my pants open and were applying tight wraps. I hadn't even felt them do it above the agony. "So," I asked, "what brings you here?"

Panos lit a cigarette and offered it to me, just like in the American movies every Greek watches. He seemed disappointed when I refused. "I wanted to see how you managed to swim that far. My men bet you would not make it. I do not earn enough to lose a wager, so I came along to help. This way, the bet's off."

"Great. Uh, what happens now?"

"I have a roadblock above to keep out the curious. And well I did so, because immediately after the explosions, five foreigners were arrested, intent on coming here. They were very upset."

"Oh? And the charge?"

"Foolish Americans. One had hashish in his pocket. We arrested them all. Naturally, they denied the charge."

"Naturally." I moaned slightly.

"They claimed to have great interest in the old church. Probably to take pictures by sunrise."

"No doubt." I grimaced, wondering how the Company would react to the agents' arrest.

"Admittedly, the evidence is sketchy, so I will release them later today," Panos said with a sigh.

I saw Dirkson being carried out. I hoped to see a sign of life, but the medic had zapped him with something. I then noticed Panos was equipped with a sizable force. There were four medical types checking bodies, and eight heavily armed uniforms.

"My people will take you to Heraklion for rest after your long fishing trip. I have influence there. Is that satisfactory?"

I nodded eagerly. "Just perfect." An attendant emptied the contents of a syringe into a vein, and I felt suddenly warmer, more relaxed.

Panos stood and began shouting orders. Four men brought in several large square boxes. They placed them against the walls and began wiring them together. "Too bad, these tourists who rent our villas," he said. "I have repeatedly warned them about the ancient heating systems in these old buildings. Poorly designed. Natural gas, you know. Very unsafe."

I was being placed on a stretcher and was drifting fast from the sedation. "The old couple down the beach," I mumbled.

"They have been moved to a safe distance. Still sound asleep." The sergeant laughed. "They missed a story to tell at the taverna!"

As my stretcher was loaded in a truck, Panos leaned over. "I have many details to finish here. It's best we not meet again. There will be...complications. Arrangements have already been made."

"How can I thank you?" I stammered. "I don't know what to say."

He looked to the building, still burning in several places. "That villa has been a disgrace for many years."

Panos turned to me. "I am only a country policeman, but I have always known who these people are, and what they stand for. But they never have broken Cretan law, and politics made us look away. I am only one man."

He stuffed the thousand dollars into my pocket. "My friend, this is also a matter of honor for me."

As the truck ground up the steep road, I was almost sleeping when the sky turned white. An explosion rocked our vehicle as the villa disappeared.

As Panos said, those tourists never listened.

# 29. HOME?

---

IT TOOK HOURS to crawl up through the smothering molasses. When I finally surfaced, the effort was too draining, so I dropped back into oblivion.

Later, conditioning took over, and I checked my inventory. First the fingers and thumbs, and then each joint. Wrists, arms, neck and face were next. Everything was going well until the legs. Left okay, right zilch. It might have been amputated for all I knew.

Sedation, tranquilizers and painkillers had infiltrated all systems. They let the downers wear off until I woke in pain, then fed me hot goo and zapped me back to dreamland.

The nurse was middle-aged, portly and kindly, but spoke no English. The first time I saw a needle approach, I protested, "Stop. No more shots. I'm okay." She chattered something, ignored me and injected with a smile.

Several times a day she entered, took my pulse, fed me and took care of my other natural functions.

I gave up any hope of answers from Florence Nightingale, so we nodded and gestured our way through the days.

The doctor was young, too young, probably an intern someplace. He arrived both early and late, no doubt before and after regular duty. When the bandages were replaced he always said, "Okay, okay, just rest."

All in all, not a bad life. It certainly was not jail, and I was being fed and mended, so why object? The room was small, with the obligatory Greek religious artifacts adorning every wall, and the bed was very comfortable. Either that, or the drugs were stronger than I thought.

"Time for a visitor," Monica said, as she appeared one day and sat beside me.

"Good morning, or afternoon, or whatever," I answered.

"I am disappointed. I thought you would be surprised to see me."

"I can hear your bar music through the wall. This had to be your building. Is it part of your extended customer service?"

"I never understand when Americans are being sincere or funny."

"Sorry. I am truly grateful. I'm alive because of you and your associates. And, uh, could you tell me about—"

"Your friend? Yes, he is fine. Younger and stronger than you."

"Thanks."

"Is the service satisfactory?"

"Perfect. Tell me, does everyone on Crete lead a secret life?"

"We Cretans have lived a double life for so long, it is normal to have secret rooms, hiding places, underground organizations. Even supplies. We have been invaded and occupied so many times, it is second nature. Part of our heritage."

"*We* Cretans?" I asked curiously.

"On my mother's side. A rare alliance between nationalities. If you ever return to Crete on a personal visit, I will tell you all about it."

"That's a promise. Tell my friend I will meet him in your bar tonight."

"Not possible, I'm afraid. Things are . . . sensitive right now. Many questions. The doctor would like you to practice with those." She indicated crutches in the corner. "When you are ready, a private plane to Karpathos will be waiting. From there, a normal ferry to Athens. It is considered wise to leave Crete unnoticed."

"Thank you very much."

"It was necessary to take money from your waist belt for arrangements. We thought you would not object."

I tried to offer more, but Monica refused. "Okay," I said. "Tell Sergeant Panos I appreciate everything."

"Who?" she answered innocently.

Two days plus countless aches later, my nurse left me a tray. On it was a note instructing me to be ready that afternoon. My clothes from the raid had been mended and dyed dark blue, the customary Greek color. There was also a bottle of Napoléon brandy on the tray, with a card saying, "Come back. M."

The two young men arrived at sundown, entering without knocking. One said something, attempted English and grabbed my crutches. The second hefted my arm over his shoulder, and we stumbled down the back stairs to a waiting car.

Dirkson was already there, and my first reaction was to clutch him, but the drained and haggard look on his face stopped me. His physical wounds were healing, but his mind still suffered.

We grinned, said something stupid, shook hands like goddamn distant relatives and sat back for the ride.

From a small field outside Khania, we took off in a modern Cessna and landed on Karpathos less than an hour later. A cab took us to the dock, barely in time to catch the ferry to Athens. The timing was perfect, and we both understood the Company had been called off. They had had a dozen chances to finish the job and burn us, but apparently had accepted the premise that by leaving Crete without police capture, we posed no threat.

There was little conversation from any of the Cretans during the entire episode. They had orders, and that was it.

We had a first-class cabin, but hardly used it during the eleven-hour cruise. Mostly we sat on the afterdeck, sipping my brandy and talking about nothing.

I recalled that all forms of human misery can be categorized into five divisions: pain, hunger, fear, guilt and loneliness. In the past weeks, I had suffered all except hunger. That probably would have driven me over the edge.

After any momentous event, one experiences an intense psychological reaction, a mental, emotional crash that often creates more stress than the actual event. The situation is problematic, with severe anxiety and depression following danger, and in direct proportion.

Dirkson was suffering that misery.

We rarely spoke of anything important, both submerged in our own thoughts. "I didn't really expect to leave alive," he finally said. "I had prepared myself."

"Maybe next time," I tried to joke, and saw a weak smile from him. "Captain Marvel will give you a vacation. What are your plans?"

"I have no idea," he mused, then laughed for the first time. "I remember an instructor at the survival course in Montana. He said if you don't know where you're going, you can never get lost."

"True," I agreed. "Unfortunately, you also don't know when you've arrived."

"Screw it. I'll leave philosophy to you old-timers."

We killed the bottle, and Dirkson bought another. "My treat," he said, smiling, beginning to look boyish again. "Why did they help us?"

"Greeks are proud people and Cretans doubly so. We removed a filthy, cancerous growth from their precious land. A Cretan will slit your throat just for glancing at his virgin sister, but never attack someone for breaking laws in another country. I think they were ashamed of harboring Trudor, but their code prevented doing anything. It had to be outsiders."

After considerable argument with the staff and security group at the American embassy in Athens, I was allowed to send a message. I had to drop several names and bureaucratic threats before permission was granted.

Buchannon
T. and several others down. Needed local cover out. All okay.

                                                              Cantrell

After the acknowledgment, Dirkson sent a message in clear to his wife. The cipher clerk asked me, "Anyone else you want to contact?"

"No thanks," I answered.

The security director, using carefully chosen words, indicated he had been in touch with Washington, and that we were reclassified as diplomatic and not to be detained. Our flight home was arranged.

It was over, all over, I said to myself on the flight back. Nothing to do but dwell on the past. It should have ended on Crete, I kept thinking, and the postmortems added to my depression.

The connections through Rome and Madrid were smooth, and twenty minutes from San Francisco I toasted Barry Dirkson. "You were great. Really great. Someday, you'll be one of the best."

He stammered for words. "Thanks. It was more than a pleasure, more like a privilege. If that makes any sense, applied to killing people."

"We did not kill, but terminated filth," I said sternly.

"I understand. That's what they said at the academy."

"And never forget it, or you'll wake up screaming."

Barbara Dirkson met us at the airport, all gushy and tearful, but did behave marvelously in not mentioning her husband's bandages and physical condition. She'll do, I thought. After some awkward introductions, they left arm in arm.

I wondered what to do next. Having no bag to collect, and assuming that everything in my refrigerator had grown green fuzz, I opted for steak, salad and real American coffee in the airport restaurant.

An hour later, I was nursing an overpriced and undersized glass of brandy in the lounge, and cursing myself for not having brought home a case.

"Do you have any idea how many bars there are in this airport?"

I stared with open amazement at Stella Evans. "What the hell are you doing here?"

"It took me ages to find you."

"How did you?"

"I called Mr. Buchannon every day, and he finally gave me your flight number. I waited by the baggage claim. You didn't show up, so I started looking."

"W-well," I stuttered, "that's very nice. Uh, how are you?"

Her eyes misted. "I even had this dress repaired by professionals for your homecoming." The mist became tears as Stella wiped them with her fingertips. "He said you were in Athens. I thought you might call . . . or something."

"I didn't know where you were," I offered.

"Mr. Buchannon did. He could have told you."

"Sorry," I muttered, feeling a fool.

"I should have known you'd want privacy, but after all we'd been through together, I thought you might let me know you were okay."

I struggled through another weak apology.

She ordered a white wine with ice and composed herself. "I had a private party, all set. I rented a fancy Cadillac limousine to take us around the city. We've got reservations at your favorite lobster house. But the car was costing a hundred an hour to sit there, so I let it go."

"Stella, that's beautiful, but I didn't know your plans. I really appreciate it, you'll never realize how much. But you shouldn't waste your time around me. You and I had something important to do, and we did it, and now it's over."

"I know we did. Mr. Buchannon told me how important."

"And I'm proud of you, but now you should be out meeting new people and planning a future. You're an incredible woman, and it's time to live your life."

"I know, and thanks to you, I will. But I want us to be friends forever, and tonight I wanted to show my gratitude and to celebrate. I was saving my surprise for later, after the cherries jubilee."

"What surprise?"

"Well, I know how much you hate your job, and I wanted to help."

"I'm afraid to ask."

"Mr. Buchannon and I made a deal," she continued slowly. "If you want, you can retire right now, tomorrow morning, with full pension. Or you can stay. Your choice!"

I tried to absorb what she was saying. Stella began to babble, and I shushed her while ordering another brandy. "I think you should tell me all about this. From the top."

"It's funny, but you said those two names so many times, Buchannon and Wainwright, I assumed when I turned myself in I would meet with them. But they brought in different people. Like you said, I was questioned about everything. I told the complete truth, but nothing made them happy. First it was male interrogators, then women trying the sisterly crap. Real assholes."

I cringed, knowing what this vixen was capable of saying. "And?"

"After two days, I was getting mad. I cooperated with everything, but they kept digging and twisting things around, trying to get me to admit things about Sam and Mateo that didn't happen. I refused to sign their papers because it made me sound guilty of all kinds of things. They wouldn't define the legal words, and I remembered your warnings. Those papers could have put me in jail!

"All of a sudden, Mr. Buchannon and Mr. Wainwright stopped it all and saw me in private. They were really very nice, and we negotiated everything. Honestly, they were perfect gentlemen. That's when Mr. Buchannon decided you could retire any time you wanted."

"Ah, Stella, what precisely did you negotiate *with*?"

"You remember those tapes I copied for you in New York? Well, I made two sets for myself and listened again when I got back here. It seemed to me that this Starkmore of Transcontinental Airlines is a very powerful man. He knows senators and important Washington people. I thought he should realize how much trouble and danger you went through, just to save his airline and keep the story from the media."

"Oh my God!" I groaned. "You blackmailed Starkmore?"

"Not really... well, not in so many words. But I remembered you people always take out insurance on yourselves.

You told me that. I merely sent him a set of tapes with a letter making suggestions. That's all. I hinted there might be other copies, and neither you nor I wanted them mailed to major papers in the country. We were not asking for anything. I made that very clear. However..."

"However?"

"However, if either of us were hassled or suddenly disappeared, or anything nasty, well, he could figure it out for himself." Stella was beaming. "Starkmore must have fast connections."

"J-Jesus," I stammered, unable to speak. "Jesus."

Stella dipped her fingers into the wine. She picked out two ice cubes and held them firmly in her palm. "I got them by the balls."

I actually worried about this child?

She smiled. "I told you, I'm a survivor."

I grinned. "Stella, can you find that driver and his limousine?"

# Spine-chilling tales of suspense, kidnapping and murder

# g novels of international
## e, adventure and suspense

---

|  |  | Quantity |
|---|---|---|
| **RECOVERY**—Steven L. Thompson<br>Max Moss must defy overwhelming enemy forces when he is sent to retrieve top-secret equipment in hostile Communist territory. | $3.95 U.S.<br>$4.50<br>Canada | ☐<br>☐ |
| **TOP END**—Steven L. Thompson<br>Max Moss attempts to recover a top-secret avionics suit, and in the process discovers a smuggling operation that has been supplying ultrasecret high-tech equipment to the USSR. | $3.95 U.S.<br>$4.50<br>Canada | ☐<br>☐ |
| **QUINT'S WORLD**—Samuel Fuller<br>An aging professional bloodhound weaves his way through the seamy underworld of Europe to locate a tape with information that could change the world. | $3.95 U.S.<br>$4.50<br>Canada | ☐<br>☐ |
| **THE SEIZING OF YANKEE GREEN MALL**—Ridley Pearson<br>A madman turns a suburban shopping mall into a center of horror as he prepares to kill thousands of hostage shoppers if his demands are not met. | $3.95 U.S.<br>$4.50<br>Canada | ☐<br>☐ |

|  |  |
|---|---|
| Total Amount | $ _____ |
| Plus 75¢ Postage | .75 |
| Payment enclosed | $ _____ |

---

Please send a check or money order payable to Worldwide Library.

| In the U.S.A. | In Canada |
|---|---|
| Worldwide Library<br>901 Fuhrmann Blvd.<br>Box 1325<br>Buffalo, NY 14269-1325 | Worldwide Library<br>P.O. Box 609<br>Fort Erie, Ontario<br>L2A 5X3 |

---

**Please Print**

Name: _____

Address: _____

City: _____

State/Prov: _____

Zip/Postal Code: _____

(()) **WORLDWIDE LIBRARY**

SUS-2